Palace
of
Lies

Also by Margaret Peterson Haddix

Full Ride
Game Changer
The Always War
Claim to Fame
Uprising
Double Identity
The House on the Gulf
Escape from Memory
Takeoffs and Landings
Turnabout
Leaving Fishers
Don't You Dare Read This, Mrs. Dunphrey

THE PALACE CHRONICLES
Just Ella
Palace of Mirrors
Palace of Lies

THE MISSING SERIES
Found
Sent
Sabotaged
Torn
Caught
Risked
Revealed

THE SHADOW CHILDREN SERIES
Among the Hidden
Among the Impostors
Among the Betrayed
Among the Barons
Among the Brave
Among the Enemy
Among the Free

The Girl with 500 Middle Names
Because of Anya
Say What?
Dexter the Tough
Running Out of Time

MARGARET PETERSON HADDIX

Palace
of
Lies

The
Palace
Chronicles
Book 3

SIMON & SCHUSTER BFYR
New York   London   Toronto
Sydney   New Delhi

SIMON & SCHUSTER BFYR

An imprint of Simon & Schuster Children's Publishing Division
1230 Avenue of the Americas, New York, New York 10020
For information about special discounts for bulk purchases, please contact Simon & Schuster
Special Sales at 1-866-506-1949 or business@simonandschuster.com.
The Simon & Schuster Speakers Bureau can bring authors to your live event.
For more information or to book an event, contact the Simon & Schuster Speakers Bureau
at 1-866-248-3049 or visit our website at www.simonspeakers.com.
Book design by Chloë Foglia and Tom Daly
The text for this book is set in Cremona.
Manufactured in the United States of America
2 4 6 8 10 9 7 5 3 1
Library of Congress Cataloging-in-Publication Data
Haddix, Margaret Peterson.
Palace of lies / Margaret Peterson Haddix.—First edition.
pages cm
Summary: "After a terrible fire destroys her home and kills her twelve
sister-princesses, Desmia must rise above those who intend to manipulate her and sieze
power for themselves—and find out the truth"—Provided by the publisher.
ISBN 978-1-4424-4281-8 (hardcover)
ISBN 978-1-4424-4283-2 (eBook)
[1. Princesses—Fiction. 2. Fantasy.] I. Title.
PZ7.H1164Pak 2015
[Fic]—dc23
2013027805

FIRST
EDITION

For Tori

Acknowledgments

With thanks to Linda Gerber, Erin MacLellan, Jenny Patton, Nancy Roe Pimm, Amjed Qamar, and Linda Stanek, for their advice about starting this book.

Prologue

Thirteen crowns glistened in the torchlight of the throne room. Twelve were newly forged, ready to be placed on the heads of the Sualan princesses whose identities had been kept secret their entire lives until now.

The thirteenth crown was mine.

I was the princess everybody knew about. The one who'd grown up in the palace, the one who stood on the balcony every day at noon and waved to the commoners crowded into the courtyard below.

The one who had always lived in danger.

Cecilia, beside me, jostled my arm in a completely unregal way, countering the effect of her satin dress and ornately upswept brown hair.

"This is so exciting!" she practically squealed in my ear. "I've been dreaming about this day forever! It's exactly like I always imagined it! Only, you know—not."

What she'd always imagined was replacing me.

For almost all of her fourteen years, she'd believed that she was the one true princess of Suala. But she had to remain hidden because her parents, the king and queen, had been assassinated, and the evildoers were still abroad in the land. Her own life was still at risk. And so, to protect her, there was a decoy princess on the throne, a mere commoner whose life didn't actually matter.

She believed that I, Princess Desmia, was an impostor.

Every single one of the eleven other newly discovered princesses—Adoriana, Elzbethl, Fidelia, Florencia, Ganelia, Lucia, Lydia, Marindia, Porfinia, Sophia, and Rosemary— had grown up believing some version of that story herself. Each one thought that she (Adoriana, Elzbethl, Fidelia, etc., etc.) was the true princess; I was the disposable fake.

They had all been lied to.

But then, so had I.

I had always believed that I was the one and only true princess. I knew nothing of the others' stories. I knew no tales of decoys and secret royal bloodlines. I knew only to fear assassins and pretenders and impostors who might show up with fake claims to my throne.

In one sense, it had turned out that all of us were impostors.

In another sense, every single one of us was right: We were all true princesses. Just not the way any of us had believed.

At least, we're all going to be true princesses now, I thought grimly as all thirteen of us fanned out across the back of the throne room, ready to step forward for the official coronation.

Was that right? Was that fair? Would the others all have been safer staying in hiding? Or—going back to it?

Of course they would, I thought, and for a moment my heart pounded as if I were the one stepping out into unfamiliar terrors and demands for the very first time.

"Psst, Desmia," Elzbethl hissed behind me. "How do you do that thing with your feet, where it looks like you're gliding when you walk? How do you keep from tripping over your dress?"

I sighed.

"I don't know, Elzbethl. It just . . ." If I said, *It just comes naturally*, that would be cruel, because nothing involving grace or coordination seemed to come naturally to Elzbethl. But I had learned how to walk like a princess so long ago I didn't remember it. I was probably taught with my very first steps. Elzbethl should have learned too. "I guess you kind of slide your feet. Don't lift your knees too high."

"Thank you," Elzbethl said, too loudly for the solemnity of the room ahead of us. "Thank you so much."

Her eyes were wide and awed, just like Cecilia's, just like all the other girls'. I could hear whispers down the line: "Did you think our crowns would be so *shiny*?" "I can't believe I'm wearing a silk dress. Silk!" "Oooo, is that courtier over there winking at you or me?"

They might as well have all been blind. They were like little kittens that didn't have their eyes open yet. They peered into the throne room, and all they could see was glitter and gold. They looked at the assembled crowd in their own silks and satins, their own velvets and gold-threaded brocade, and the only things my new sister-princesses saw were beauty and adoration and pride. They didn't see any of the scheming or conniving or greed. They didn't see any more lies.

They thought all the danger was past.

The royal trumpeters sent out a series of blasts on their horns. It was the same royal refrain that had announced Sualan royalty for generations. I had been hearing it all my life, but the others gasped and gaped.

"Hear ye, hear ye," the royal herald announced from the front of the room, from beside the newly arranged lineup of thirteen thrones. "Presenting . . . the thirteen princesses of Suala."

The other girls around me stood frozen, overcome. It would be unroyal and undignified for me to poke Cecilia in the back and hiss, *Proceed!* But for a long moment I feared that I would have to resort to that. Finally Adoriana, in the lead, stepped forward and began stumbling toward the thrones. After only a brief pause, Cecilia bounded up behind her. I waited a decent interval, then followed along.

"I still don't get how she does that gliding thing," Elzbethl whispered behind me, probably to Fidelia.

I resisted the urge to turn around and see how Elzbethl would fare strolling (or, more likely, galumphing) down the long purple carpet leading to our thrones. Faces leered out of the crowd at me, and I catalogued the expressions behind their expressions.

Was that man secretly working for Lord Throckmorton all along? I wondered, my gaze lingering on a particularly pompous, preening face. *Should we have arrested him, too?*

My gaze shifted to the next minister, the next adviser, one after the other.

What is that one plotting now? How about that one?

The other girls thought we had nothing else to worry about. After all, we'd triumphed over our worst enemy, Lord Throckmorton—and put him and his minions under lock and key. The other girls had never lived in a palace before. They didn't understand how new enemies could spring up overnight. Or do their evil in secret for years. I'd seen that happen too.

Elzbethl distracted me from my thoughts by stepping on the hem of my dress.

"Oh, sorry! I'm so sorry! I got too close, didn't I?" she cried, turning a tiny *faux pas* into a spectacle for the entire assemblage to gawp at.

I turned, partly to make sure there wasn't any damage to my dress, partly to get her to stop screeching.

She backed away so dramatically that she almost fell over.

I gave my most gracious bow.

"It is no matter," I said softly. "I pray, put it from your mind."

I didn't say, *And, from now on, watch where you're going!* Even though I was thinking it.

I turned forward again and kept walking toward the thrones.

Behind me I could hear Elzbethl giggle nervously and recount to Fidelia, "She was even nice about it! Back in my village, when I was pretending to be a peasant, the other girls would have punched me if I'd done something like that."

Truly? I wondered. But I was also secretly celebrating. *Yes, Elzbethl, that's right. Learn to be suspicious of false kindness.*

But did I want her to be suspicious of me?

This question absorbed me as we all settled onto our thrones, an array of glittering girls with a table full of glistening crowns before us.

It was unprecedented for so many princesses to be crowned—or, in my case, recrowned—at the same time. It was highly abnormal for princesses to rule at all, let alone multiple princesses who were all only fourteen years old.

We had jointly decided that becoming a kingdom with thirteen ruling princesses made more sense than having all of us designated queens. The others argued that we were making everything up as we went along, anyway—why not call ourselves whatever we wanted?

Secretly, I thought that they were all so happy to finally be able to call themselves princesses out loud, in public, that they didn't want to give up the title too quickly.

Was I being unfair? Were they really that shallow? How vulnerable did that make us all?

Why did any of us think this would work? I wondered in despair, as I stared out at the crowd. I was surer than ever that the assembled courtiers were all calculating and conniving. Was

t there who wasn't scheming to take
n's old role as the power behind the
princesses to manipulate?
he way to the far right, to the section
rom the neighboring kingdom of

Jed. They aren't scheming. They're people

lediah Reston was the ambassador
dom had been at war with Fridesia
ber. Until now. The other girls and
princesses to be signing a ceasefire
with Fridesia. And then, as soon as possible, we planned to
work out terms of a lasting peace treaty that would end the
war once and for all.

Even though he was still technically my enemy, I trusted
Jed. And I *really* trusted his fiancée, Ella Brown, who sat
beside him clutching his hand and positively beaming up at
all of us.

Does Ella believe thirteen girls can really rule as co-princesses? I
wondered. *Or is she just being nice? Or just supporting us and Jed,*
because that's the way to get Jed's dearest dream of a peace treaty?

So of course Ella and Jed had ulterior motives too. Did it
even matter that their ulterior motives were noble?

The royal herald stepped to a podium near the center of the
stage, between the thrones for Florencia and Ganelia.

"Be it known," he began, "that on her deathbed fourteen

years ago, Queen Charlotte Aurora designated not just one but thirteen baby girls as her royal heirs."

The other girls and I had struggled so over the wording of that sentence. Sophia and Fidelia in particular wanted to hide the fact that none of us actually possessed a drop of royal blood. The only thing that made us royal was the queen's secret deathbed writings. Otherwise, we were all of us just ordinary orphans—ordinary orphans raised by knights who were themselves tricked into believing we were princesses.

Why did it have to be my knight, Lord Throckmorton, who found out the truth first? I wondered for the umpteenth time. *So I was the one manipulated and preyed upon, instead of being protected and cosseted and . . . and loved?*

Unexpectedly, tears sprang to my eyes. But I knew the trick to holding back tears: You stare at whatever you're afraid of and remind yourself how much worse it would be if you showed any weakness.

I learned that from Lord Throckmorton. For fourteen years, he was the one I feared most.

Now I made myself stare out at the crowd of calculating, scheming courtiers again. Not a single face registered surprise at the herald's words. No flurry of astonished whispers began. That made me certain that all the courtiers already knew—or thought they knew—everything about us. They'd already heard the stories; they'd undoubtedly been gossiping for days about how Cecilia hit Lord Throckmorton over the head with a harp, about how the other eleven girls and their knights were freed from the dungeons and the torture chamber, about how I had proposed sharing the throne.

And do they say I was a fool? I wondered. *Do they think all of us are silly, preening girls easily played, easily used, easily . . . destroyed?*

I wished Elzbethl would sit up straight. I wished Marindia would hold her head higher. I wished Cecilia would stop fidgeting with one of the ruffles on her skirt, where there seemed to be a rip. She was only going to make it bigger, more noticeable. That was how it went with rips.

You all have to act royal, look royal, seem royal . . . or else no one will believe that any of us deserve to rule, I wanted to tell them, each and every one. *You have to start doing that right now.*

The others didn't look like princesses. They looked like little girls playing dress-up, or lowly servants guiltily trying on their mistresses' fancy gowns. Or maybe like baby mice who didn't hear the snakes rustling in the grass behind them.

What have I done, allowing them to join me as princesses?

What else could I possibly have done?

The royal herald went on with his pronouncement of carefully constructed sentences, giving the sanitized version of why we all deserved our crowns. But in my head, I began making up my own version: *Once upon a time, there was a girl who grew up in a nest of vipers.*

It was true, wasn't it? Truer than anything the herald was saying, anyway.

The herald was still talking, so I went on with my own story in my head.

Then one day, the girl found out she had twelve sisters—sisters who'd grown up in safer places, hidden from snakes. All twelve of the sisters came to live in the vipers' nest with the girl. But the sisters didn't know the rules for surviving in a vipers' nest. They didn't know you had to dodge the fangs. They didn't even see the fangs.

The girl knew how to protect herself from the snakes. But what could she do to keep her sisters safe from harm too?

I imagined standing up, pushing the herald aside, telling my story instead. Would my sisters finally understand what they had gotten into? Would they learn to be wary too?

It seemed more likely that the courtiers sitting before us would understand—and would see who needed to be eliminated first. Me. It wasn't as though all the advisers and ministers and counselors out there would stand up and peel back their lips and reveal venomous fangs and start attacking right then and there, but . . .

Well, maybe they would, I thought.

And there was an echo to that thought, one I didn't want to think: *What if it turns out that some of the other princesses have fangs too? What if it turns out that they are secretly snakes as well, and I've made a fatal mistake in trusting them?*

"Princess Desmia," the herald said, then again, a little softer, "Princess?"

I was jolted to realize that I'd missed the end of the herald's explanations. I'd also missed watching the crowns placed on the heads of Adoriana and Cecilia. Both of them were back on their thrones now and smiling so broadly you'd think their cheeks would split. I gave a gracious, congratulatory nod to both of them, then rose. I walked four steps to the heavy stone coronation altar that had been used for the past eight generations of Sualan royalty.

"We are only reaffirming Princess Desmia's coronation, as we all know that she has been wearing the crown for years," the herald intoned.

I had no memory of my original ceremonial crowning. Probably Lord Throckmorton just slid a tiny crown onto my infant head the very day the queen died, and went out before all the other gentlemen of the court proclaiming, "See, the queen entrusted the baby princess to my care! Henceforth I shall make all decisions in her name. I am in charge now. That's right—bow down to me!"

And then he probably sloughed me off to the nearest servant the instant we were out of sight of the court. Or perhaps I cried and he slapped me, even way back then.

Everything's different now, I told myself.

"And we are declaring Princess Desmia's right to rule, now that she has reached the age of majority," the herald continued.

Like all the other princesses, I was only fourteen. Fourteen was the age of majority only when there were no trustworthy adults available to act as regent.

Was that true? Was no one worthy of my trust?

I knelt at the altar. The royal priest, a man I barely remembered seeing at the palace before, stood before me, holding my old familiar crown.

Did Lord Throckmorton banish him, back in the days when Lord Throckmorton was in power? Is that why I've seen him so little? I wondered. *Does that mean he's someone I could trust? Eventually? Someday? Or is he just another conniving courtier, only disguised in a priest's stole?*

How was I supposed to survive if I didn't even know who my enemies were?

The priest placed the jewel-encrusted crown onto my head. There were ridges on my scalp from my previous years of wearing a crown, and it settled right into place. I didn't have to glance at any of the mirrors lining the throne room to reassure myself that my crown, unlike Cecilia's and Adoriana's, wasn't tilting precariously, wasn't about to slide off.

I looked at the mirrors anyway.

For the briefest of instants, I could see the reflection of everything around me the same way the other girls saw it: the glitter, the gold, the excitement. Beautiful girls in beautiful dresses and crowns; a crowd full of beautifully dressed people watching us, all in a beautiful room.

Then my vision swung back to seeing everything the way Lord Throckmorton had taught me, and I knew it was all an illusion.

Something bad is going to happen, I thought.

And there was nothing I could do to stop it.

1

"Somebody has to go to Fridesia for the treaty signing," Cecilia announced at our Princesses Council meeting. "I'll do it."

"No—" I gasped, and instantly cut myself off, because I knew better than to react like that, without thinking. But Cecilia was the sister-princess I came the closest to trusting. Back when she still thought I was a decoy princess, she'd come to the palace partially to rescue *me*. That had to be worth something.

How could she leave?

All the other princesses stared at me from around the vast wooden table we used for our council meetings. The ministers and advisers we allowed to sit along the wall behind us stared too. For a moment all that registered was the sheer number of widened, stunned eyes peering at me. Then I automatically started searching for guile and craftiness in those eyes.

Why couldn't I tell who was scheming what?

We were in a formal meeting, requiring a strict code of conduct, but Cecilia playfully bumped her shoulder against mine. She had to twist herself halfway out of her heavy wooden chair to do it.

"Aww," she cooed. "Are you saying you'd miss me? How sweet."

She grinned, the tiny gap between her two front teeth making her smile seem whimsical and cute, as always. And oblivious.

Doesn't she understand the danger of leaving? I wondered. *The way she'd lose power being away for weeks, just when the rest of us are forming alliances, jockeying for position . . .*

It had been one week since our coronation. Already we'd signed the ceasefire and hammered out details of a peace treaty that Jed assured us the Fridesian royal family would be willing to agree to. The thirteen of us had approved it unanimously.

But I still couldn't shake my feeling of impending doom.

Was this the first true sign of trouble? Would the ministers and advisers and counselors who might be plotting against us see this as their opportunity? Not that it would be that much easier to strike against twelve princesses than thirteen, but . . . this was *Cecilia*. For all her whimsy, she was the most formidable of the new princesses.

Wouldn't our enemies see that?

I swallowed hard, barely managing to keep the action from sounding like a gulp.

"I only meant . . . regardless of my fondness for you, of course, Cecilia . . . the problem is that while you are in Fridesia, that will leave only twelve of us on the Princesses Council," I said. I hoped my solemn tone conveyed that I was back to speaking thoughtfully.

Several of the other girls kept staring blankly. But Lydia nodded knowingly.

"We can't have an even number on our council, because that could lead to tie votes," she agreed. "Desmia is correct."

I could tell that she wanted to sound solemn and thoughtful and learned too. But Lydia had a faceful of freckles, which gave her a comical air. She always tried too hard to be taken seriously. It usually backfired.

I heard giggles around me.

Cecilia just waved away the complaints.

"Well, that's an easy problem to solve," she said, shrugging. (Did I have to mention that royalty should never ever shrug?) "I could have one other princess go with me. Or three or five . . . Heck, in this kingdom, we could have ten princesses off signing treaties, and still have more rulers left behind to govern than in any other kingdom around us!"

I expected her to grin again and let someone else take up the argument. Instead, Cecilia hit me in the shoulder once more—this time with a playful fist—and asked, "So, Desmia, how about it? Want to come?"

I froze. I could feel the counselors and ministers and advisers behind me watching even more intently. They probably didn't actually narrow their eyes—they were too crafty to be so blatant—but they'd undoubtedly narrowed their focus. They were probably already doing calculations in their head: *With both Cecilia and Desmia gone . . .*

I couldn't go to Fridesia. Not now. Probably not ever.

"No, thank you," I said. I was trying for my kindest princess voice—letting Cecilia down gently. But like Lydia, I was a little off. Even to my own ears I sounded too stiff and prim.

Cecilia shrugged again. But the motion wasn't so carefree this time.

Is she actually . . . hurt? I wondered. *Offended? Did she truly want me along?*

"Your loss," she said. "I was thinking we could time the trip so we sign the treaty *and* go to Jed and Ella's wedding. You know they've invited us all. Come on, girls—a *wedding*! Who wouldn't want to go to that? Who's with me? Desmia, don't you want to reconsider?"

I was the first to shake my head and gently murmur, "Sorry." But the other eleven girls did the same, one after the other.

Do they understand after all? I wondered, glancing around. *Are they plotting now too?*

All eleven of them were shame-faced and peering down at the table. And then I remembered how Cecilia was different from all the other sister-princesses. Back before any of us knew the truth about ourselves, Cecilia had come to the palace to find me and meet her fate on her own—or, actually, with her friend, Harper—but still, without any adults.

The other eleven had been captured and imprisoned by Lord Throckmorton's forces. They'd spent time in the dungeon. They'd had to rely on their knights—and, indirectly, Cecilia and Ella and me—to rescue them.

They were all terrified of going to Fridesia. They were terrified of stepping foot in a kingdom whose subjects had been killing Sualans for longer than any of us had been alive.

Did Cecilia think I was just being a coward like all the others?

Was I?

Cecilia's gaze swept the room.

"All right, then," she said, and I could tell she was trying to sound nonchalant and unaffected. "All of you will be missing out. Don't worry—I'll sign the treaty with my fanciest script. No blots! I'll make us all proud. And I'll write down what everyone is wearing at the wedding. I'll even try to draw sketches of Ella's dress." This was directed at Porfinia, the sister-princess who was both the best at drawing and also the most interested in fashion. If she had her way, all of our proclamations would be about clothes.

"But . . . it wouldn't be proper for you to travel all that way by yourself," Florencia said, sounding shocked. "You're a young maiden, and now a princess, too. . . . It simply isn't done. And it's not as though we have dozens of extra servants on retainer we could afford to send along with you. Remember, even the palace budget has its limits. . . ."

Florencia was the prissiest of the sister-princesses. She was also obsessed with the palace budget.

"Don't worry," Cecilia said, brushing aside Florencia's concerns. "I'll only need to take a few servants with me. And Harper's going too. I've already asked him."

She said this almost defiantly, as if daring Florencia to object. Florencia's face did go pale, but she didn't get a chance to declare how scandalized she was that Cecilia would take along a boy—and a commoner at that—of uncertain relationship. Sophia spoke up first.

"You and Harper walked most of the way across Suala on your own, before. I'm sure you'll be fine," she said, as if trying to butter up Cecilia with her praise. "But the notion of tie votes in your absence *is* a concern. Is there one of us you'd like to designate as your proxy while you're away? That is, someone you would trust to vote on your behalf?"

She fluttered her eyelashes in a way that I'm sure she thought was engaging.

"Good idea!" Cecilia agreed. "I want my—what's it called? Proxy?—to be . . . Desmia."

Sophia's face fell. Clearly she'd thought it would be her, since it had been her idea. Everyone turned to me again. I could count the number of disgruntled expressions around me: Eleven, just among the princesses. I couldn't see all the advisers and counselors without turning around—which I wasn't going to do—but the mirrors on the wall before me showed that at least several of them looked disturbed too.

Was Cecilia trying to make the others hate me, giving me two votes to everyone else's one?

Or was she maybe . . . possibly . . . conceivably . . . treating me like a friend?

2

I drifted along the edge of the ballroom. We'd decided to throw Cecilia a farewell party—over Florencia's objections that it was too much expense after we'd just thrown a similar good-bye banquet and ball for Jed and Ella and the other Fridesians only the week before.

"Why couldn't we have planned ahead and just said good-bye to everyone at once?" Florencia had argued.

"Because . . . not everyone is leaving at once?" Sophia argued back. "And would you want to make Cecilia feel like she's just an afterthought to Fridesians?"

Sophia evidently planned to keep lobbying for Cecilia's proxy vote right up until the moment Cecilia left. Either that, or she was trying to stir up animosity again toward the Fridesians.

Is there any reason she'd want us to go back to war? I wondered. *Are there any sword makers or armor makers paying her off, or . . . is there some other reason I'm not even thinking of?*

I couldn't be sure. I'd been ruling with the other girls for a full month now, and still the only one I was even close to trusting was Cecilia.

Is there any way I could convince her not to go? I wondered.

I'd felt melancholy at the good-bye party for Ella and the other Fridesians. Tonight was even worse. Tomorrow I'd be without Ella, Jed, Cecilia, *and* Harper. I might as well be alone.

You were alone for fourteen years, I told myself. *You can handle it.*

That didn't help. Something was gnawing at me tonight, something that went beyond missing Ella or bracing myself to miss Cecilia. Some instinct, some intuition, some . . . fear. I found myself watching the dancers before me with the same kind of anxiety I'd always associated with standing on the palace balcony hoping that the palace mathematicians had calculated correctly, and no archer's arrow really could soar high enough to pierce my heart.

One, two, three, four, five, six, seven . . . It was hard to keep track with all the whirling and spinning and leaping, but I thought I saw twelve tiara-style crowns gleaming out in the midst of the dancing. So all the other princesses were out there. All of them had already paired off.

I should have warned them, I thought. *Do they all understand that a dance with a princess is never just a dance? Do they know that they need to be on guard for entreaties and double-talk and deviousness even between dance steps? Do they know that their choice of dance*

partners is never just a girl's whim, but a decision the rest of the court
will be discussing and dissecting and probably disdaining the rest of
their lives?

My gaze swept over the dance floor again, giving me a
quick glimpse of Lydia's freckled face, beaming; Porfinia's
lovely green eyes, glowing with excitement; and Adoriana's
exquisitely tiny hand, cupped over her mouth as she laughed
and laughed and laughed.

Even if I trusted all my sister-princesses enough to speak to
them with complete honesty, how could I destroy all that joy?
How could I ruin their innocence, their happiness like, like...

Like Lord Throckmorton ruined yours? my brain offered.

"Don't tell me you of all people don't know how to dance
the galliard!" a voice exclaimed behind me.

I spun around, the broad bell of my skirt twisting a little
too vigorously before settling back into place.

"Cecilia!" I cried. "Never mind me—why aren't *you*
dancing at your own ball?"

I tried to hide the panic I felt at finding out I'd miscounted
the number of princesses dancing.

Hardly a disastrous mistake, I counseled myself. *Don't look*
out and count again. Focus on Cecilia. It's all right for the two of you
to be seen speaking together.

"What, you want me to *start* the trip to Fridesia with a
broken leg?" Cecilia joked. "That's how all that leaping would
end for me."

"It's just the *cinq pas*—five steps—then a cadence, the

leap, and then the posture, the landing," I said, narrating as the dancers before us swept through each motion. I refrained from adding, *It's easy*.

"Easier said than done, I'm sure," Cecilia said, almost as if she knew what I had been thinking. But Cecilia also flashed me a grin that wasn't dignified enough to be fake. Or particularly regal. It was too wide, too open, too . . . happy.

I was strangely tempted to blurt out, *Why did you give me your proxy vote? Do you consider me a friend? Will you miss me in Fridesia? Whom should I trust while you're gone?*

But of course I couldn't say any of that. Fourteen years of palace life had taught me the importance of being circumspect.

Like all the other princesses, Cecilia had also gotten fourteen years of royal training. But it was all at night, in secret—the rest of the time Cecilia had to pretend to be an ordinary peasant girl. I couldn't figure out if Sir Stephen, Cecilia's royal tutor, wasn't a particularly effective teacher, or if Cecilia was just too good at pretending to be a peasant.

If you didn't count servants, I'd never actually met any peasants, so how would I know?

Cecilia started giggling.

"Can you imagine if Sir Stephen *had* tried to teach me court dancing, rather than just showing me pictures?" she asked, gesticulating so wildly that she hit me in the arm. Again—very nonroyal. And yet . . . endearing.

"Perhaps he intended to," I murmured diplomatically.

"With his arthritic gait?" Cecilia gave a very un-princess-like snort. "And perhaps with Nanny Gratine helping?" Cecilia's nanny, who had also raised her, was just as ancient as the former knight Sir Stephen. "I would have thought the dance properly went like . . ."

Cecilia began a shuffling imitation of the steps of the galliard. In place of the leap, she lifted her shoulders and grimaced and looked down at her feet as if she couldn't understand why they hadn't flown up from the floor.

Cecilia had just as much of a talent as Lydia did for being comical, and she didn't mind showing it. Two or three people standing nearby began to chuckle. Out on the dance floor, the six couples closest to us began dancing exactly as Cecilia had: just as stiffly, just as humorously. I was sure I'd see this version of the galliard in the court jester's act soon—and probably in ballrooms the rest of my life.

Do you not see how everything we do is watched and imitated? How nothing is private? I wanted to snarl at Cecilia. *Do you not understand how completely this is the Palace of Mirrors?*

But scolding Cecilia would be like kicking a puppy. My only experience with dogs was one time when a maid smuggled a spaniel puppy into the palace, just to let me see. It was one of those rare moments in my childhood when someone tried to be kind. But the maid was caught, and Lord Throckmorton had . . .

Never mind, I told myself, because it would not do for one of the thirteen princesses of Suala to be seen at a ball with tears welling in her eyes.

I turned slightly, to block Cecilia's view of the dance floor, and to check the nearest mirror to make sure my troubled thoughts left no outward sign or blemish in my expression.

Cecilia jostled me just as she had at the coronation, just as she did so often at council meetings.

"Yes, silly, you still look absolutely, breathtakingly beautiful," Cecilia teased. "Like always. And, no, you don't have a single hair out of place, and neither your rouge nor your powder nor the balm on your lips has smudged . . . Don't worry. You're still perfect."

"It is hard to glance anywhere in this palace without seeing a mirror," I murmured, looking down.

"Perhaps you all should banish mirrors at the next council meeting," Cecilia suggested. "So that when I come back, I won't have to see that *my* hair is perpetually mussed, and my crown is always crooked . . . and right now it looks like I'm even sweating—no, *perspiring*, I mean—"

"And you still look stunning, no matter what," Cecilia's friend Harper said, coming up behind her. He handed her a crystal goblet of punch, and I understood that the only reason I'd had those few moments of talking to Cecilia alone was because he'd temporarily left her side to bring her something to drink.

I liked Harper. The way Cecilia told the story of their misguided journey to the palace to rescue me, Harper deserved far more credit than she did for worrying about me from the very start. But somehow, standing alongside the two of them tonight reminded me of an odd sort of math, where two plus one didn't equal three, but stayed starkly separate: a couple and an outsider.

Cecilia put her free arm around Harper and drew him close, so both of them were leaning toward me.

"Can we tell you a secret?" Cecilia asked in a near-whisper. "We're not going to announce anything as official as a betrothal yet, but... Harper and I are going to get married. Someday. Not too far into the future."

"If she'll have me," Harper added, beaming. Clearly he was confident that she would.

"Congratulations!" I said. "Felicitations!"

I tried to smile sincerely. Shouldn't I be happy for them? Not . . . feel lonelier?

I told myself my problem was just that I could hear in my head how Lord Throckmorton would assess the situation: *Harper's just a boy, and a common one at that. How could a princess marry him? He talks like a peasant and he thinks like a peasant and he acts like a peasant, and putting him in courtier's clothing doesn't change that . . .*

The truth was, even in his formal waistcoat, Harper still looked like a peasant. He just looked like one who happened to be wearing a courtier's clothing. He had even more freckles than Lydia, and his hair stuck up in a cowlick at the back of his head. And he'd pushed up his sleeves as if he were a common laborer in a cotton workshirt. Didn't he know how easy it was to crush the pile of velvet?

Can't you focus instead on how much they adore each other? I asked myself.

"It will be wonderful to have a wedding here in Suala," I said. I decided to tease a bit. "Is *that* why you were so insistent on going to Jed and Ella's wedding? To get ideas?"

"I would have wanted to go, regardless," Cecilia said. "They're my friends."

She clapped her hand over her mouth, as if she'd suddenly realized that that could have been viewed as insulting. Ella and Jed were my friends too, and I wasn't going.

"Anyhow, don't tell anyone else our secret. It's just between us." Cecilia seemed to be hoping I hadn't noticed her gaffe. She angled Harper toward the mirror, as if to let him admire himself. "Doesn't Harper look handsome tonight?"

I nodded, even though it seemed that Cecilia and Harper were now too busy gazing at each other in the mirror to notice. This was not the time to say, *I'll miss you when you're in Fridesia,* or, *Are you sure you have to go? Can't you change your mind?*

"Well, everyone should get an eyeful of me now if they want it, because I won't wear anything like this on the road to Fridesia," Harper said. "Five whole weeks with no monkey suits!"

"You will take your harp with you, though, won't you?" I asked, to head off any debate about his attire once he reached the Fridesian court.

"Of course he will. Ella asked him to play at her wedding,"

Cecilia answered for him. "She loves his new style of music!"

Cecilia and Harper acted as though Harper had been tortured because his mother forced him to take music lessons his entire childhood. But his mother had just been appointed music master for the palace.

Is she *someone I could trust after Cecilia and Harper leave?* I wondered.

I barely knew the woman.

"Everyone loves Harper's music," I murmured, for politeness. But my gaze wandered back toward the great crowd of dancers.

One, two, three, four, five, six, seven . . .

This time I really was certain that all of the princesses were accounted for: eleven whirling out on the dance floor, only Cecilia and me standing off to the side. The crowns of the eleven dancing princesses glittered more brightly than ever. It struck me that there was something odd about how dramatically all those crowns glowed, as if the ballroom was lit by something more than candlelight reflected by dozens of mirrors.

At the same time, I heard the panicked scream from across the room: "Fire!"

3

"Let's get you two out of here, then I'll help put the fire out," Harper said, grabbing both Cecilia and me by the arm.

I realized he was showing more chivalry than the actual, true royal courtiers I saw abandoning their dance partners and scurrying for the nearest door.

Harper tugged on my arm, but I stood firm, watching the flames. They were reflected so many times in all the mirrors that it was easy to be dazzled by them, and hard to see where they had begun. But all of the draperies along the north wall were ablaze now. The tapestries along the east wall were starting to sizzle and burn too.

Did a dozen candles slip and fall from the sconces on separate walls all at the same time? I wondered. *In such a way that each one of the candles just happened to land on flammable fabric?*

It was a ludicrous thought. It was impossible.

"The fire's been set!" I hissed. "Somebody started those fires. They're still starting them!"

Even as I spoke, the first of the south-wall draperies went up in flame too.

The three of us were standing by the west wall—the only one still untouched by flame.

"Quick—the secret passages!" I cried.

Now I tugged on Cecilia's and Harper's arms—and the two of them resisted.

"You don't hide inside a wall when a fire breaks out!" Cecilia protested. "You go outside! Where it's safe!"

"I don't think it's safe outside right now," I argued. "I think that's where they want us to go!"

I didn't think I needed to spell out who *they* were—the unknown, unseen people starting the fires, the source of the hidden danger I'd known was there all along.

Only, now it had burst out into the open.

Cecilia and Harper were both still staring at me blankly. Oh—they hadn't heard me over the crackling flames and the screaming crowd. Even in the midst of a fire, I'd automatically used my carefully modulated bell-like, palace-approved voice.

Panicked dancers swarmed past us; the dance floor was now engulfed in smoke. The smoke was like something alive: hunching, stretching, advancing, retreating . . . Even if the flames at the bottom of the draperies and tapestries were beaten back, the smoke bearing down on the crowd could still win. The smoke spun, trailing behind dancers frantically fleeing the dance floor, and for an instant I had a clear view of one of the girls in the shiny golden crowns. It was a

sister-princess with dark hair, one in an aquamarine dress—
Rosemary? Fidelia? I wasn't close enough to see a face; in the
panic and smoke and fear, I couldn't remember who had been
wearing which dress.

I have to get her out through the secret passages too, I thought,
actually stepping toward the flames and smoke.

The smoke swirled; my next glimpse showed two men
sidling up beside Rosemary/Fidelia and putting arms around
her shoulders.

Oh good, somebody else is taking care of her, I thought. *So I
don't have to worry.*

Except that, in the next instant, the princess in the
aquamarine dress crumpled to the floor, and the two men
moved away as though that was what they'd intended all along.

If thirteen princesses die in a tragic palace fire, what then? I
wondered. *Who would dare to question it? Who would risk offending
whatever ruler replaces us?*

I was still clutching Cecilia's and Harper's arms. Something
pounded in my heart, a feeling too intense for the palace.
Even if I failed at everything else—even if I myself died—I
had to save Cecilia and Harper. They were so innocent, so
good, so out of place in this palace of smoke and mirrors.

A surge of strength flowed through me, and I shoved
Cecilia and Harper toward the wall.

"Go!" I screamed, all modulation gone from my voice
now.

All three of us slammed into the stone wall—had we

been running too fast? I let go of the other two just long enough to run my fingers along a familiar crack in the stone, to spring a release that almost nobody else knew about. A door in the stone appeared, the opening just wide enough to squeeze through.

I glanced back quickly. The smoke had grown in the past few moments; now it rose like another wall behind us. But I was grateful for it now. Since I couldn't see anybody clearly through the smoke, surely that meant that nobody could see me.

I shoved first Cecilia, then Harper through the opening to the secret passages.

"Save Cecilia!" I screamed in Harper's ear. "Go down two flights of stairs, there's a way out to the street . . ."

I was relieved that there was no hint of smoke in the secret passageway. Flames and smoke rose, didn't they? Wouldn't Cecilia and Harper be safe climbing downward?

"Oh yes, through the torture chamber," Cecilia shouted. "I remember now! I know the exact door!"

"Then go straight on to Fridesia," I commanded. "Leave immediately! There's something going on here, some danger none of us knew about. . . . Save yourselves!"

It was terrible that sending them to the land of our former enemies seemed the best way to save their lives.

"Tell Ella and Jed!" I added, taking a step back. "Get their advice! Let them help you figure everything out . . ."

I began easing the door shut between me and Cecilia

and Harper. Harper's face went pale behind his freckles, and Cecilia's eyes grew wide, as if it were just now occurring to both of them that I didn't intend to escape through the secret passageway with them.

"Desmia!" Cecilia screamed. "You come too!"

"I'll meet you in Fridesia!" I screamed back, still shoving on the stone door. "It'll be safer if we travel separately! In disguise!"

Stone met stone with a subtle click; the door to the secret passages was hidden once more.

Harper will care most about getting Cecilia to safety, I told herself. *And Cecilia will want to make sure that Harper stays out of danger. . . .*

My heart twisted as I turned to face the smoke again. I couldn't have said if it was because of fear or hope or just the longing to have somebody, someday, love me the way Harper and Cecilia loved each other. Could the other two possibly believe that I would meet them in Fridesia? Could they believe it enough that they'd manage to save their own lives?

The other princesses, I reminded myself. *They need to be rescued, too . . .*

The smoke was so thick now that it was impossible to see more than a foot or two in any direction. My eyes stinging, I hunched over, because the smoke seemed to thin a bit lower down. Was that the glint of a golden crown off through the tendrils of smoke? Was that a girl in an aquamarine dress still lying on the floor?

You knew there was still danger, I chided myself. Even I hadn't known to fear fire, but at least I'd known to be on guard. *You should have warned the others; you should have told them a ball is always more than just giggling and dressing up and dancing.You let them stay too innocent and now you owe it to them to save them . . .*

It was undignified and unroyal to crawl—not to mention, incredibly difficult in a ball gown. But I dropped to my knees anyway. I took a deep breath and held it, then lumbered forward even though the smoke hid my destination from view. I bumped into something that might have been the fluffy layers of an aquamarine dress covering an unconscious princess.

Not dead, I told myself. *Surely not dead yet. . . . Surely those two men didn't actually kill her. . . .*

I grappled for ankles or wrists, hands or feet—something to pull on, anyway. I could check for a pulse later, when the unknown princess and I were both safe. A shoe came off in my hands and I wasted time staring at it stupidly for a moment, noticing the arch of the heel, the golden filigree meant to loop daintily from ankle to toe.

"We'll take care of her, princess," a man's voice said from behind me. "We'll take care of you both."

How did he know I was a princess from behind, in all this smoke? I wondered.

Then I remembered my own crown, still glistening on my head.

I'd been an idiot. In a ballroom where people were setting

drapes and tapestry on fire and going around knocking princesses unconscious—or dead—I should have taken my crown off first thing, disguised my identity before taking a single step in any direction.

I spun to face my supposed rescuer—or assailant. I hoped I would be able to tell the difference at a glance. But I was still holding my breath. The thoughts, *You're running out of air! You're going to have to take another breath!* pounded in my head, making me dizzy. I couldn't see the man before me very well; his hulking shape seemed to waver in and out of focus.

"Princess," the man purred, patting my arm.

I couldn't decide which threatened me most: The lack of air in my lungs? The overwhelming smoke around me? The stinging sensation on my arm?

And then I couldn't decide anything, because everything went black.

4

I awoke.

In . . . a bed, is it? I wondered groggily, feeling what could have been soft cotton sheets tucked around me.

I heard no crackle of flames, no shrieks of panicked courtiers in fear for their lives. So it seemed I was in no imminent danger from fire, at least.

But maybe . . . from something else . . . ?

I decided it might be wise to learn as much as I could before tipping off anyone else that I was awake.

I let my eyelids flutter, not as if I were waking up, but in the manner of someone suffering from a horrific nightmare. This also gave me a reason to thrash about a bit, to gauge the width of the bed, to snatch quick glimpses of the room on either side of the bed. I let a soft moan escape my lips—the moan of someone deep in sleep, deep in the grasp of a dread-filled dream.

"Princess Desmia?" a woman's voice murmured softly

from the left side of the bed, the same side as a heavily draped window.

Of course I didn't answer. I turned toward the right, still pretending that it was only because of my nightmare thrashing. Then I pretended that I found the sound of my own name comforting, that I was settling back into a soothing slumber.

Actually, I was staring at a wall.

Plaster, not stone; whitewashed, not painted . . . I'm not in the palace anymore, I told myself.

That alone was a shock.

Because my supposed parents, the king and queen, had been murdered, the threat of danger from the unknown assassins had hovered over my first fourteen years. As long as Lord Throckmorton was my guardian, I couldn't remember ever being allowed outside the palace, except to stand on the single balcony high above the adjoining courtyard.

Which meant that, in reality, I might as well have *never* stepped foot outside the palace in my first fourteen years.

And in the month since Cecilia and the other princesses arrived, and Lord Throckmorton and his evil cohorts were unmasked and imprisoned—since everyone else thought the danger was over—somehow there was always too much to be done or watched over within the palace walls for me to take advantage of my new freedom and go outside.

But now I was outside the palace. Now I was exposed.

You're still in a house—still in a structure of some sort, I reminded myself, because my stomach was roiling, my throat was growing tight, my vision was threatening to go dark again. *And, remember, it's not as if being in the palace kept you safe, anyway . . . not as if sharing the palace kept the other princesses safe . . .*

Thinking about the other princesses steadied me a bit. But it also made me too impatient to focus on cataloging the level of ornateness of the pitcher and bowl on the table beside the bed, or to bother with covertly scanning the wall for artwork that might provide clues about my location. Those details wouldn't help me find out what I really wanted to know.

I took a sudden breath as if I'd been startled awake, possibly even by my own dreams. I jerked, and rolled back again toward the left.

"Where . . . am I?" I groaned. "What . . . happened? My sisters—where are my sisters?"

"Shh, princess. Calm yourself."

The voice came from beside the bed again, from a location that seemed to be hidden behind one of the cloth-draped pillars holding up the canopy of the bed. But it was followed by a muted creaking—was the woman sliding forward in her chair, standing up, moving toward me?

She's called me princess twice now, I reminded myself. *Would someone who intended to harm me continue addressing me by my royal title?*

I remembered the princess in the aquamarine dress— *Fidelia,* I thought now, *it had to have been Fidelia*—collapsing between the two men in the smoke-filled ballroom; I remembered the two men stepping past Fidelia's crumpled form as carelessly as if she'd been a dropped handkerchief. I also remembered the man standing over Fidelia and me and saying, *We'll take care of you both.*

There were various ways to interpret that. I'd heard it as a threat.

A woman's face appeared at the edge of my vision, just past the regal swoop of cloth hanging from the canopy.

I couldn't place this woman. She wasn't someone from the palace—I was sure of that. I would have recognized at least the face of all but the lowliest palace servant, and this woman was clearly not a lowly servant.

You always knew there were plenty of people in the world outside the palace as well, I chided myself, though that was a matter I'd only taken on faith for most of my life.

This woman's air of dignity seemed suited for palace life, anyway. Her silver hair was pulled back in a distinguished style, held in place by matching combs that might have been pewter—an interesting choice: expensive without being flashy, understated without being dull. Her skirt and blouse were deceptively simple; perhaps only someone like me, who'd been raised with the finest of goods, would be able to see that they were of the highest quality, stitched together with extreme care.

"Who . . . are you?" I asked, and was dismayed that a tiny frisson of panic sounded in my voice.

I wasn't accustomed to meeting new people without

being fully briefed ahead of time. Or—without spying on them first.

The woman cleared her throat reprovingly.

"You may address me," she said, "as Madame Bisset."

I had to feign a sudden, overwhelming weakness that demanded I close my eyes again. I couldn't let this woman see that I recognized the name: my Fridesian friend Ella had told stories of clashing with a woman named Madame Bisset back home in her kingdom's palace.

Could it possibly be the same woman? I wondered. *Or a sister? Or . . .*

A sister would not have the same last name as a *Madame* Bisset. Perhaps it was a sister-in-law? Or not a relation at all? For all I knew, Bisset could be an extremely common name in some other part of the world.

But it wasn't in Suala. I had heard the name only in connection with the villain in Ella's stories. Even though Ella, telling it, had admitted, *Oh, how Madame Bisset would have loved you, Desmia! Because you are neat and tidy and careful and polite and everything else Madame Bisset thought a princess should be . . .*

I decided it best to go on pretending the name meant nothing to me. If Ella and Madame Bisset hated each other, mentioning Ella's name wouldn't help. I forced myself to open my eyes again, struggle a bit higher on the pillows, and extend my hand.

"My apologies," I murmured demurely. "I find my mind

is still so . . . foggy. It is a pleasure to meet you, and I thank you for watching over me so carefully. My last memory is of collapsing in the smoke at the ball. . . . To whom shall I address my thanks for rescuing me? Could you please summon my sisters so we can make a statement of gratitude together?"

Now it was Madame Bisset's turn to hide her expression as she took my hand. Madame Bisset bowed her head slightly—it was probably meant to look respectful, but the motion made me distrust the woman even more.

"Alas, my dear princess, what you request cannot be granted," Madame Bisset said. The heavy sorrow in her voice gave me chills.

"Why ever not?" I had to work to keep a calm tone. My voice was still as bell-like as always, but I let it also contain a hint of a threat: *Do as I say, or else! You do not cross Sualan royalty!*

Madame Bisset patted my hand.

"My dear child, you cannot be ready to hear this," the woman murmured. "Rest yourself awhile longer yet, then perhaps . . ."

I noted the shift in terminology. I was no longer a "dear princess," only a "dear child."

"Tell me," I commanded, my voice steely.

Madame Bisset blinked back something that might have been tears. Or at least the pretense of them.

"Poor, dear Desmia," Madame Bisset crooned, shaking

her head despairingly. "Do you not yet grasp the tragedy? You were the only princess to escape that ballroom." A kind person would have left it at that. But Madame Bisset did not. She clutched my hand and drove the awful news home: "All of your sister-princesses are dead."

5

I don't believe you, I thought, and though I had fourteen years of experience being controlled and restrained and cautious, it was all I could do not to scream at this woman, *You lie! Stop your vicious lies this instant!*

I lowered my head, because that would be expected of me. But I was sure my eyes glinted with anger, not grief, so it was a relief to hide that.

I know Cecilia escaped the ballroom, I reminded myself. *I saw it with my own eyes. I shut the door behind her. She was safe! Or, in any event, if she ran into further danger, it wasn't in the ballroom....*

Only, was it possible that after I walked away, intending to rescue Fidelia, perhaps Cecilia and Harper came back out of the secret passageway, back into the burning ballroom? Could they possibly have returned intending to rescue me?

No! screamed through my head. *They couldn't have! Harper wouldn't have let Cecilia risk her life like that....*

But hadn't Harper and Cecilia risked their lives thinking they would save mine once before?

No, no, no, no, no, no, no . . .

Tears dripped down my face—*As they should*, I told myself. *You are only pretending, behaving the way this horrible woman expects you to. You are hiding knowledge she doesn't know you have. You are protecting yourself, and Cecilia and Harper as well, because they won't be able to escape to Fridesia if you tip off anyone about where they are going. . . .*

A tiny voice inside my head whispered, *But what if any part of what Madame Bisset told you is true? Aren't you sad if any of your sister-princesses are dead?*

I couldn't let myself feel anything. Not until I knew what was truth and what was a bald-faced lie.

"Please," I whispered, and maybe the despair in my voice was pretense; maybe it wasn't. "Please. I must see my sisters. See their . . . bodies. I must bid them farewell. I must hug them good-bye."

Madame Bisset's grip on my hand began to feel like a trap. A cage.

"You are delirious with grief," Madame Bisset said. "You do not know what you are asking. I cannot permit you to see your sisters as they are now. The flames . . . Well, 'tis better for you to remember them as they were before the ball. Not disfigured and . . . charred."

The "charred" seemed like a deliberate cruelty. It felt like a sword thrust, meant to loosen any remnants of my self-control. It appeared to be carefully designed to send me into true delirium and total, babbling grief.

But I had lived with fourteen years of Lord Throckmorton's cruelty, both his casual, unthinking, everyday sort and the premeditated scheming that controlled all those around him. It was not that I was immune to such heartlessness, but I did know how to gird myself against it, how to pretend to be unaffected.

Does she already know that Cecilia escaped—and maybe others, too? I wondered. *Is she trying to shock me into telling her everything I know, just because I'd want to deny the possibility that what she's telling me is true?*

I couldn't yet piece together why anyone would have set the ballroom on fire in the midst of Cecilia's farewell ball. I couldn't see any benefit to the crime, unless it eliminated all thirteen girls. But I could see a scenario building in my mind, one built of equal parts hope and fear:

Suppose every single one of us—except, perhaps, Cecilia—was rendered unconscious and then dragged from the flames, I thought. *Suppose all over the city the other sister-princesses are waking up in houses like this, being told by strange women, "You are the sole remaining princess."*

Suppose our reactions are being gauged and compared, and all of us will be killed except for the one who is judged the most malleable, the most easily controlled. . . .

It did not seem like such a far-fetched idea. Was this so very different from what had happened back at the beginning, when all of us were babies?

I will not be the pawn this time, I told myself. *But I have to keep pretending. . . .*

"I must go to the palace!" I cried as I jerked my hand back from Madame Bisset's grip and threw off the coverlet weighing down my legs. "I must assure the Sualan people that *they* are safe, even in this time of tragedy. I must assure them that their government is yet strong, in my hands, and that the other princesses they loved will be remembered well. . . ."

I had to bite my tongue to keep myself from adding, *And that the miscreants who set this fire will be caught and punished—* because what if I shouldn't even acknowledge that I knew the fire had been deliberately set?

Madame Bisset put her hand over my wrist this time— encircling it, pinning it to the bed. With her other hand, Madame Bisset tugged the coverlet back into place over my legs.

"Spoken like true royalty," the woman murmured admiringly, even as she held me back from taking any of the actions I'd listed. "To think of the people of your kingdom, even at this time of grief . . ."

"Then let me go!" I insisted. I tried to assume the tone of Sophia, who was the best of any of us at ordering people around. "I command it."

Madame Bisset looked down mournfully. But she didn't let go of my wrist.

"My dear girl," she said. "Why do you persist in forcing me to tell you all the bad news at once? Your people will understand that you need time. . . . Can you not simply lie back and rest, and let yourself recover from one shock before requesting another?"

How can anyone who's been told there's more bad news not demand to hear it immediately? I wondered.

"Tell me," I said through gritted teeth. I glanced down, already thinking of the impression I'd need to make, stepping back into the palace. I'd have to leave no doubt that I was in charge. I would have to start someone hunting down the arsonists. I'd have to find out what portion of the story Madame Bisset had told was true—or if any of it was.

But I wouldn't make much of an impression sweeping into the palace in a nightgown.

"Tell me fast—and then send a servant child over to the palace, to bring me a daydress to speak to my subjects in," I added.

"I can't," Madame Bisset said.

This was not simply clutching a wrist a moment too long. This was insubordination, clear and certain.

If I didn't punish it instantly, there was no telling what Madame Bisset might do next.

"Because there is no palace anymore," Madame Bisset continued.

I stared at her. The woman sighed and turned to the heavy drapes behind her. She whipped them aside, revealing a scene of still-smoking rubble in the incongruously bright sunlight.

"I am so sorry," Madame Bisset murmured. "The palace burned completely to the ground."

6

Madame Bisset seemed to expect me to be more distressed about losing my palace than losing my sisters.

And I was more . . . stunned, anyway.

Because I still have hope for my sisters. And I was worried about them all along. I knew they were fragile and unprotected. But the palace . . .

The palace had survived hundreds of years of Sualan royalty living and dying, being born and growing old. It had outlasted twelve generations of the people I still thought of as my ancestors.

But I couldn't deny that it was gone now.

Unless . . .

"That's not the palace!" I protested. "You're just showing me . . . some other building that burned!"

Even as I spoke I could see a courtyard between me and the rubble: It was the same courtyard that I'd faced every day from the palace balcony. I was just on the other side of it now.

I must be lying in one of the houses across from the palace.

The yellow one with the gingerbread trim? I wondered. *Or the red one with the outline of dragons on the roof?*

I was amazed that I could still think of such frivolous things as gingerbread trim and fanciful wooden dragons. What did it matter which house I was in?

Because . . . you're going to have to escape, I thought.

This was a big shock too. But it made sense. Somebody had put the other girls and me in danger—maybe even killed some of the others. Somebody had burned down the Palace of Mirrors, the only home I'd ever known. Somebody had deposited me with this strange woman who may or may not be Ella's worst enemy.

Was it an overreach of logic to suspect that the first two crimes probably meant that I was still in danger here and now?

"Desmia?" Madame Bisset said softly, and I recognized the tone. This was how Lord Throckmorton often operated: Just when he'd driven me to the brink of madness with his conniving, he'd turn around and be unexpectedly kind.

Except, I had quickly learned that his kindness was always fake. It was like a velvet glove on the hand that beat me.

Madame Bisset doesn't yet know that I consider her my enemy, I reminded myself.

"How . . . ?" I began, and I didn't have to fake the tone of shock. "How did it even start? How is it possible that *everything* is gone . . . my sisters, my palace . . . and the others who were there that night? How many of the courtiers, the servants, are . . . are . . ."

I acted like I couldn't bear to speak the word, "dead." Only, I wasn't sure that it was an act. Maybe I really couldn't.

"No," I moaned. "Don't tell me about the others. Not while I'm still absorbing the news about my sisters. . . ."

I was dangerously close to admitting a truth. I couldn't think about anyone but the other princesses right now.

Madame Bisset patted my hand, as if rewarding me for my shocked, stunned, humbled tone.

Shocked, stunned people are probably easier to fool, I thought darkly.

I made myself listen carefully to Madame Bisset's answer.

"It is believed that one of the ribbons festooning the ballroom came loose, and perhaps blew into one of the candles," Madame Bisset said. "There was a devilish breeze last night—did you notice?"

How could anyone believe that story? I wondered. *How could one loose ribbon set three long walls of draperies and tapestries on fire in the blink of an eye?*

But it was probably like everything else in the palace— people tended to believe whatever gave them an advantage, whatever gave them greater power or diminished their enemies'.

Probably everyone in Suala would believe this story of the ribbon and the devilish breeze if they felt they needed to.

"But . . . people can escape from fires," I said. I didn't have to work very hard to keep my tone of being stunned senseless. "There were windows. And . . . the palace servants are trained to start a bucket brigade when there's a fire. . . . They *practice*. How could all our safeguards have failed completely?"

"Not completely—*you* survived," Madame Bisset reminded me.

I winced. Was Madame Bisset trying to make me feel guilty? Or powerless?

Madame Bisset began to toy with a loose thread on my coverlet.

"It turns out that there were secret passageways honeycombed throughout the castle," Madame Bisset said. "Perhaps the knowledge of them vanished decades ago. But the flames found those passageways—they climbed from one level of the palace to another, and the people fighting the fire had no hope of following. They could not understand why the flames kept popping up in new places—and once the new outbreaks were discovered, it was too late. So . . . everything burned."

I sank deeper into the pillows.

Cecilia . . . I thought. *Harper . . .*

Had the secret passageways already been burning when I sent my friends into them? Had I actually condemned them to death when I was trying so hard to save their lives?

The secret passageways didn't smell like smoke, I reminded myself. *And flames climb up. Cecilia and Harper were climbing down. I saw where the fire started. In the ballroom.*

Wasn't I right?

"Desmia?" Madame Bisset said. "You've gone pale. This is too much for you to hear, while you're still so fragile yourself."

I could feel the color draining from my face. I could see how my dainty hand nestled in the sheets was just as white as my bedding and nightgown. But my time in the palace had taught me that "fragile" was a word that could be used like handcuffs. It was meant to make me feel frail and useless and trapped. It was meant to keep me from thinking I had any power or control.

"I would like to be alone with my grief," I murmured, which was the only way I could think of to fight back.

A gentle half smile played across Madame Bisset's face. It was probably supposed to look sympathetic and kind, but I saw glee behind it.

Madame Bisset thinks I have given up, I thought. *She thinks I will be malleable now. She thinks she can use me.*

The question was, what did Madame Bisset want to use me *for*?

7

Madame Bisset left the room.

I took that as a sign that I'd acted sufficiently devastated by all the bad news; I'd fooled her into thinking that I was so fragile and frail and mind-numbingly grief-stricken that I would be incapable of coming up with any plots of my own.

What if I am so mind-numbingly grief-stricken that I'm incapable of coming up with any plots of my own? I wondered.

My heart throbbed. I hadn't known it could do that: hold so much pain and regret and fear that the agony seemed to come in waves.

Potential pain, I told myself, fighting back again. *It's still possible that everything Madame Bisset told you was a lie.* I glanced out the window, toward the smoking devastation that only last night had been the most impressive palace in six kingdoms. *Except the part about the palace burning down. But just because the palace is in ruins, that doesn't mean that anything else Madame Bisset told you is true.*

I wanted to slide down deeper under the coverlet. I wanted to cry and cry and cry. I wanted someone—not Madame Bisset, but someone who truly cared, someone sincere—to pat me on the shoulder and say, *There, there. Everything's fine. All you've lost is a palace, and those are easily enough rebuilt. . . .*

I imagined Ganelia, the sister-princess who was fascinated by everything architectural, actually being delighted to have a chance at designing a new palace. I imagined Florencia arguing over the cost of all the frills and furbelows Ganelia would want to include on a new palace. I imagined both of them—and the other ten—still gloriously alive.

I have to act to Madame Bisset as though I believe they're dead, I told myself. *But for myself, to keep from plunging into the depths of grief, I have to hold on to the faith that they survived . . .*

And what did I have to do to make sure that I myself stayed safe? So that, if it was still possible, I could rescue the others from wherever they were being held?

Was I safe enough in this house that I could take time to cry?

No, I told myself.

I shoved back the coverlet and the sheets. Chilly air rushed at me, and for a moment I hesitated.

This Madame Bisset might not actually be the same evil woman that Ella told me about, I thought. *It might be that everything Madame Bisset told me is true, and she really does have my best interests at heart. . . .*

I had lived with liars and conniving schemers my entire life. I recognized the signs.

I knew when I was in danger.

Just think about escaping, I commanded myself. *Then you can think about everything else.*

I put one pale, bare foot down on the wood-planked floor.

Splinters, I thought disjointedly. *Shoes.*

I looked around, but there was nothing in the room but the bed, the chair, and the bedside table with its porcelain bowl and pitcher.

I am in a box, I thought, with rising panic. *A cage.*

I shook this off and forced myself to place my other foot down on the floor. I reminded myself that, coming to the palace, Cecilia and Harper had made shoes for themselves by cutting up a felt cloak and sewing the pieces back together in the general shape of footwear. They'd been hideously ugly shoes, but surely they'd given some protection against splinters and nails and the kind of burrowing insects that liked to crawl into feet.

I didn't have a knife or a needle. The sheets or the coverlet would make a poor substitute for felt.

Before they made their ugly felt shoes, Cecilia and Harper walked barefoot all the way to the capital city from their tiny village out in the middle of nowhere, I reminded myself. *They walked barefoot for days.*

Cecelia—and all the other girls—had spent pretty much their entire childhoods totally barefoot, and they'd survived.

Truth be told, even in the palace the twelve of them were constantly, secretly slipping their shoes off, complaining about how shoes pinched and bound.

You can do this, I told myself, putting full weight on my feet, even though nothing lay between them and the surely splinter-filled wood floor.

I could hear a mocking voice in my head—Cecilia or Harper, perhaps, or maybe Rosemary, who was the most sarcastic of the sister-princesses—saying, *Ooo, Desmia, you've managed to stand up all by yourself! Congratulations!*

At this rate, even if the others hadn't died in the palace, they would be dead by the time I found them: dead of old age.

This thought propelled me forward, though I stepped cautiously: afraid of splinters, afraid of creaking floorboards . . . My choice of escape routes was either the door Madame Bisset had exited through, or the window that looked out on the palace ruins. I had an image in my mind of Madame Bisset sitting right outside the door, listening at the crack.

So your only possible escape route is the window, I told myself, trying to be brisk and decisive, when really I felt more like a girl who was terrified of splinters, terrified of making a noise, terrified that I might really have lost practically everyone I'd ever cared about.

I found myself at the windowsill. I appeared to be on the second or third floor, but the roof below the window sloped downward in a way that made it seem possible for someone to shimmy down, clutch the eaves at the bottom of the roof, and then drop safely to the ground from there. I could imagine Ella or Harper or Cecilia doing that—or even one or two of the other sister-princesses—Lydia? Marindia, maybe?

I couldn't actually imagine myself climbing over shingles and eaves.

Think about what Ella had to do to escape from her Madame Bisset in Fridesia, I reminded myself.

Ella had had to dig her way out from a dungeon, starting from the . . . well, hadn't she called it a "crap hole"? Was it possible that chamber pots weren't available in dungeons? Shouldn't I be glad that I would just have to climb down a roof, not through bodily waste?

I wedged my fingertips against the bottom of the window and began trying to raise it.

It didn't budge.

Belatedly I noticed the matching padlocks on either side of the window. Both of the empty keyholes stared tauntingly back at me.

Of course there were padlocks. Of course the keys were missing. Of course Madame Bisset and whomever she was working with would want to keep me locked in my cage— and they could easily pretend that they were just trying to keep me safe.

Locks can be picked, I reminded myself.

This was actually something I was good at—I'd learned in the palace. All I needed was a hairpin, and . . .

I patted my head. I didn't have any hairpins. My dark hair

flowed down my back long and loose and unencumbered, because I'd been put to bed, treated like an invalid.

This, too, could be easily justified. Hadn't Madame Bisset said I needed time to grieve and recover before making myself presentable and going out in public? Hadn't I myself asked for time alone to mourn?

It wouldn't make sense for me to ask to have my hair done in the midst of grieving.

A creaking noise sounded outside my room, beyond the door Madame Bisset had left through. I pictured her sitting in a chair right outside the door, and shifting her weight ever so slightly just to remind me, *I'm out here. I'm listening.*

I pulled my hands back from the window. If Madame Bisset came in, I could say, *I'm just looking at my former palace. I'm trying to see if there's anything left, any memento of my sister-princesses I could ask to have retrieved and preserved. . . .*

Would Madame Bisset instantly understand what I was really doing?

No second creak sounded. The door didn't swing open.

I let out a breath I hadn't realized I'd been holding.

I could fall to my knees and sweep my hands across the floor and hope that some woman who'd stood in this room before me had lost a hairpin that had gotten stuck in the floorboards. Then, assuming there was a hairpin, I could only hope these padlocks were similar enough to palace padlocks that I could open them, and do it quickly enough to flee before Madame Bisset returned.

All of that seemed entirely too painstaking and time-consuming. There wasn't a blazing fire roaring toward me or great clouds of choking smoke spinning in my direction—as far as I knew—but I felt just as much urgency as I had the night before, when my palace was burning before my eyes. I had to know what had happened to the others. If any of them were still alive, I had to find them.

I cast my gaze about the room once more—bed, chair, table, pitcher, bowl. Dashing across the room, heedless of splinters or creaking, I snatched up the porcelain pitcher.

It was heavier than it looked. There was no question that this pitcher could shatter a window.

But—how loudly? I wondered.

I reached back and pulled the sheet from the bed, then wrapped the sheet around the pitcher. There. That would muffle the sound. But would it muffle it enough?

I wished I could somehow test my plan ahead of time before swinging the pitcher at the window full strength, with all my might. I liked practice and preparation and planning things out. But once the window shattered, there'd be no turning back.

I went back to the window and raised the sheet-wrapped pitcher high over my head. As I swung the pitcher forward, I thought of another way to hide the noise: I began wailing, "Oh, my sisters. Oh, I miss my sisters . . ."

It was entirely too easy to start myself wailing and weeping. Breaking the window wasn't as successful: The pitcher bounced back. I'd been too afraid of noise to hit hard enough.

So I did get a test case, I thought.

But I wasn't cautious. I didn't quickly put the pitcher back in place and scramble back into bed and wait to see if Madame Bisset opened the door. Instead, I raised the pitcher again and moaned even louder, "My sisters . . ."

This time I swung the pitcher as hard as I could. Spiderwebs of cracks began spreading across the window, and I held the trailing edge of the sheet up against the window casing to catch the shards of glass as they fell.

"My sisters, my sisters . . ." I sobbed, and to my own ears the sobbing sounded as loud as a roaring fire, as overwhelming as a shattering window.

But I hadn't been thinking straight: Of course the broken glass fell forward, rather than crumbling illogically backward so I could catch it silently with the sheet. The shards of glass slid down the roof, making a sound like cracking ice; even if Madame Bisset didn't hear the noise over my sobbing, how long would it take for someone to notice the broken glass starting to pool on the ground below?

You were an imbecile for doing this in bright sunlight, I told myself. *You were an imbecile for thinking this could work at all. . . .*

I stepped out onto the roof and added a third criticism:

You were an imbecile for doing this barefoot . . .

But I was on shingles now, and there was no turning back. I sat down with the sheet folded beneath me and edged forward, hoping the sheet would work like a sled over ice.

Cecilia wouldn't necessarily have done this any better, but she would have had Harper helping her out, suggesting improvements in the plan, I thought. *They would have figured out together how to do this without getting covered in blood and broken glass....*

I reached the bottom edge of the roof a little too quickly. I had to scramble to find something to hold on to—a gutter? An eaves trough? I barely got my hands around something stone and solid.

Oh, a gargoyle, I thought, looking at the gruesome beast as I slid past.

But my grip was tight around the gargoyle's neck, and though my arms jerked painfully in their sockets, I kept holding on. I came to a stop, my body dangling down from the gargoyle.

For a moment I was filled with love for that gargoyle. His ugly scrunched-together face seemed like the loveliest sight I'd ever seen.

Then I realized that, in my white nightgown in the bright sun, I might as well be a flag or a beacon. Granted, the few people out and about in the courtyard all seemed to be gazing toward the still-smoking ruins of the palace. But it would take only one quickly turned head, one glance toward me, and there'd be screams and shouts and a growing crowd.

So should I use that? I wondered. *Should I cry, "Help! Help!" and get the people's attention and tell them everything?*

There was a follow-up to that thought: *What if they don't*

believe me?What if they think I'm just some crazy girl in a nightgown?

My subjects had seen me only high above their heads, standing on a lofty balcony with a veil over my face. The only people who would recognize me were either possibly dead—like my sister-princesses—or possible enemies.

Like everyone else from the palace, I told myself. *And Madame Bisset.*

If Madame Bisset had heard anything of the breaking window or the falling glass, surely she'd already burst into my room; surely she'd already discovered me missing; surely she was right this minute rushing down the stairs of the house to see where I'd fallen.

I looked down.

I was only six or eight feet off the ground, close enough that, if I'd had shoes on—solid ones, anyway—I would have dared to just let go and drop to the cobblestones below. But my feet were still bare, and I could already see blood on them. And if I dropped straight down from the gargoyle, I'd land directly on shards of glass.

If I jump down into that, I'll drive glass into my feet and legs so forcefully that, that . . .

That I could die.

I gulped. My hands began to sweat, holding on to the gargoyle's neck. I swayed slightly, and then began swinging back and forth, as I frantically tried to keep a grip on the gargoyle. My big toe scraped against a pillar at the front of the house.

Had I already lost so much blood that my mind wasn't working properly anymore? I kept thinking, *Pillar, pillar, pillar . . .*

Oh. I could wrap my legs around that pillar and slide down it slowly and safely. Or, at least, more slowly and safely than jumping into a pile of glass.

From above my head, I heard a faint voice call out, "Desmia?"

Is Madame Bisset just calling to me from outside the room? I wondered. Or has she gone back into the room and found me missing? If she looks out the broken window, can she see my hands on the gargoyle?

How long did I have before Madame Bisset came racing out the front door of the house and discovered me dangling from the gargoyle in my nightgown?

Quickly, I swung my body forward, toward the pillar. On the first pass, I did nothing but scrape my heel on the pillar, leaving behind a smear of blood.

This time you have to swing harder—and let go! I told myself.

I took one hand off the gargoyle and hitched up my nightgown to free my legs. It was shameful and horrifying, but this time when I swung forward I got both legs around the pillar, and locked my ankles together on the other side.

The gargoyle felt less stable in my hand. I threw my arms forward instead, wrapping them around the top of the pillar just as the gargoyle separated from the roof and went crashing down into the pile of glass below.

Even if Madame Bisset hadn't heard anything amiss before, she had to have heard that.

Probably even some of the people gazing into the palace ruins had heard that, and were right now whirling around to see what the latest catastrophe was. But I didn't have time to worry about them. I just focused on scrambling down the pillar, hand over hand, bare legs scraping against the stone. I left streaks of blood everywhere, but I didn't care about that, either.

Finally I was on the ground, in a space that had been protected from the glass by the overhang of the roof. I crouched down and slipped into a space between the house I'd just left and the one next to it.

I did it! screamed through my mind. *I escaped!*

And then arms wrapped around me, pulling me down to the ground.

"I got her!" a voice cried, right in my ear.

8

I struggled blindly to get away. I jerked against the arms clasped around my shoulders.

"No, no, we're here to save you!"

This time it was a voice in my other ear.

I didn't stop struggling, but I twisted around, trying to see who was holding me.

Two pairs of grubby hands, bony wrists sticking out of ragged sleeves . . .

I turned my head. On my left was the scrawniest little beggar boy I'd ever seen.

On my right was . . . I blinked. It *looked* like the same boy, with the same tousled brownish hair and green eyes that gleamed in a dirty face. But right-side boy was bigger. And maybe his shirt had more patches on it, in more variety of colors.

"Look, you try to run away with those bloody feet, *anybody* could follow your trail," right-side boy argued. "We'll get you to safety." He grinned, his white teeth a surprising break in the filth covering his face. "Princess."

He knows who I am? I thought anxiously. Princesses could be captured and held for ransom. Whereas girls who were crazy and running around outdoors in their nightgowns but were otherwise unremarkable . . .

I didn't know much about it, but I guessed that they wouldn't exactly be safe either.

And then the younger boy leaned in closer, and I had trouble remembering what I'd been thinking.

"Here, give me some of that blood, and we'll make it look like you just ran to the house next door," the younger boy said.

He didn't wait for me to agree. He just ran his grubby hand along the bottom of my foot. This made me realize that there were perhaps several small pieces of glass still in the foot, that his touch drove even deeper, bringing out more streams of blood.

"Ow—" I only started to scream; I was already choking it back when right-side boy clapped his hand over her mouth.

"See?" the younger boy said, lightly pressing his hand down onto the packed dirt beside my feet.

He left a smear of blood on the ground, then a second and a third slash of blood leading back out of the alleyway. He disappeared around the corner of the neighboring house. In no time at all, he appeared at the opposite end of the alley, clearly having circled the neighbor's house.

I was still sitting there stunned. I realized I'd just missed my opportunity to run away when there was only one boy holding on to me.

But . . . *he was right about the blood,* I thought dazedly. Maybe I was a little dizzy because I'd lost so much of it. *How could I avoid leaving a trail?*

How was I going to avoid it now? Even with the fake trail of blood leading the wrong way, it wasn't like I was safe and hidden right now.

"No one saw me," the younger beggar boy bragged to the older one. "And no one's come out of the prison house yet."

Prison house? I thought.

"Then we'll try the rug, not hide her in the rain barrel," the older boy said.

He turned and pulled down a curling sheet of . . . well, it was some sort of cloth, wasn't it? Or, it once might have been cloth, before it got so threadbare and filthy that now it could really only be categorized as garbage.

"Climb in," the younger boy said. "Quick!"

I didn't move. Did they mean *me?* Did they mean I should have anything to do with that filthy, rotten, stinking shred of garbage? Was I supposed to touch it? Be *wrapped* in it?

It was bad enough just sitting three feet away from it. Even at that distance I could catch its reek of rotted fish or pus-filled sores or maybe just the world's stinkiest feet.

"Desmia?" I heard Madame Bisset call from around the other side of the house.

Hands shoved me toward the rotting rug, and I didn't resist, not even when the two boys curved the two sides of it around me.

"You've got to lie down flat!" the older boy hissed, and I heard the urgency in his voice, the fear.

They're probably risking their lives, hiding me, I thought, and that made it easier for me to straighten out my legs and let the boys press the filthy, stinking rug tighter against my face.

And then they hoisted me in the air. I could guess from the tilt of the rug that each of them had one end balanced on his shoulder—the bigger boy at the front, the smaller one behind.

"Maybe we'll make it safely away," the older boy murmured.

Just then a voice cried behind them: "Stop!"

It was Madame Bisset.

9

I froze. I held my breath, which had the bonus effect of keeping the reek of the filthy rug out of my nostrils. But it made it so that my hearing seemed to go in and out. It was already muffled enough by the layers of rug wrapped around me.

"Yes, mistress?"

Wasn't that the older boy's voice? But it carried such a tone of innocence that it made him sound much younger.

By the motion of the rug, I could tell that both boys were swinging around to face Madame Bisset.

"Where have you come from? Did you see a girl in a nightgown running past?" Madame Bisset asked.

"In a *nightgown*, mistress?" the younger boy asked. And somehow he sounded even more innocent. He made even me wonder if it was possible for girls in nightgowns to go wandering about at mid day—and I'd just done that myself.

I also noticed that he didn't answer Madame Bisset's first question.

The older boy did instead.

"We'uns are taking this rug from a house over by Downtree to another house in Cordelstaff. The owners couldn't make payments on it, mistress," the older boy said. "Begging your pardon, mistress, for mentioning such places as Downtree and Cordelstaff to the likes of you."

The front part of the rug shifted, and I could imagine the older boy making an apologetic bow, the kind of motion that would accompany the doff of a cap, if the boy actually had a cap.

Madame Bisset sniffed loudly enough that I could hear her through three layers of filthy rug.

"The likes of you should not be in this area of the city," she said haughtily.

"Yes, mistress. We know, mistress," the older boy said, backing away slightly. I recognized this motion too: It was what servants did in the palace, bowing and scraping to proclaim with their every movement, *I am less than you. I am not worthy to be in your presence. I am not qualified to breathe the same air as you.*

Cecilia had practically laughed her head off the first time she'd seen one of these little pantomimes at the palace.

"Seriously?" she'd cried. She'd put her hand on the servant's shoulder and burst out, "Aren't you kind of laughing inside every time you do that? The lower you bow—isn't that secretly a sign that you're mocking us that much harder?"

I had never thought of such a possibility. *Did* servants ever secretly laugh at royalty and courtiers? How could they get away with it? How was it that Cecilia had noticed it immediately, while I'd been totally ignorant my entire fourteen years in the palace? Was Cecilia just smarter than me? Did that mean that she and Harper *had* managed to escape from the fire?

Stop thinking about Cecilia, I told myself, because now there was a lump in my throat that threatened to make me gulp noisily. Maybe it was threatening to make me cry.

And I was missing the older boy's long, convoluted explanation about how his little brother had wanted to see the palace, and so they'd swung through the royal courtyard, "and how sad is it for my little brother that the day he finally gets to see the palace, it's nothing but a pile of smoking stones down on the ground?"

"You better not have been searching through the rubble for items to steal!" Madame Bisset snapped.

"No, mistress. Of course not, mistress," the older boy said. "Once we saw the palace was gone, we didn't even go near."

"We didn't want our rug to catch on fire!" the younger boy added.

"I should have my guards search through your pockets just to be sure," Madame Bisset snarled. Her voice was harder to hear at the end, as if she was turning around, searching for her guards.

"Say, that girl you be looking for . . . might she have had

blood on her feet or shoes?" the little boy asked. "Because, look, there are bloody footprints coming into this alley, and then you can tell, they go back out . . ." The back end of the rug dipped perilously low, and I had to dig my fingers into the filthy, unraveling cloth closest to my hands, just to keep from sliding down. "Look—feel it. The blood isn't even dry yet."

He touched it? He actually thinks Madame Bisset would touch it too? I thought in disgust. Though I didn't know why this should bother me: He'd already touched my blood in order to plant the appearance of fake footprints.

I accidentally let myself breathe out and in again. This brought in such a reek of rot and unthinkable bodily functions that it was all I could do to hold back a gagging noise. I forced myself to concentrate on Madame Bisset's response.

"Ah yes, I see. . . . Guards! Come quick! Follow this trail!" Madame Bisset called out. I could guess that the woman was backing away from the offered chance to touch blood. Then her voice went even louder, as if she'd turned back to face the two boys directly. "And begone with you, beggars! Don't let me see you in this part of the city ever again!"

"No, mistress. Of course not, mistress. We'll be out of your sight directly, mistress," the two boys said, their words running over top of one another.

I felt the rug around me spinning in the other direction. The boys seemed to be settling it back on their shoulders; they seemed to be walking out the rear of the alley at a brisk pace.

I went back to holding my breath. When it came time that I either had to take another breath or faint, I judged that we'd moved far enough away from Madame Bisset and her "prison house."

"Let me out!" I whispered to the section of the rug that I guessed might be closest to the older boy's ear.

"It isn't safe yet!" the boy hissed back. "There are soldiers and guards everywhere! And we don't know who they're loyal to . . ."

"I'm going to faint!" I complained.

"Then faint if you have to!" the boy whispered. It came out more like, "ain i' oo have oo," so I guessed that he was trying to speak without moving his lips. "We'll wake you up when we get where we're going."

I was about to ask, *And where's that?* when the boy hissed, "And stop talking! You aren't safe yet at all!"

Was this true?

I had no way of knowing. I'd been trying to keep track of the path the boys seemed to be following—*right turn, left turn, right turn, right*—but I'd never seen anything of the capital city, Cortona, beyond the palace courtyard, so I wasn't sure if it was likely that there were guards and soldiers about or not. I drew in a measured breath. I could at least try to stay alert, even if I couldn't be sure if it was wisdom or foolishness to trust the two ragged boys.

"Fresh fish!" someone cried nearby. "Get your fresh fish here!"

So are we close to the river? I wondered. *Do the fishmongers sell the fish straight out of the water?*

The voice calling out about the fish blended into another one bragging, "Freshest apples in the market!"

So are we just walking through some large, open market where all sorts of goods are on sale? I wondered. *Could I slide right out of this rug and blend into the crowd?*

I had very little idea of what the common people of Cortona looked like—I'd only ever seen them from behind a veil, from high over their heads. But I suspected that it'd be hard to blend in wearing nothing but a nightgown.

And a nightgown fit for a princess, at that, I reminded myself. I'd marked the difference between the two boys' patched, tattered clothing and the snowy-white perfection of my own garb.

So I'm stuck in this filthy rug until the boys decide it's safe for me to come out?

The horrific odor of the rug seemed worse than ever. The bristly surface pressed painfully against my body; the places where I suspected I had cuts and bruises hurt worse with every bit of jostling. And I had no idea where we were going. Even if I asked, I had no guarantee that the boys would tell the truth. I'd just heard how skillfully they'd lied to Madame Bisset.

In the palace, when I had grown most panicky and despairing, I'd taken to skulking through the secret passageways, listening secretly at hidden doors.

You're already hidden now. So pay attention. Listen.

For a while there seemed to be nothing to hear but vendors plying their wares. Then I started noticing an occasional undercurrent of whispers.

"Get your fresh-baked bread here! Fresh bread!"

"—burned to the ground—"

"Grapes! Pears!"

"—heard nobody found out until—"

"Walnuts! Almonds!"

Why isn't anybody talking about what happened to the princesses? I wondered.

Or were they talking about it, and I just missed every reference?

It was incredibly frustrating to catch only bits and pieces of the conversations around me.

And then we evidently left the marketplace behind, because the voices of the shouting vendors faded. Now it was quiet enough that I could hear the older boy breathing beside me.

It was strange to listen so intently to another human being breathe. I had never done that before. It was too . . . personal. Private. I felt like I had back when Cecilia and Harper first came to the castle, and I'd watched them without their knowing it. That was when I believed that I was the one and only true princess of Suala, and they were impudent interlopers—perhaps even treasonous interlopers. I'd trapped them in my tower, which I thought was the only safe thing to do. And yet, listening to them talk, I felt like I was doing something wrong, in a way that I never worried about when I eavesdropped on the various royal advisers and ministers.

Older raggedy boy was starting to breathe hard. He was probably carrying the bulk of my weight. They'd probably been walking for nearly an hour since they'd left Madame Bisset behind.

"You're going to wear yourself out," I started to say, because I'd learned at the palace that sometimes you could get people to do what you wanted by convincing them you only had their selfish interests at heart.

But at the same time, the little boy started giggling.

"Did you see her face when I touched that blood?" he asked.

"Shush, Herk," the older boy said. "I know it looks like there's nobody around, but, remember, sometimes the walls have ears."

"Fraidy-cat Tog-dog," the younger boy mocked—Herk? Was his name Herk? I guessed that was probably right. I wasn't sure what to pull out as the older boy's name. Surely his parents hadn't named him "Dog." "I'm just talking about the blood I told that lady about. It's not like the walls are going to hear anything I didn't tell her straight out. Was she half-blind? I thought she was never going to see it."

"The likes of her, they're not used to seeing things like blood," the older boy countered. "They're not like us. They pretend messy things don't exist."

"Blood, pee, poo, guts . . . We've seen it all, haven't we, Tog?" Herk crowed.

I felt slightly queasy. Were people even allowed to say words like that on a public street? Hadn't someone in the palace passed a law against it?

I made myself focus on the fact that the younger boy must have just revealed the older boy's name: Tog. It had to be Tog.

"But, by pointing out the blood, you could have made that lady think you were the one who put it there," Tog said. "Like you were trying too hard to make her see it."

Tog's smart, I thought, and this surprised me. Cecilia and Harper had looked a lot like ragamuffins too when they arrived at the palace just over a month ago, but Cecilia had been screaming, "I'm the true princess! I'm the true princess!" pretty much the whole time.

Tog and Herk had seemed perfectly fine with Madame Bisset assuming they were not just filthy beggar children, but stupid as well. Why hadn't they protested?

Oh. Because that would have made it harder for them to rescue me, I realized.

I had plenty of experience with people pretending to be something they weren't. But usually they were pretending to be richer, wiser, craftier, prettier . . . better. Everyone at the palace always pretended to be better than they were.

So Tog and Herk pretended to be worse than they are to rescue me because . . . because . . .

For the life of me, I couldn't figure out why they would

care. It was as big as mystery as what Madame Bisset wanted
to use me for, or what had actually happened to all the other
princesses.

"Oh, that lady would never have suspected me of anything,"
Herk was bragging. "I make my voice go like this"—it shot
up, high and innocent—"and people think butter wouldn't
melt in my mouth."

"We'd have to have some butter, first," Tog muttered.
"Anyhow, Mam always sees through you."

Herk didn't argue with this.

Mam, I thought. *So even these beggar boys have what I've always
been missing. A mother.*

The front of the rug dipped down, and even with my
face wrapped tightly in the rug, I could tell by the deepening
shadows that the boys were stepping out of the sunshine and
into a darker area. Perhaps they were descending stairs into
a basement?

They stopped and there was a creaking noise—a door
opening? And then I felt the rug around me sliding lower,
lower, lower . . . Was I on the ground now?

"We found her, Mam!" Herk cried, his voice so jolly that
I could imagine him doing a jig for joy. "We found her! She's
alive!"

"Praise the Lord!" a woman's voice called back to him.
"Where? What are the fortifications like? Would it be possible
to rescue—"

"Mam, we already rescued her!" Tog said, and his voice

was even merrier than Herk's. "She's right here! In the rug!"

And then I found myself spinning out of the rug. Eager hands rolled me out into the light. The last bit of the bristly, reeking rug came off my face, and I found myself practically nose to nose with a beaming young woman. She crouched down and threw her arms around my shoulders, lifting me up into a seated position to be swallowed in a huge embrace.

"I've missed you so much!" the woman cried. She held me at arm's length for a moment, then drew me back into an even tighter hug. "And you've grown so since the last time I saw you . . ."

When had this woman ever seen me? From high overhead, on the balcony of the palace? And why would that make this woman think she had to right to touch me, let alone hug me? Nobody hugged me in the palace. Actually, Cecilia and one or two of the other sister-princesses had tried, but it always felt strange. Unnatural. The last time someone had pulled me this close, it had been Lord Throckmorton trying to strangle me.

I pushed back at the woman, shoving her away.

"Who *are* you?" I demanded.

The woman looked . . . hurt. Was she some sort of lunatic who didn't understand the rules of polite society? Or was she just as much of a beggar as Herk and Tog, and that was why she didn't understand how to behave?

Her clothes were clean but awfully ragged. She was dressed as simply and poorly as the boys, with a threadbare dress and apron and kerchief. Her long dark hair seemed to be tied back with a raveling string.

"Desmia, don't you remember me?" the woman gasped. She still had a hold on my shoulders, but it was shakier now. Less certain. "I know I've changed in the past ten years, but . . . I'm Janelia."

Something about that name burrowed deep into my brain. Or sparked something in my mind. But it was just a momentary flash and then it was gone, and I could do nothing but stare blankly at the woman.

The woman slipped her hands down to clutch my arms, one on each side. It was hard to say if she was trying to steady herself or me.

"I'm Janelia," the woman repeated. "Desmia—I'm your sister."

10

I jerked back, breaking the woman's hold on me.

"I'm an orphan," I said numbly.

It took me a moment to realize that that wasn't a denial—orphans could easily have brothers or sisters.

"All my sisters are the same age as me," I said. I resolutely kept myself from wondering how many of my sister-princesses were still alive. *They're all fine*, I told myself. *They're all fine, and you're going to find them. . . .*

I went on with my explanation.

"We all came from the orphanage," I said. This part of the story had not exactly been released to the public, but somehow I felt I had to tell it now. "The queen secretly sent her servant girl out in search of little baby girl orphans she could pretend were the true princess, because her own baby had died—"

"Desmia, you should know the rest of that story," the woman—Janelia?— interrupted. "I was that servant girl."

I blinked. Was it possible? Could the servant girl herself have been from the orphanage too? A month ago, when I had learned the truth about my origins, there had been twelve other fake princesses to keep track of, along with twelve knights who were so protective of each of their princesses. I had had no time to think of minor players in the story. Or, really, I hadn't believed the servant girl was worth thinking of, because undoubtedly Lord Throckmorton would have had her killed to keep her from ever telling her story. He could have done that before I lived more than a day in the royal nursery.

I peered more intently at Janelia. The woman's ragged clothes and too-thin face made her look older, but perhaps she had lived only a dozen or so years past my fourteen. She was the right age, then, to have been a servant girl when I was a baby.

"But . . . but . . . how—" I sputtered.

Janelia's expression shattered. The hollows in her cheeks sagged; her heavy eyelids dropped, shuttering the joy that had been glowing forth from her gray eyes.

"You forgot," she whispered. "I tried so hard to make sure you remembered—well, as much as I could safely tell you—and you . . ."

"Mam, she was only four," Tog interrupted. "You tell Herk and me things all the time that we don't remember."

"But she knew this was important," Janelia said, speaking slowly, as if still dazed. Or horrified. "I was so sure that she understood. . . ."

"So what you tell us *isn't* important?" Herk said, plopping down on the floor in a cross-legged position. "Hurray! We don't have to listen anymore!"

I was glad that Herk at least thought this was funny. He started giggling. And there was something about the sound of a child's laughter, something that went with Janelia's voice. . . .

Do I remember her? I wondered. It was like I almost did, or almost thought I did, or almost could be convinced that I did. But the almost-memory kept slipping away, like a fish that couldn't be caught.

Why would I even think about catching fish? I was a princess. I'd never gone fishing. I'd heard Cecilia and Harper talk about their fishing exploits, but for myself— never.

Unless, maybe, with Janelia, when I was almost too young to remember . . .

The almost-memory was gone again. I winced and closed my eyes momentarily.

"Mam, maybe you should look at her wounds first?" I heard Tog say. "I think she's still bleeding."

Janelia gasped. I opened my eyes and looked down. The nightgown I'd been thinking of as snowy-white perfection was smeared with blood. Some of the blood had dried to a brownish color, but other spots were fresh and bright red.

It looked like the gown of a murder victim.

"Oh, you poor, dear child!" Janelia cried. "Did they stab

you when you were escaping?" She looked frantically up at Herk and Tog. "Were either of you injured? Are you sure nobody followed—"

"*Nobody* could have followed us, the way we went," Herk bragged.

Janelia turned her frantic gaze back to me.

"I had to break a window to escape," I said. Just saying those words made me dizzy. "I didn't have shoes. I stepped on some glass. Oh, and slid down a pillar."

It already seemed impossible that I had done those things.

Janelia nodded, a troubled bobbing up and down of her head.

"It could be worse, it could be worse," she muttered. She scooted back and peered more directly at my bloody feet. "Tog, put on the kettle so we'll have hot water to clean the blood away."

I remembered how much it had hurt when Herk touched my foot.

"I think there might still be some glass left inside," I said hesitantly.

Janelia kept nodding.

"We'll get it out," she said. She lifted the bottom of my nightgown slightly, looking at my scraped legs. "Boys, while I'm helping Desmia, I'll need you to go to the market to purchase—"

"Mam, there's no money left to buy anything," Tog said,

backing away from a fireplace where he'd just hung a kettle. "If you want us to leave so we don't see a girl's leg—the leg of a girl we just *rescued*, remember?—just tell us to leave."

Herk scrambled up.

"Bye, bye," he said.

And then both boys walked back out the door.

I missed them.

Maybe I was dizzy from losing so much blood. Maybe it was just too strange to have lost my palace, lost the girls I thought of as sisters, endured so much to get away from danger—and now have this strange woman claiming a relationship I was supposed to remember. Or, was the strange part that I almost did remember?

While Janelia busied herself pulling out cloths and watching the kettle, I made myself focus on looking around the small room.

Dirt floor, I thought. *Bedding over in the corner—do all three of them actually* sleep *on the floor? Table that looks like it would fall apart if someone put his elbows down on it, three rickety stools . . .*

I had never seen such a poor-looking space. Of course, I'd never seen inside any home except the palace and the "prison house" where Madame Bisset had kept me, so for all I knew, maybe most of my royal subjects lived like this. Or maybe, by the standards of ordinary Sualans, this was actually a fine home, an upper-class living space.

I doubted that. I couldn't imagine anyone living in a

worse place than this. Not if they intended to survive.

Janelia brought a steaming bucket of water and a pile of rags over beside me. I was relieved to see that she piled the rags on one of the rickety stools, not the dirt floor.

"It's not your fault you don't remember me from when you were little," Janelia said, though I could tell from the way she bit her lip that it still bothered her. "And—from the other things I tried, trying to get a message to you. I shouldn't have expected so much. I just wanted so much to believe . . ."

"*Why* did I know you when I was four?" I asked. "How—"

I stopped myself before I could ask, *How is it that Lord Throckmorton didn't have you killed?* even though that was one of the things I wanted to know. Maybe what I wanted to know most. I was working out an odd sort of equation in my head: *If poor servant-girl Janelia managed to survive in spite of Lord Throckmorton's murderous ways, doesn't that make it more likely that Cecilia and Harper and all my other sister-princesses managed to survive the fire and whoever might have been trying to kill them?*

Janelia dabbed at my right foot with a dampened rag.

"Oh good, a lot of this is just dried blood on unbroken skin," Janelia said. "It looks worse than it is—you don't have wounds *everywhere.*"

I winced anyway.

"But, oooh, here's a cut and there's still glass in it and it's deep . . . Brace yourself," Janelia said. She seemed to be speaking through gritted teeth. A moment later, she looked up. "How is it that you aren't screaming?"

"Sometimes when you know things are going to hurt, you just make yourself stop thinking about them," I said.

And once again I had the sensation that Janelia might be familiar, that I might remember her . . . but then it slipped away again.

Would there have been any reason that I might have made myself forget? I wondered.

Janelia was watching my face too carefully. I felt the same kind of squeamishness I'd felt listening to Tog breathe. Janelia was too close. It was like she actually knew me, knew me so well she didn't even see me as a princess anymore.

Nobody knew me that well.

"Go on taking the glass out," I said, and without meaning to I sounded imperious, with a tone of, *Do as I command, servant!*

"I'll tell you the story I've always wanted you to know," Janelia said. "While I work. It might . . . distract you."

"As you wish," I said stiffly.

Why did I feel like hearing the story might be as painful as having my wounds cleaned?

11

"'Twas odd that I was given over to serve the queen," Janelia began.

"Odd?" I murmured, holding back a wince. Just when I had bragged about how good I was at not thinking about pain, the tactic failed me. Maybe it didn't work as well on physical pain as on other types. It was starting to feel like Janelia was rooting around under the skin of my feet with razors and knives and swords.

"Before that I'd only ever been a scullery maid," Janelia said. "Plucking feathers from chicken and geese, scrubbing dirt from potatoes . . ."

"The lowest work a servant girl could have in the palace," I agreed.

"Oh, no," Janelia corrected me. She paused to brush away a curl of hair from her forehead. "Cleaning out chamber pots is *much* worse."

"But a royal person's own maid or butler does that," I protested.

"Right, and so in the *palace*, everyone acts like it's a better job," Janelia said. "Because you're close to the royalty, see? If they like you, they give you treats and favors, they tell you secrets. . . . You've got *prestige*."

I tried to remember if I'd ever given servants any treats or favors. I was certain I'd never told them any secrets.

Secrets shared had a way of escaping, of spreading further than the secret-teller wished.

"So you agreed to be the queen's servant girl for the prestige?" I asked.

"No," Janelia said. She reached back for a rag that wasn't covered in blood. "I was chosen to be the queen's servant girl because everyone else was afraid. And . . . I was too stupid to know that I should be afraid too."

I flinched, and I couldn't have said if it was because of what Janelia had said or because of the way Janelia was digging into my wounds.

"But the queen—everybody loved the queen," I protested.

This had always been treated as gospel truth around the palace. The queen's universal appeal had played a huge part in the lies I'd originally believed about myself, as well as the fuller story that emerged once all of us "true princesses" got together and began comparing stories.

"The queen was dangerous," Janelia said, dropping a large sliver of bloody glass onto a bloody rag.

That was in my foot? I thought, suddenly so queasy that I thought I might vomit or faint.

Janelia evidently misunderstood the expression of dismay on my face.

"Oh, of course, Queen Charlotte Aurora was also beautiful and gracious and kind, and all the servants loved her," Janelia hastened to say. "I can't speak for the likes of Lord Throckmorton."

I kept silent. If I tried to speak I would surely scream or wail or maybe even curse.

"But the queen was . . . reckless," Janelia said. "She was so good herself, she didn't understand that other people could be evil through and through. She just thought they were misunderstood."

"Like Lord Throckmorton," I muttered. Saying his name was almost like cursing. "The queen didn't know he was evil."

Janelia nodded. She paused, looking off toward the door.

"Servants hear things," she said. "They may not understand it all, but . . . everybody knew the king and queen were in danger. The queen was pushing for the end of the war, and she couldn't see why it wasn't easy. She didn't see that . . . that some men would kill to keep the war going. Because *they* were profiting."

I shivered. Had the other girls and I been as reckless as our supposed mother, the queen? We had wanted to end the war too; *we* had actually accomplished a peace treaty. Well, all but the formal signing of the document. I knew for a fact that Lord Throckmorton had made a fortune from the war, as had some of the other advisers we sent to prison. Were there others we didn't know about who still had reason to want war? Who were willing to kill to get their way?

Someone burned down our palace—is that proof that warmongers are still out there? Someone knocked out at least Fidelia and me in the middle of the fire—was that because of the peace treaty? I wondered. *If Madame Bisset is to be believed—which she isn't! She isn't!—then someone made sure that all the other princesses besides me are dead. Because . . . because . . .*

A great sob rose inside my throat but I didn't let it out. I clamped my lips together and hoped that Janelia thought I was grimacing only because of my wounded feet.

"Fourteen years ago, none of the other servants wanted to serve the queen because of the rumors," Janelia said. "Some said her enemies would strike in the middle of the night; some said they'd strike by day and they'd probably kill everyone in the room with her, to kill all the witnesses. . . ."

"Lord Throckmorton did kill all the witnesses," I said. "Even the men who'd worked with him to kill the king."

Janelia shook her head, ever so slightly.

"Not *all* the witnesses," she said softly.

My eyes widened, and for a moment I really did forget the searing pain in my feet.

Janelia gave a heavy sigh.

"The queen's last chambermaid quit in hysterics the same day the queen gave birth," she said. "The rumors . . . I didn't know this at the time, because the girl peeling potatoes is always the last to know anything. But everyone believed that the assassins wouldn't strike until a new prince or princess was born."

"Until there was an heir," I said bitterly. "Until there was a tiny royal baby who would be totally dependent on her advisers for years to come. A tiny royal baby who could be molded and shaped and manipulated . . ."

I knew now that I hadn't ever been the *real* true princess—the one with the actual blood of her parents running through her veins. But I had played that role long enough to know how this part of the story went.

"Yes," Janelia said, She seemed to be concentrating hard on my wounds. "I'm not sure how many girls they asked to attend the queen, but eventually they worked their way down to me. And—I was a foolish child. All I knew was that the queen had just given birth and was seriously ill, and I'd seen my own mother give birth, and I thought . . . I thought the queen needed me."

"You were brave," I whispered.

"I didn't know any better," Janelia said. "And—it gets worse."

For a moment she was silent, focused on washing away blood. She inched my nightgown up to an indecent level, and even though I'd been used to servant girls washing me and dressing me all my life, I felt strangely exposed. Was it because I worried about Tog and Herk coming back too soon? Or was it because Janelia seemed to be laying bare her own soul?

Being washed and dressed by servant girls only worked well if the servant girls were anonymous, impersonal, practically unnoticed.

"Oh, this isn't so bad," Janelia said, dabbing now at the scrapes on my legs from sliding down the pillar. "None of these wounds are deep—they'll be healed before you know it."

Did that mean that the wounds on my feet would take a lot longer?

I felt better when Janelia pulled the skirt of the nightgown back down and moved to attending to my left foot.

"Pray, go on with your tale," I said.

"I hauled bathing water for Queen Charlotte Aurora," Janelia said. "I washed her brow when she turned feverish. I listened to her babble about the king, the baby, the king, the baby . . ."

"Did you see the dead baby?" I asked. "The . . . corpse?"

I felt cruel asking that question. But it'd been a point in the story I'd always stumbled over. Who wouldn't want proof?

Janelia shook her head no.

"I was given to believe that other servants were caring

for the child," she said. "A wet nurse, a nursemaid, a nanny . . . And the queen was too ill to hold an infant, so it was no surprise to me that the child was never brought to her to admire and coo over and dandle."

"But didn't *you* want to see the new princess?" I asked.

"I was the queen's only servant girl," Janelia said. "I didn't have time to do anything but tend her. Day *and* night. I even slept on her stone floor, an hour or two at a time, no more than she herself was able to sleep. . . ."

"So you were there the night the assassins killed the king?" I asked in horror. "They killed the king, they killed his guards, they left the queen with fatal wounds . . . How is it that you survived?"

Janelia had stopped gingerly dabbing at my feet, and was just staring now at all the blood.

"I fear that another servant girl died in my place," Janelia said in a hollow voice. "I've learned that one servant girl looks much the same as another to men like Lord Throckmorton—unless she is unduly beautiful, which I was not." She swallowed hard. "And neither was Lena."

Janelia stopped talking, and I had to prompt her: "Lena?"

Janelia winced and took a deep breath.

"Lena . . . my friend . . . I had asked her to bring more wood for the queen's fire right before midnight," Janelia said. She seemed to be looking off into the distance, at something I couldn't see. "Lena tarried coming up the stairs. If she had just gotten there faster, put the wood on the fire, and been out of the room again before the last chime of midnight, before the assassins arrived . . ."

Janelia dragged her gaze back to me now. Her eyes burned.

"Lena tried to defend the queen," Janelia said. "The way her body fell near the bed, not over by the fireplace—I'm sure that's what she was doing." Janelia swallowed hard, a shamed expression on her face. "And I—I lay frozen, half under the bed. I couldn't move. It was like I was under some evil spell or something . . . the spell of cowardice. And the assassins never knew I was there because they never came around to that side of the bed. That's the only reason I lived. Because I was a coward."

"Who wouldn't have been afraid?" I murmured. I remembered how terrified I'd always been of Lord Throckmorton. And, until the very end, it had been in his best interest to keep me alive.

Suddenly I realized that Janelia had spent the past fourteen years thinking about that night the wrong way.

"I'm sure the assassins knew you were there," I said. "They were experts—they would have been watching. They would have kept track of who entered and left that room. They probably killed that other girl—Lena?—because she saw them. Even if they were wearing masks or disguises, she could have described their stature, their physiques. But you . . . you didn't see them. You only heard what happened. And . . . it was in their interest to leave a witness, as long as she didn't know too much. So you could spread the terror to everyone else in the palace."

Janelia gaped at me.

"I—I never thought of that," she said.

I shrugged, as if knowing the minds of evil men was something to be modest about.

"I know how Lord Throckmorton and his minions thought," I whispered.

Janelia still didn't go back to cleaning my wounds.

"So I was supposed to *not* be terrified, as well as not a coward?" she asked bitterly. "I have more to feel guilty about?"

"Or less," I said. "You shouldn't think Lena died in your place. It was her own fault for tarrying on the stairs."

I felt clever saying that. But Janelia snapped, "Don't you dare ever tell Lena's son that! He thinks his mother died a hero!"

I didn't think there was much chance I'd ever meet the son of a dead servant girl from the palace from fourteen years ago—especially now that the palace had burned down.

And what of your sister-princesses? a cruel part of my brain asked me. *If they are dead, are you going to remember them as dying heroic deaths? Or as being at fault?*

"I don't want to hear anything else about the murders right now," I said. My imperious tone was back, simply because I was trying so hard not to cry. This tone had always sounded perfectly fine in the palace—it was something I'd aspired to and practiced when I was younger, and it didn't come naturally. But the tone felt out of place in Janelia's hovel, when my blood was soaking into her dirt floor. And when my palace was gone and my sister-princesses might be dead and some enemy I couldn't even identify had apparently tried to kill me, too, and I had had to rely on Janelia's ragamuffin sons to rescue me from Madame Bisset . . .

"You were brave later on," I told Janelia, trying for a tone of kindness. It came out sounding condescending. "Even after the assassins, you stayed on as the queen's servant. Even as she lay dying."

Janelia picked up her rag again and started scrubbing away at the blood caked on my left foot.

"*Is* it bravery when your only other choice is starvation?" she asked. "When you're the only one bringing in money in your family, and you don't want to watch your little brothers and sisters starve too? Or watch your new baby sister die?"

I remembered that Janelia had claimed that the two of us were sisters. Maybe I had lost too much blood; maybe it just seemed too incredible. What Janelia had said just kept floating out of my mind.

Does she mean . . . Is she saying I *was the new baby sister she didn't want to see die?* I wondered.

"But surely at the orphanage . . ." I began. I had little

notion of what orphanages were like. I tried again. "Surely the food was adequate, even if it wasn't as elegant as palace fare . . ."

Janelia gave me a look that I wouldn't have been able to identify even a month and a half ago, before the other girls arrived at the palace. It was a look of pure incredulity, the same look that my sister-princesses almost always gave me when I made any supposition about life outside the palace.

It made me feel like a fool. It made me wonder, *Has everyone at the palace thought me foolish all along? How is it that everyone except my sister-princesses—and Janelia—have always been able to hide those looks from me for the past fourteen years? And . . . is this proof that Janelia really is another sister?*

"Children starve to death in orphanages and outside them," Janelia said. And maybe her rag hit another hidden piece of glass in my foot, because an extra jolt of pain shot through my body. "Especially babies. That's one of the things the queen was so upset about. That's one of the reasons she wanted to stop the war."

Belatedly I remembered that the queen herself had written about her concern for orphans in the letters she'd left for all the sister-princesses.

Janelia dug at the glass in my foot.

"But you and me and the rest of our family . . . we were never in an orphanage," Janelia continued.

I jerked back not just my foot, but my whole body.

"What?" I protested. "But I saw the queen's account

myself, in her own handwriting . . . She said *all* of us princesses came from the orphanage!"

Janelia kept her head bowed, her focus on my foot.

"The queen thought she was telling the truth . . . ," she murmured. She let out a deep sigh. "I thought I was doing the right thing. I thought I was just helping you stay alive . . . if I could keep you alive . . ."

I felt chills that had nothing to do with the blood I'd lost or the fact that I was sitting on a dirt floor.

"What did you do?" I demanded.

Janelia winced but went on.

"The queen was dying," she said. "I thought it might be her last day, and maybe you can't believe this, but I was genuinely fond of her. In spite of the danger she put me in. I wanted to do anything I could to keep her happy. So she could . . . die in peace. She sent me to the orphanage with instructions to bring back thirteen orphan baby girls of no more than a month or so old."

"Did she tell you what she was going to do with all those babies?" I asked. I could listen to this story only as long as I didn't think about who the babies really were: me and Cecilia and Fidelia and all the other sister-princesses: Ganelia with her love of architecture and Florencia with her love of numbers and Lydia with her freckles and Elzbethl with her desire to walk without stumbling . . .

Stop, I told myself. *Stop thinking about who the babies grew up to become. Or about what happened to them last night.*

Think of them as nameless, faceless, anonymous orphans. . . .

"Queens don't explain themselves to lowly servant girls," Janelia said stiffly. She wrung out a bloody rag and went on with the story. "As much as I thought about it, I guess I thought that her own baby had been sent far away, for safety, and she wanted other babies around her in her last moments as a reminder of new life, even as she slipped away into death."

From what I had heard about the queen, that sounded like a reasonable guess.

"It took me most of a sleepless night to get all the babies," Janelia said. "Sneaking in and out of the castle, to and from the orphanage, bringing back a basketful of babies each time. But the queen had been specific—she wanted *thirteen* babies. And there were only twelve baby girls at the orphanage that night."

"So why did you not grab a boy for the thirteenth baby?" I asked. "Surely there were boy babies in the orphanage too."

"Plenty," Janelia said drily. "But I knew even a dying queen could tell the difference between a baby boy and a baby girl."

I knew so little of babies that this had not occurred to me.

"And—I had made arrangements to bring in wet nurses for all the babies," Janelia said.

"Wet nurses?" I repeated numbly.

"Babies have to eat," Janelia said. "Especially little babies—they cry for food every few hours. And when babies are orphans, of course they don't have mothers of their own to give them milk. . . ."

My jaw dropped. This was another part of the story I had never thought about. Maybe I had heard somewhere that babies couldn't eat regular food. But if Janelia brought wet nurses into the palace to feed the babies, that meant even more people knew at least part of the true story from the very beginning.

And there were undoubtedly guards who saw Janelia walking back and forth from the nursery, carrying her mysterious basket, I thought. *And probably people at the orphanage who saw what Janelia was doing, who heard her explain the queen's request . . .*

How was it that anything about my sister-princesses and I had stayed secret for longer than five minutes?

How many people had Lord Throckmorton had killed to protect his own claim to power?

How had Janelia survived?

"My own mother was very ill," Janelia went on. "*Our* mother. She'd been sick since giving birth to you, and her milk dried up. Whenever I went home, you cried and cried and cried, and I knew that you were starving. . . . I knew that there were wet nurses in the palace with lots of milk, and I knew the queen wanted one more little baby girl to gaze upon before she expired. . . . Can you see why I thought it was an easy decision to bring you to the palace as a stand-in for the thirteenth baby orphan? Can you see why I thought, *It will make the queen happy and it will get my baby sister a full belly for the first time in her life and of course this is the right thing to do?* Can you ever forgive me my mistake?"

Janelia's voice was anguished and her face twisted as she spoke the word "mistake." Her hands dripped with blood.

I found that I could not look at Janelia.

I could not look at my sister—was she truly my sister?

Whether I believed her or not, I needed to act as if I did.

"But then the queen began giving the babies away," I said, and my voice came out sounding convincingly tortured. "The next morning. Didn't you see? Knights of the royal order kept coming in secretly, one by one, and the queen handed each one a baby and told him, 'This is my child. Please take care of my child.' She convinced each and every knight that he alone had the one true princess. When really he had only an orphan girl. How could you not understand what was going on? How could you not stand with your ear to the door and listen as one baby after another was taken away? How could you have let me go to the worst man of all, Lord Throckmorton?"

I glanced up only long enough to see that Janelia was peering down into the bucketful of bloody water.

"I kept you in the royal nursery until the very last," Janelia whispered. "I did . . . I did listen at the queen's door. I heard everything. But I didn't know how many knights were in the royal order. I don't know—I guess I didn't think each and every one of them would come for a baby. I didn't think the queen would live long enough to give away every baby. I was just thinking about making sure you got as much milk as possible. I was going to leave you suckling until the very last minute, and then, if I had to, I was going to confess to the queen that you were the one baby in her royal nursery who wasn't an orphan."

"You never confessed," I said accusingly.

Janelia peered straight back at me.

"Because, when every other baby was gone from the nursery, a messenger came for me," she said. "To tell me that my own mother had just died."

I could imagine Janelia fourteen years ago, standing alone in the hallway of the palace, weeping over her dead mother. I could imagine this so easily because the palace walls had absorbed so many of my own tears, before I had learned that crying did no good.

"But then . . ." I murmured. "Didn't you have a father who wanted his youngest child back after his wife died? Didn't I—Don't I—?"

It was too much of a stretch to work out the connections, to lay claim to a stranger who might once have been father to both Janelia and me.

Janelia was shaking her head anyway.

"Our father died while our mother was yet pregnant with you," she said. "He died in the war."

I didn't know what to say to that. Janelia seemed to be

trying to work her face into something resembling a weak smile.

"So the truth is, you *were* an orphan by the time the queen gave you to Lord Throckmorton," she said.

"Fitting," I muttered.

Janelia's expression turned beseeching.

"I didn't know what Lord Throckmorton was like," she said. "Not then. I just saw that I had given you to the one knight who was going to keep his baby in the palace, where I could see you. And that I had guaranteed you would continue to get milk and food. Don't you see that you would have died if I hadn't let the queen give you away? Died, like . . ." Her eyes darted about, as if she couldn't find a single place to let her gaze rest comfortably. "Died like our other brothers and sisters when I couldn't take care of them?"

I winced. I had thought the palace a hard place to grow up, but at least nobody there had talked about death so bluntly. Nobody there had dared to let pain show as nakedly as Janelia was doing right now. Everything bad and ugly at the palace had been muted, prettied up, covered over, hidden.

I had no idea what to do around anyone else's pain. I closed my eyes. Perhaps now would be a good time to pretend to faint?

I was just thinking about the best way to lower my torso back to the dirt floor without actually hitting my head, when a loud *bang* startled me into opening my eyes again.

The door of the basement room had swung open so violently it slammed against the wall. Herk and Tog were scrambling back into the room.

"Mam, Mam!" Herk cried, as Tog shoved the door shut again behind them. "They're saying in the marketplace, they're saying—"

"They're saying all the other princesses are dead!" Tog finished for him.

I braced myself, locking my elbows into place.

You already knew from Madame Bisset that this is the rumor the palace officials are spreading, I told myself. *That doesn't mean it's true. Remember? Palace officials always lie.*

But the boys weren't done.

"And," Herk said breathlessly. He gulped. "And they're saying Desmia's the one who killed them!"

12

My arms buckled and my shoulders slammed against the ground. Was this a real faint? My mind felt so vacant all of a sudden that it seemed possible. But I didn't lose consciousness. I could see a spider crawling across the beams above me, spinning its web.

I couldn't be imagining that, I told myself. *I couldn't make up a spider with such intricate detail. . . .*

A moment later, Janelia's face floated into view, hovering above me.

"Desmia, we know that isn't true," Janelia said. "We know you wouldn't have done that."

How do you know? I wondered. *How is it that you think you know me at all? Just because you say we were sisters fourteen years ago—before you gave me away? When you weren't able to protect me any more than I . . .*

I tried to hold it back, but the thought came anyhow . . . *than I could protect my sister-princesses?*

Janelia wrapped her arms around my shoulder, pulling me back to a seated position. Or, no—was she just trying to hug me?

Herk pulled on my right arm, wrapping it around his own shoulder to help in raising me. Tog stood off to the side watching curiously.

I had a million questions flooding my mind, but I didn't have the chance to ask any of them before the door to the basement room banged open yet again, and other ragamuffin boys began streaming in.

"Mam, we have news!"

"Mam, I heard—"

"Mam, I have to tell you—"

"Shh! Not until you shut the door!" Janelia called back.

But the door kept banging open again, revealing yet another boy shouting that he had news.

I recoiled, just as I would have if the basement room had been overrun by rats.

"How many sons do you have?" I murmured to Janelia.

It was Herk who answered.

"Oh, none of us are her *sons*," he answered. "We just started calling her Mam because she's the only one who'd take care of us after the orphanage closed."

My mind stumbled over his words, *after the orphanage closed*. I didn't want to think about that right now.

"But you all look alike," I protested. "Are you at least all brothers?"

"We don't look alike!" Herk laughed. "Tog has darker hair than me and Jake has crooked teeth and Arno has a big nose, and . . ."

I lost track of all the other differences Herk pointed out. I could see now that the boys did indeed have a variety of features and hair colors and textures—even Herk and Tog, whom I'd at first seen as different-sized versions of the same boy, actually bore little resemblance to one another, except that they were both dirty and dressed in rags.

And, really, hadn't that been the only thing I'd noticed?

I stopped examining the roomful of boys. Because suddenly they were all examining me.

The door slammed shut a final time. All the boys fell silent. And then one of the smallest ventured, "Is that—"

Janelia beamed so radiantly she practically glowed.

"Yes, this is Desmia," she announced joyously. "After all these years of having you all watch over her, we have her back."

"Years of w-watching . . . ," I stammered.

Janelia turned back to me.

"I didn't quite make it to that part of the story, did I?" she apologized. "For years I've had at least one of the boys posted as a sort of guard near the palace, doing the best they could to watch for you. I tried to get notes to you too, but . . ."

But I never got any of them, I thought. *Wonder who always intercepted them?*

It had to have been Lord Throckmorton.

Janelia had moved on to a more cheerful topic. She went back to addressing all the boys.

"Herk and Tog saw where Desmia was taken after the fire," she told them. "And then they rescued her!"

Well, I kind of rescued myself, starting out, I thought with unusual crankiness. *At least the part about getting out of the prison house.*

I didn't say anything to the boys but a shy, "Hello." Several of them dropped to their knees before me, either as a worshipful gesture or as a way to let the boys behind them catch a glimpse too. I was reminded of something out of a fairy tale—maybe that one about the lost princess being greeted by dwarves and woodland creatures?

And how is it that I even know fairy tales? I wondered. *Who in my childhood would have taken the time to tell me fanciful, purposeless stories like that?*

Why did it seem that it might have been Janelia?

"It would be nice to make introductions," Janelia said. "To let Desmia know how all of you have been helping me—and her— the past several years. But first—you all say you have news?"

"I heard that Marindia is still alive, and she's being taken to Fridesia," the tallest of all the boys said.

"And Elzbethl is alive and being taken to Fridesia," a curly-haired boy beside him said.

"And Sophia is being taken to Fridesia," a crooked-toothed boy—perhaps Jake?—agreed.

"Let's make this go faster," Janelia said, holding up her hand. "Did all of you hear that the princess you'd been assigned to is still alive and being taken to Fridesia?"

Heads bobbed up and down, the motion lasting long enough that I had time to count . . . *eight, nine, ten, eleven* . . .

Were they each nodding about a different princess? Did that mean that all the other princesses were accounted for except Cecilia—and I could assume that Cecilia was safe because she was with Harper and already planning to go to Fridesia?

"And did any of you besides Herk and Tog actually *see* the princess you were assigned to find?" Janelia asked.

Now all the bobbing boy heads changed their motion from up-and-down to side-to-side.

"Did any of you see *any* of the other princesses?" Janelia asked.

This time the heads just kept shaking side to side. More nos.

"So there's no proof any of this is true," I heard Tog mutter, off to the side. "This could be more palace lies."

"Palace can't lie when it don't even exist no more," the tall boy who'd reported on Marindia taunted.

"The people who burned down the palace could still lie," Tog retorted. "There can still be palace liars without a palace."

Back at the palace, I had been taught to have the patience to practice minuets and études on the pianoforte for hours on end. I'd been taught to have patience to make small talk through court dinners where each course could last an hour. On my own, I'd learned to have patience to hide for entire days in the secret passageways, spying on meetings of palace officials where the one detail I wanted to know could be buried in boring discourses about the rising price of flaxseed or the productivity of tin mines.

But I found I had no patience for listening to these two boys argue. Not here. Not now.

I started to rise up by pushing back against Janelia and Herk.

"If the rumors are either that I killed all my sister-princesses—which I know isn't true—or they are all still alive and being taken to Fridesia," I began, "then I'm going to Fridesia to find them. And rescue them!"

It had been awkward enough sitting in front of all these boys in nothing but a nightgown. But I felt even more ungainly trying to squirm into an upright position when every motion made my legs and feet scream with pain. I managed to raise myself onto my left knee and gingerly began sliding my right foot back into position.

Is it safe to put any weight on the ball of my foot? I wondered. *The heel? The tips of my toes?*

Just touching my foot to the ground brought such stabbing pain that I lost my balance and toppled over backward.

Janelia, Herk, and Tog dived to catch me.

"Desmia, you can't go to Fridesia right now," Tog told me, clinging to my arm. "You can't even stand up!"

I lifted my chin—evidently the only part of my body I was capable of lifting without pain.

"Then," I said, "someone will carry me."

13

The room exploded in chatter—how could these boys talk so loudly in such a small room? Were they agreeing or disagreeing? Who could tell?

It didn't matter. I knew I was going to get what I wanted as soon as I saw Janelia's face.

She feels guilty for leaving me in Lord Throckmorton's clutches when I was a defenseless baby, I told myself. *Whether or not the story she told me is true, she seems to believe it. And she needs to act like she believes it. So I can use that to get her to do anything I want.*

I felt guilty thinking that. Back at the palace, everybody manipulated everybody else; it was as natural as breathing. You figured out who had power and who had secrets and who could accomplish what you wanted—and if you didn't have enough power to get what you wanted, you used your knowledge of the secrets your target wouldn't want revealed. Lord Throckmorton had been the cruelest and most extreme manipulator in the entire palace, but manipulation might as well have been the coin of the realm. I had seen maids manipulate submaids, chefs manipulate sous chefs. I'd always assumed that the lowest of the low—the stable boys who mucked out the palace horse stalls, perhaps, or the scullery girls who peeled potatoes down in the kitchen—simply took their manipulation out of the palace, lording their palace positions over the peasants outside who were never allowed past the palace gates.

But Janelia had been the lowly scullery girl peeling potatoes in the kitchen, and even though she now seemed to run an entire network of ragamuffin boy spies, somehow I couldn't believe that she'd used manipulation to achieve that position.

No, Janelia somehow seemed . . . sincere.

Should I believe her?

You can think about all that later, I told myself. *After you've rescued your sister-princesses in Fridesia. After there's no reason for anyone to suspect you of murder.*

I realized all the boys were arguing about who deserved to go to Fridesia with me. Who was worthy to carry a princess.

"I'm the strongest!" one bragged.

"But I can run the fastest!" countered another.

"But I know the most about traveling in the wilderness!" argued a third.

"You're scared of ants!" a fourth boy sneered at the third.

"Herk and Tog will take me," I said. "And Janelia."

I couldn't evaluate the usefulness of the attributes the boys were arguing about. I didn't even know how to judge whether the boys actually were strong or fast or knowledgeable, or whether they were just making hollow boasts. I was simply looking for another trait: loyalty. Herk and Tog had already rescued me once, at risk to themselves. And if Janelia's story was true, she'd spent the past fourteen years wanting to make amends for her mistake when I was a baby.

Show quiet authority, I told myself. *Don't go on explaining. That would just leave an opening for someone to argue against you.*

I shot a glance at Janelia and saw there was no need to worry. Janelia was nodding.

"If you wish," Janelia said. She gazed out at the crowd of boys and narrowed her eyes warningly for a moment. "I'll expect that all of you will stay out of trouble while I'm gone. And watch out for one another." Then her face eased back into a more thoughtful expression. "But I think we should have one other person go with us so we can switch off more with the carrying—Terrence?"

The tall boy who'd bragged about being the strongest made his hands into fists and pumped them up and down.

"Told you," he crowed to the boys around him. "Told you I'm the best!"

"It's not necessary," Tog muttered through gritted teeth. "Me and Herk can handle—"

"This journey won't be easy," Janelia muttered back. "We don't know what dangers we'll face. And Terrence doesn't get scared."

"Even when he should," Tog muttered again. This time he spoke so softly that I may have been the only one who heard.

I looked away from Tog and studied Terrence, now in the center of a crowd of boys slapping him on the back.

If nothing else, at least he has a proper name, I thought. Somebody named Terrence wouldn't have been out of place at the palace.

Like the other boys, Terrence was dressed in rags, and his shirt contained just as many crazily placed patches as Tog's or Herk's. His light brown hair was just as haphazardly cut; his feet were just as bare and filthy. But somehow he didn't seem quite so much like a beggar.

It's how he carries himself, I thought. *He looks like he's ready to say to anyone who might challenge him, "You think you're better than me? Oh, yeah? Well, you're not!"*

Terrence's stance would have fit right in at the palace, too.

Terrence turned his head and caught my eye—caught me staring at him. He raised an eyebrow, quite cockily. Invitingly.

Quickly I looked away.

It's not like you think, I wanted to explain to anyone who might listen. *I'm not staring at this beggar boy the way certain ladies of the court stare at certain, uh . . . particularly handsome . . . courtiers. I'm just looking more the way a stable master might look over a horse, to make sure there's little chance of it going lame on a long journey."*

Something seemed wrong about thinking that way too.

To cover my confusion, I turned to Janelia.

"How quickly can we leave?" I asked. "I assume the others will be going by carriage, and they might have even left already. To catch up, we should hire the fastest horses we can find, and—"

"Desmia, we've no money for the hiring of horses!" Janelia protested.

"Maybe there's enough for hiring a cockroach," Herk said.

I guessed that was a joke. But I didn't see how anyone would think it funny.

"Could you perhaps . . . ," Janelia began. She stopped, cleared her throat, and began again. "Do you think there's any safe way for you to get money from the royal treasury? Anyone you trust who could help you pay for the journey?"

I considered this. Until my sister-princesses began reigning with me, I'd never given a thought to money. Everything I'd needed or wanted had simply appeared: dresses for the palace balls, food for the palace feasts, even new exotic birds for the cages in the palace tower. It was only because of Florencia always going on about the royal budget that I understood that hiring horses might cost a lot of money.

I thought about Lord Oxnard, the chancellor of the treasury. He was a short, fussy man who had taken over after Lord Throckmorton and his minions were unmasked as traitors. Florencia had worked with him closely. But did she actually trust him? Should I? Could I trust anyone who'd been at the palace the night of the fire?

You've been ruling with the other sister-princesses for a month, and you still don't fully trust any of them but Cecilia, I reminded myself. *And you just think of her as the one you trust the most.*

Somebody had burned down the palace and endangered all of us. Somebody had done that on purpose. And I didn't even know whom to suspect.

That fact made it impossible for me to trust Lord Oxnard. It made it impossible for me to ask anyone for money from the royal treasury.

"Perhaps . . . perhaps you could get a loan from someone *you* trust?" I asked. "And then after we've rescued the other princesses and restored the palace, I can have the royal treasurer pay them back?"

Beside me, Herk snorted as though this was the funniest suggestion he'd ever heard.

"As if anyone we know has any money!" he laughed. "As if anyone who has money would loan it to us!"

I decided it was good most of the boys were still so busy congratulating Terrence that probably only Janelia, Herk, and Tog had heard what I'd said.

Janelia seemed to be trying very hard to smile encouragingly at me.

"I'm afraid that idea won't quite work," she said, in such a carefully tactful tone that both Herk and Tog snorted even more derisively. "But perhaps it will turn out that we're safer and maybe even faster walking. We can go cross-country undetected. Horses would attract a lot of attention that we won't want."

Beggars on horses, she means, I thought. *They'd look out of place.*

But for all I knew, maybe *any* travelers with horses were rare in the remote parts of Suala and Fridesia.

"You've forgotten I can't walk until my feet heal," I said, and too much of my despair seeped into my voice.

"And you've forgotten you asked to be carried," Tog said, and there was something in his voice I didn't like. Disdain? Contempt?

I looked down at the rug I was still sitting on, the one Herk and Tog had used to carry me away from Madame Bisset's prison house. Janelia had slid it back so at least my feet and shins hadn't continued to bleed on it as Janelia cleaned my wounds. But, just in the time I'd lain hidden in the rug, my blood had left rust-colored stains all over it, along with the less-identifiable blotches of equally unsightly colors.

"Wrapped in this . . . all the way to Fridesia . . . ," I murmured. "I can't. I'm sorry. I just can't."

I could feel my nose wrinkling up; even without a single mirror, I could tell how haughty and disgusted and ungrateful I appeared.

"Don't worry—we'll have to sell this rug to have money for food, anyway," Tog said, and there was definitely scorn in his voice this time. There was.

"We'll come up with a different system for carrying you," Janelia assured me. "Something more comfortable. Or, at least . . . cheaper."

I couldn't imagine anyone being desperate enough to buy the filthy rug. I couldn't imagine how much worse being carried in something cheaper would be.

"Isn't there anything else you'd want to do before leaving the capital?" Tog asked.

I looked back at him blankly. Then I glanced down at my bloodstained nightgown.

"Oh, of course. I need decent clothes," I said. "Especially for once I'm at the palace in Fridesia. But . . ." It seemed a little tactless to say, *But if you're worried about money for food, how can you afford the gowns a princess like me deserves?* An idea occurred to me that made my whole face light up. "But I only have to worry about traveling clothes. I'm sure when I get to Fridesia, I can have Ella help me with the more impressive gowns. My friend Ella Brown, I mean, whose fiancé was the Fridesian ambassador who negotiated the peace settlement . . ."

"We know about that," Herk said, crossing his arms stubbornly. "We're not stupid!"

I thought about apologizing: *I've never been around beggar children before, so I've got no idea what you would or wouldn't know.*

Somehow I didn't think that would help.

Tog hadn't actually crossed his arms, but he looked just as insulted.

"I meant, are you going to leave Suala without letting your royal subjects know if you're dead or alive?" he asked. "Letting them know which rumors they should or shouldn't trust?"

I hadn't thought about my royal subjects. I was used to palace opinion being the only thing that mattered, and the palace was gone.

But the people who burned it down will be watching and listening . . . and feeding the rumors that help them, I thought.

I jerked my chin up again.

"You're right," I said. "There's a way to fight back against my enemies even before I get to Fridesia. I'll need a quill pen and high-quality black ink and four—no, five—sheets of the finest sheepskin paper. The kind we used at the palace for royal proclamations."

"Do you know how much money that would cost?" Tog exploded.

He had his hands out like he was about to grab my shoulder and shake me. I shrank back from him. I'd forgotten about the other boys in the room—they'd been so loud and raucous their voices had become background noise. But Tog's voice soared above the others', and everyone else fell silent. Now they all stared at Tog and me. I felt the full weight of more than a dozen pairs of questioning eyes.

I didn't know these boys. Despite the promised possibility of an eventual introduction, the only ones I could identify right now by name were Terrence, Tog, and Herk. Of course these boys were, as Tog had put it, my royal subjects. But they were also completely alien—beggars, not royalty; accustomed to life in the filthy streets, not the palace. I warranted that any random resident of the palace in Fridesia would seem less foreign than these boys.

And yet I felt like I knew what each of them was thinking: *This is the princess we're supposed to be revering? What's so royal about her? She's as dirty and bedraggled as we are right now. She's just as much of an orphan. She would have been just as poor as us if it hadn't been for Janelia's mistake. She doesn't even have a good answer for a beggar boy ranting about money! Why should we do anything to help her? What's in it for us?*

"I—" I began, and the one word stuck in my throat, blocking whatever else I might want to say.

And then Janelia leaned in and put a hand over Tog's hands, gently pulling them away from me. With her other arm, Janelia hugged me close.

"We'll get what you need," Janelia promised. "We'll find a way to work it all out."

14

I lay flat on my back with a sheet over my face. This was the solution Janelia and the ragamuffin boys had settled on for carrying me until my feet healed: They had put together an improvised stretcher for me, with a narrow length of canvas held between two poles. Tog and Terrence walked along carrying opposite ends of the poles.

Tog had told me this was how the men who'd fought in the Fridesian War carried wounded soldiers off the battlefield. Corpses, too.

And, at least until we left the capital city behind, I had to pretend that I was also a corpse—just the ordinary dead body of someone whose family was too poor to pay for burial and so was sending the corpse to be thrown onto the paupers' bone pile outside the city. Janelia and the boys had decided this was the best way to keep anyone from seeing me and figuring out who I was. Nobody would look too closely at a supposedly dead body hidden under a sheet.

I had never thought before about how corpses on battlefields were disposed of. I'd never thought before about burials or paupers. I'd certainly never known that there was a bone pile just outside my city walls.

Are there people in this city right now who think I deserve to land in that bone pile for real? Who wish I really were dead? Was that why someone set that fire? I wondered, as Tog and Terrence jostled the stretcher up and down. I had had no trouble back in the palace sitting through interminable meetings, pianoforte practices, and court dinners. But somehow it seemed to take every ounce of self-control right now to force myself to lie as still as death on this stretcher.

Because you're thinking about death. . . . Because you don't want to die and you so easily could have, back in the palace fire. And you don't want your sister-princesses to be dead either. And you don't know who burned down the palace or what Madame Bisset was planning. . . .

I decided to occupy my mind instead by listing the people who might even now be wondering if I was alive or dead, who would rejoice when they found out the truth: Cecilia, of course. And Harper.

And the other sister-princesses?

I decided to skip over the rest of them for now and move on to people who wouldn't have heard about the fire yet but who would absolutely wonder and worry about me when they did: Ella Brown and her fiancé, Jed Reston. And . . .

And is that it? Is that really all the people who care whether I live or die?

"When the sheet slides around, I can see your hands clutching the sides of the poles!" Tog's voice hissed in my ear. "Stop it! A real corpse wouldn't hold on! Either make your body absolutely stiff, like rigor mortis has set in, or let your limbs go all floppy. But don't hold on!"

And then, probably to provide an excuse for bending down low enough to put his mouth near my ear, he pulled the sheet slightly to the right.

I let go. I didn't think I had it in me to flop around right now—especially with so many wounds on my feet and legs. The wounds throbbed even without movement. So I concentrated on holding my body rigid instead.

See, Tog must care if you live or die, I told myself. *Janelia does too. Janelia cares a lot. And probably Herk and Terrence do too. . . .*

Somehow none of those names seemed particularly comforting except Janelia's. For all I knew, Tog and Herk and Terrence were protecting me just to keep Janelia happy.

Or to have an adventure, I thought. *Hasn't Terrence been acting like this is all a great adventure?*

With my face covered by the sheet, I had no more idea of what parts of the city they were carrying me through now than I had the day before, when I was wrapped in the rug. It had taken all afternoon, evening, and most of the night for Janelia and the others to make arrangements for the trip. They'd conjured up the stretcher and paper and shoes and a dress for me. The dress was every bit as worn and ragged as Janelia's, but at least I wasn't wearing a nightgown anymore.

The others had mentioned buying food, too, but I hadn't seen much of it. By the weak slant of sunlight filtering through the heavy sheet, I could tell we had met our goal of leaving at sunrise. And by the general silence around me— interrupted only by the slap of Tog's and Terrence's feet against the cobblestones—I guessed that sunrise was not a particularly crowded time on the streets we were passing through. I couldn't even hear Janelia and Herk behind us, because they'd decided to follow at a goodly distance so they could rush forward to help if Tog and Terrence got caught, rather than everyone being captured all together.

Are we in danger of being captured? I wondered. *Are my enemies so plentiful that everyone we pass might be a threat?*

I strained so hard listening that my ears rang. Was that a horse's whinny off in the distance? The lapping of water along the riverbed? The cry of merchants in some marketplace four or five blocks away?

And then suddenly I felt the stretcher beneath me twist around a corner, and there was crowd noise for the first time, people whispering and muttering and exclaiming.

"What's everyone looking at?" I heard Tog ask. I thought I could detect the same tone of faked innocence in his voice as he'd had talking to Madame Bisset.

"A letter from the princesses posted on the wall," a man's voice replied. I pictured him middle-aged and paunchy and prosperous, like a lot of the ministers and advisers and counselors at the palace. Already I didn't trust him.

I trusted him even less when he sneered, "Not that we can believe it's from an actual princess. Not that anybody would tell *us* the truth." He paused for a moment, as if looking Tog and Terrence up and down. "Not that the likes of you would be able to read it."

I was pretty sure Tog could read, because I'd seen him looking over each copy of the letter I'd written out in my best hand the night before. And his eyes had scanned the words just like someone reading. But I heard him reply in a perfectly affable tone, "Then maybe it's best you tell me what the letter says." He swung the poles of the stretcher slightly, as if bringing it to the middle-aged man's attention. "Because no one in this crowd wants us pushing past them with *this*, trying to see the letter."

The man sighed, sounding aggrieved, but intoned, "'Be it known, royal subjects of Suala, that we, your rulers, are safe despite the appalling attack upon our palace. We are temporarily in hiding until such time as the evildoers are brought to justice. But rest assured, the evildoers will be brought to justice.' And then it's signed, 'The thirteen princesses of Suala.'"

"It's good to know they're safe," Tog said mildly. He didn't just sound innocent now; he also sounded slightly stupid. "I heard some of them were real pretty."

There was a smacking sound, and the stretcher swung oddly to the side. I put the sound and the motion together and realized what had just happened: The man had hit

Tog so hard he'd almost dropped onto the stretcher.

"Fool!" the man said. "This letter doesn't mean anything! Except that someone *wants* us to believe that the princesses are safe. Probably so we don't start rebelling. Probably so we'll go on acting like sheep, doing whatever the palace tells us. Even with the palace gone!"

People talk openly of rebellion in the streets of the capital? I marveled. *Standing right in front of a letter from their rulers? From* me?

I wanted to jump up from the stretcher and cry out, *This letter is true! Look at me! I'm your princess! I yet live! I'm safe! Guards, arrest this man for treason!* Except—what if I *wouldn't* be safe if I did that? What if there were no guards within earshot? Or . . . no guards who would obey me? What if the rest of the crowd felt the same way as this malcontent man, and they didn't actually care if I was alive or dead either?

What if they were on the same side as the people who'd set fire to the palace?

What if they killed me?

I waited for Tog or Terrence to speak up on my behalf— or even Janelia or Herk, if they were close enough. But the stretcher lifted and fell as if both boys were shrugging.

"Guess I'd have to take bodies out to the bone pile no matter who was in charge," Tog said, just as mildly as before.

I felt the stretcher start moving forward again. Now it was harder than ever to lie still. I waited until the crowd noise faded in the distance, and I could hear nothing but

Tog's and Terrence's footsteps once more. Then I took the risk of sliding my hand secretly past my head—out from under the sheet—and tapping Tog on the leg.

For a moment I thought he didn't notice or understand, but then he called to Terrence, "Hold on. I think the body is about to slide off."

The stretcher lowered to the ground, and Tog reached under the sheet as if he needed to center my body on the stretcher once more. I could tell by the shadow across the sheet that he also bent his head close to mine.

"Could you tell—did the rest of the crowd agree with what that man said? Or did they believe the letter?" I whispered urgently. "If there's going to be rebellion, I need to stay here. I need to call up my soldiers. I need to . . . I need to . . ."

"That man was just talking," Tog whispered back. "Nobody paid him any attention. But—nobody believed the letter, either."

"What? Why?" I demanded.

Tog nudged my shoulders gently toward the center of the stretcher.

"You should have just signed your own name, not anyone else's," Tog said. "Should have stuck to what you knew for sure. People are more likely to believe the truth."

And then he grasped the poles of the stretcher once more, and he and Terrence lifted me again, carrying me farther and farther away from any possibility of calling up soldiers (How would I do that? Would they obey if it was just me alone?) or just going back to the ruined palace and proclaiming, *Look! I'm here! I'm still your ruler! See for yourself!* I didn't have to struggle to lie rigidly anymore, because Tog's words alone made me stiff with fear.

Surely he just meant that nobody believed all thirteen princesses could have survived the fire and gone into hiding together. If we'd all survived and were all together, we'd be stepping forward and taking charge. We would have already found and punished our enemies; we'd be starting on plans for a new castle. We wouldn't have needed ragamuffin boys to secretly post cryptic letters around the city in the dark of night. We'd be in control.

But it's still possible the others are all alive, even if we're not together, I told myself. *It is. It's still possible that I can rescue them and we can come back in triumph. Everyone will believe then. They will. They have to.*

But why did I have to work so hard just to convince myself?

15

"State your business," an official-sounding voice called out, after Tog and Terrence had carried my stretcher a long way farther in silence.

"Headed to the bone pile, sir," Tog said, with a shrug that lifted and lowered the stretcher. "Another pauper died."

I expected a grunt of assent from the guard at the city gate—for surely we were at the city gate now, weren't we? Wasn't that who would challenge our progress? I didn't think even the gate guards would be too concerned about Tog and Terrence. The guards were supposed to challenge people *entering* the city, not leaving it.

But I heard no approving grunt; though I braced myself for moving forward again, the stretcher stayed still.

"You're not the usual bone boys," the guard said, and I could hear suspicion in his voice.

The stretcher rose and lowered again, this time at both ends. That made me think both Tog and Terrence had shrugged.

"The usual bone boys got sick." I recognized Terrence's voice. "Lot of people are sick down on Spittle Trail Street. This corpse here was the first to die. Want to look at it so you'll recognize the oozing sores if they break out on your own skin?"

Now the stretcher moved in a different direction: Terrence seemed to be swinging it closer to the guard.

I heard the guard take a step back, the heel of his boot clicking against the cobblestones.

"Move along," he said. "And don't come back in through this gate after you get rid of that body. Take your sickness-carrying selves to the south gate."

"Yes, sir," Terrence said mockingly, and I wondered that he didn't get his ears cuffed for disrespect.

Then again, the guard probably didn't want to touch a boy who'd touched a corpse with oozing sores.

The stretcher began moving again. Tog and Terrence took only about a dozen more steps before Terrence began snickering.

"Did you see his face when I said, 'oozing sores'?" Terrence chortled.

"Did you think about the people on Spittle Trail Street?" Tog replied. "Did you think about what they're going to do when soldiers come in and burn down their houses to get rid of the sickness—which doesn't even exist?"

Would that actually happen? I wondered. *Would my soldiers do that? In my city?*

"Enh, no soldier's going to care about Spittle Trail Street," Terrence said. "They'd be scared to go there. Anyhow, the soldiers don't burn houses for illness anymore. One of the princesses issued an edict stopping it. Marindia, I think."

She did? I thought. It was possible—and Marindia was the likeliest to have done something like that secretly, without telling the rest of us.

How many of us even knew things like that happened? I wondered, and my discomfort had nothing to do with the way I'd been holding my body stiffly for so long.

"Still," Tog told Terrence. "You don't know how things are being done now. And you didn't need to say the name of any street."

"And you don't have to try to tell me what to . . . Janelia!" Terrence said, his voice shifting from defiance to more of the obsequiousness I was used to hearing at the palace.

"We made it out of the city safely!" Janelia's voice was close and full of joy. "We all did! Thank you both!"

Janelia and Herk must have decided it was safe to catch up. That probably meant we were far enough outside the city that they weren't worried about anyone stopping us.

"Well, the guard gave us a hard time, but I talked my way out of it," Terrence bragged.

I didn't hear anyone answer. By the shadow falling across the sheet, I could tell that Janelia was bending down close.

"Desmia—are you all right?" Janelia asked. "Your wounds don't hurt too much, do they?"

"I'm fine," I said. My voice came out just as bell-like and pure as it always had back at the palace. I was a little amazed that I could sound so calm.

"We'll go on a ways, and then the maps say the land will get flat and we should be able to see anyone coming toward us a long ways out," Janelia said. "I think it will be safe for you to sit up then. We'll take the sheet off your face and you won't have to pretend to be a corpse anymore."

I held back a shudder, thinking about the oozing sores I was supposedly covered with. And about the real wounds that covered my feet and legs and kept me from walking on my own.

"That sounds good," I said, just as calmly.

"Will there be any snakes where we're going?" Herk asked. "Or wolves, or, or—"

"Don't we have enough troubles without you making up more?" Janelia asked.

"I just want to know, because if there are snakes or wolves or other wild animals, I'll carry a stick and beat off anything that gets too close to Princess Desmia," Herk said. "I want to be ready!"

"How about you take a turn carrying the stretcher instead?" Tog asked.

The stretcher tilted, and I could tell that Herk had taken over one of the poles near my head.

"I can carry two poles!" Herk said. The stretcher careened dangerously. But I didn't think Tog would actually let me fall.

"You know what?" Tog asked. "If I go from carrying both poles to carrying nothing, my muscles are going to freeze up. Let's ease you in and me out kind of gradual-like, all right?"

I guessed that Tog was just making sure that Herk could carry the stretcher safely. I liked the way he'd phrased his explanation to save the younger boy's pride.

"You want me to take your end?" Janelia asked, evidently speaking to Terrence.

"Nah, I'm good," Terrence said. "Tog gets tired quicker than I do."

But—*Tog was just doing that to make Herk feel useful*, I thought. *Wasn't he?*

It felt strange to analyze the words and actions of beggar boys the same way I'd always done with palace officials'.

They walked on, the stretcher lurching beneath me a bit less steadily than before. Time passed, and I thought I might as well sleep—what else was there to do? But sleep didn't come, not when the wounds on my feet and legs screamed with pain with every jostling. Not when the sun rose higher, and seemed to bake me through the sheet. Not when my brain raced, *And when we get to Fridesia, I'll need to get in touch with Ella first thing. I'll need to find out if any of my sister-princesses are there for real; I'll need to* . . .

"This would be a good place to stop for lunch," Janelia said. "See how those rocks over there would shelter us from the road?"

From the shadow that appeared across the sheet, I could tell that Janelia was pointing.

"I'll check first and make sure nobody else is there," Tog volunteered.

He means thieves, bandits, brigands . . ., I thought.

"Tog's right," Janelia said. "It's good to be cautious. And we can put down the stretcher while we wait."

I felt the stretcher descending. Then I could feel twigs and pebbles beneath me.

"All's clear," Tog called from off in the distance.

"And there's no one in sight on the road . . . Desmia, I think it's safe to take the sheet off your face," Janelia announced. "I know this will be such a relief for you!"

Janelia tugged at the sheet and it slithered away, bringing almost unbearably bright light to my eyes.

What I saw first was sky, a vast dome of it that arced impossibly high overhead. Of course I had seen the sky before from the palace windows—and from my daily trips to the palace balcony to wave at my subjects in the courtyard below. But the sky had never appeared so large before; it had never seemed so overwhelming.

"Here. You must be dying to sit up," Janelia said, reaching for my arm. "Let me help you."

Dazedly, I let Janelia pull me up by the shoulders, let Janelia bend my waist. I might as well have been a doll.

A new scene appeared before my eyes: Not just sky but a horizon-to-horizon stretch of dust and rock, broken only by

the road curving off into the distance. I felt dizzy. I couldn't
have said if the road I was looking at was where we'd just been
or where we were going.

"Desmia?" Janelia prompted.

My ears rang, turning my name into something almost
unrecognizable. My heart pounded faster and faster, barely
finishing one thump before the next one sounded. It felt
like my heart was running, maybe even trying to escape my
chest. Sweat poured off me, soaking my hair and clothes and
sliding into my eyes so I couldn't see. My eyesight was going
dark, anyhow, as though I was about to faint. But somehow
the image of that awful open sky and that awful stretch of
empty dust and rock stayed burned onto my vision.

I gulped air into my lungs and fought to stay alert.

"Desmia, what's wrong?"

"What happened?"

"Desmia?"

The voices seemed to come at me from a million miles
away. Or from as far away as the distance between my balcony
and the people who always stood down below on the ground,
back at the palace.

"Was she poisoned?"

"How could she have been poisoned when she ate the
same food as the rest of us last night and this morning?"

"Desmia, you didn't eat or drink anything else, did you?"

I couldn't tell who was saying what. But the mention
of poison and eating made me notice that my stomach was
roiling. I gagged.

"Go ahead—throw up if you have to!" This was Janelia's voice.

Still gagging, I leaned over the side of the stretcher. I closed my eyes so I didn't have to see if anything came out.

"Ugh, that's how a *princess* behaves?"

Terrence's voice, I thought. *That was Terrence.*

Someone was wailing, a long, drawn-out howl of pain.

Oh. That's me, I thought. But I couldn't seem to stop it.

"This isn't a princess! This is just some crazy girl!"

Terrence again.

"Desmia, just tell us what's wrong! Just tell us what we can do to help!"

Janelia? Tog? Herk?

It was strange how I couldn't separate those three voices, couldn't tell them apart, even though I could recognize Terrence's.

I still couldn't stop the wailing coming from my mouth, but I found I could shape it, direct it, turn it into words.

"The sky, the sky, that awful, open sky . . ."

"I think I know what's wrong!"

That was Tog, wasn't it?

He was still talking.

"I think I know what to do! She was never out of the palace before yesterday, right?"

"Not for years, I don't think. . . ."

And that's Janelia, answering Tog, I thought.

It was amazing how much better I felt, just to identify the voices around me.

"Let's carry her over by those rocks, then," Tog said, a note of confidence back in his voice.

I felt myself being lifted on the stretcher again and rushed away from the road. After a moment the overly bright sunshine stopped pounding mercilessly against my eyelids. I dared to open my eyes a crack. The stretcher was sliding downward. They were lowering me into a dim cave, maybe, or just into the shadowed space between rocks. I reached out and put my hand against the nearest rock and it was so blessedly cool that I thought just the touch of it could bring down a fever, if fever was what I had.

Solid, I thought. *Strong. And closed up and hidden and safe.*

I found that I could finally stop screaming.

16

I lost track of time. Was it only a moment or hours that I lay silently, the palm of my hand pressed against solid rock? Was it a moment or hours that the others sat silently staring at me before Janelia murmured beseechingly, "Desmia, please—are you all right? Can you tell us what's wrong?"

I gulped, tamping down nausea and revulsion. *This* was more like me. This was the control I was used to having over my body.

"I'm sorry," I whispered. My voice came out a little ragged, but I was able to clear my throat and make it right again. "I'm so sorry. I don't know what happened. It was like . . ."

Like I was afraid that the ground would open up and swallow me whole. Like the sky was too big and too confining, both at the same time. Like I couldn't think. Like I wasn't me. Like something I couldn't control took over my body.

I turned and looked at Tog.

"How did you know bringing me back here between the rocks would help?" I asked.

He shrugged, and it actually seemed like a show of true modesty, as if he really didn't believe he deserved credit. But I couldn't be certain—in my time in the palace, I wasn't sure I'd ever seen any modesty that *wasn't* fake.

"I just guessed," Tog said, spreading his hands wide, a gesture of both innocence and ignorance. "I've seen soldiers back from the war who act like you, and they always want to get somewhere safe. You were screaming about the sky, and I thought maybe you needed to get away from it. So it wouldn't scare you anymore. And I thought, if you've lived your whole life between stone walls, a rock cave would be the next best thing."

I wasn't scared, I wanted to say. *I am nothing like soldiers who have fought in the war. I am nothing like soldiers, period.*

But I hadn't been able to stop screaming on my own. If the other four hadn't moved me away from the horrible sight of that dome of open, empty sky and the open, empty landscape beneath it, I might have still been screaming.

"I get scared sometimes too," Herk whispered, leaning in to pat my arm. He glanced quickly back toward Tog and Terrence. "I just don't usually tell the big boys."

For the first time I thought about what I was asking Herk to do—what I'd so carelessly drawn him in to when I announced back in Janelia's basement, *Herk and Tog will take me. And Janelia.* Herk was just a little kid. I hadn't thought to ask or even guess at his age before, but I did now: Was he maybe nine? Eight? Only *seven?*

Herk didn't actually look any more scared or stunned or worried than Janelia or Tog, sitting on either side of him. I couldn't tell about Terrence, the one who was supposedly never scared. He had his face turned, and he seemed to be gazing off into the distance.

For a moment everyone sat frozen in those positions, pinned in place by Herk acknowledging he was afraid. Or maybe their sudden paralysis was my fault. In the palace, I hadn't gotten as much leadership training as all my sister-princesses had in their hiding places: Lord Throckmorton hadn't actually wanted to turn me into a strong leader. He'd wanted me to be a spineless puppet he could manipulate however he wanted. But Cecilia, at least, had told me about what she'd learned. I knew the first rule of leadership was to look decisive and unafraid no matter what.

I had just failed that test of leadership.

But what could I do about it when I was still shaking, still drenched in sweat, still barely able to hold myself back from wailing even more?

Janelia broke the spell by reaching out and putting her arm around Herk, drawing him close.

"I get scared sometimes too, Herksy," she said. "You're being really brave, going with us to Fridesia. I think you're braver than any of the big boys were, when they were your age."

"Hey! Don't insult my courage like that!" Tog said. "I was brave when I was a little guy too!"

I could tell he was only pretending to be offended. I wasn't sure Herk noticed, but Tog's joking tone made me feel better.

Terrence didn't join in the joking. He was still peering off into the distance, his gaze roaming across the landscape that had terrified me.

"Cold water would help, wouldn't it?" he asked. "I think that's a river beyond the rocks. I'll go fill our water gourds."

"Good idea. Take these three, and I'll give Desmia the rest of what we have left," Janelia said. "She should probably start out with lukewarm water, anyhow, until her stomach settles."

Janelia took gourds from Herk and Tog and carefully poured all the remaining water into one. She handed the empty ones to Terrence, who started toward the river even as Janelia held the full gourd up to my mouth.

They're treating me completely like an invalid now, I thought. *Or like a small child or a pet. I'm the princess and they're beggars and yet they're acting like I can't think for myself.*

Considering that I still didn't quite trust myself to open my mouth without screaming, I didn't see how I could protest. I let Janelia trickle a thin stream of water down my throat, and it did help. I was parched; my mouth tasted of dust and vomit and fear.

The water seemed to wash all that away.

"Better," I murmured, when I finally stopped drinking. "I feel better. Thank . . . you."

Royalty was almost never supposed to show gratitude—it was as forbidden as regret or apologies or any other show of weakness. What I had learned from Lord Throckmorton was that you should only show appreciation in order to manipulate someone into feeling obligated. That was the strategy I had been trying for with Madame Bisset back at the prison house. But now I felt the words "thank you" slip out almost without my thinking about it.

Because of the sister-princesses, I thought. *I picked up the habit from them. None of them could remember that they weren't supposed to say thank you.*

My vision blurred again, and I forced myself to concentrate on looking at the solid rock around me.

"If you think you can keep it down, food would be a good idea too," Janelia said. "Why don't we start eating? I doubt that Terrence will mind. We can let him take a shift of not carrying the stretcher, after lunch, so he can get his break then. . . ."

Janelia seemed to be babbling, saying anything to fill the gap of silence.

"What's for lunch, what's for lunch, what's for lunch?" Herk chanted. It seemed as though he, at least, had recovered from his fear.

Janelia and Tog both laughed.

"This might be one of those meals you want to pretend is something else," Tog suggested.

Janelia glanced apologetically at me.

"We're going to eat up the bread first, before it goes bad," she said. "And it was stale to begin with, because we didn't have the time or the money to wait for fresh this morning. Later we'll catch some fish and maybe rabbits or fowl as we go along. And I have an idea for a way to make money to buy more food in the villages we pass—the meals will get better after this, I promise."

I wanted to be noble and gracious and murmur something like, "Oh, I'm sure it will be delicious"—and somehow sound sincere. But the thought of stale, hard bread made my stomach churn once again. I thought I was showing great nobility and graciousness just forcing myself to hold out my hand to take the small chunk of bread Janelia dropped into my palm. The bread felt as dense as a stone and no more appetizing.

Tog and Herk tore into their chunks of bread as if they hadn't eaten in days. Janelia smiled apologetically and began gnawing on her own piece, which I noticed was by far the smallest portion.

Somehow that detail made it possible for me to lift my hand to my mouth and at least try to start nibbling the bread.

In no time at all Herk had gobbled down his bread. He glanced pointedly at the piece Janelia had laid aside on a clean kerchief for Terrence.

"How long will it take Terrence to get back?" Herk asked.

"It looked like a ways to that river," Tog said. He shoved the bread on the kerchief a little farther from Herk. "Why? You know Terrence won't share."

"I know," Herk said. "I'm just thirsty. And—I thought we could play a game."

Janelia pushed my gourd toward Herk.

"There's a few drops left in that," Janelia told him.

But—I'm the princess! I thought. *Nobody except other royalty or the official taster would share a princess's drinking goblet!*

I reminded myself this was a dried-out gourd Janelia was offering Herk, not a goblet. I kept my mouth shut.

"And, Herk, we talked about this last night," Janelia said, fixing Herk with a stern gaze as he upended the gourd into his mouth, gathering perhaps three or four drops. "Until we get to Fridesia, nobody will have time or energy to play the running-around games you like so much. We have to focus on getting there as fast and as safely as we can."

"I didn't mean *that* kind of game," Herk protested. "I just thought, since Princess Desmia didn't see anything we passed this morning, we could have a competition. Each of us can tell the best things we saw, and then she can judge whose story she likes best."

Tog and Janelia glanced anxiously at me and then at each other, as if they were both thinking, *Doesn't he get that the scenery we passed this morning would have terrified Desmia? Doesn't he understand that she wouldn't even want to think about the world outside this circle of rocks right now? Who's going to tell him that?*

But Herk was peering at me so eagerly, I suddenly couldn't bear to see him quashed.

"Let's hear your story," I said. "I'm already sure it'll be best."

"No fair saying that yet!" Herk said, sticking out his bottom lip. "Now I know you're just going to let me win!"

What had I done wrong?

"Oh, no," Tog soothed Herk quickly. "The princess *won't* think that after she hears my story. You just *think* you have the advantage."

"I know I can't compete with the two of you," Janelia said. "So I'll go first, and get out of the way. I saw . . ." She lowered the small sliver of bread she still held, and tilted her head thoughtfully. "I saw a family of butterflies, right after sunrise, flying over a field of flowers. There were five of them, just like there are five of us, and it looked like they were watching over one another. They sparkled in the sunlight and it felt like a promise or something, that they would be safe, and we would be safe, all the way to Fridesia. . . ."

"You're making that up!" Herk protested.

Janelia held up her hand.

"God's honest truth," she said. "It's what I saw. What I felt."

She had her eye on me. I looked away, embarrassed.

"Well, I saw these two bees, and it looked like they were racing each other to land on the same flower," Herk said, all in a rush. "And they flew so fast that when they landed on the flower they flipped over and fell off. The ground wasn't that far away, but their faces were so funny, looking at each other. I know bees can't talk, but if they could, I bet they would have said, 'You pushed me!' 'No, you pushed me!'"

"And then they would have punched each other, and it

would have been just like you and Augie back home," Janelia said.

"Maybe," Herk admitted.

Butterflies, bees . . . Once I would have dismissed all creepy-crawly things as equally disgusting and unpleasant. Knowing that there were insects around would have made me even more panicked this morning as I hid under my sheet. But maybe I'd managed to catch a little bit of the awe and humor Janelia and Herk had seen in their stories. I kept my face carefully neutral when the others turned to me.

"My story's the best so far, isn't it?" Herk asked. "Tog, tell yours, then Princess Desmia can really judge."

But Tog was standing up.

"Doesn't it seem like Terrence has been gone too long?" he muttered.

"You want to go look for him, while Herk and I stay with Desmia?" Janelia asked quietly.

Tog nodded.

"Just—be careful," Janelia said. "Stay hidden as much as you can. And we'll stay quiet until you come back."

Tog nodded and slipped silently away. Herk bit his lip, as if that was the only way to hold back his usual torrent of words. But he didn't make another peep. Janelia popped her last crust of bread into her mouth, and stood up with a studied casualness, as if she wanted Herk and me to think she was only stretching.

I could tell that Janelia was actually keeping watch over

Tog as he threaded his way around the rocks and out of sight.

All that screaming I did . . . did I summon bandits or blackguards, brigands or thieves? I wondered. Have they already killed Terrence and thrown his body away, and now they're just waiting for the right moment to attack the rest of us?

Why hadn't I been able to control myself? Why hadn't all of us been quieter?

What could we do to save ourselves now?

Herk slid one small, grubby hand into mine, and I was amazed at how comforting that felt.

"Your face is turning white again," Herk whispered. "Don't worry. Tog and Terrence are the best fighters. Except, mostly they just fight with each other."

They're just boys, I wanted to say. *Beggar boys, without a single weapon besides their own fists.*

I craned my neck and started to look off in the same direction as Janelia. But that put me back in view of a huge expense of sky, which made me feel dizzy again. I looked back down at the rock, and focused on nibbling the bread. The bread was so hard it required concentration, and probably stronger teeth than I had. After a moment I gave up.

"I'm not very hungry," I lied in a whisper to Herk. "Do you want the rest of my bread?"

Herk's face lit up.

"*Could* I?" he asked. He glanced toward Janelia, as if waiting for her to intercede. But she was still staring off into the distance, watching for Tog and Terrence.

I nodded at Herk and handed over the bread.

"I'll take half," Herk whispered. "And I'll give half to Tog and half to Terrence and half to Janelia."

I wondered if I should tell Herk that was too many halves, or if I could leave that for Janelia to explain. But suddenly there were shouts in the distance, from the direction of the river.

Is it Tog? Terrence? Someone else? I wondered.

The shouting came nearer, and I could tell: It was Tog's voice.

And then I could make out the words.

"He's gone!" Tog screamed. "Terrence ran away!"

17

Janelia bolted down through the rocks, toward Tog.

"Are you sure?" she called to him. "What if he's in danger?"

Tog had just climbed into view. Now he stopped with his back against a rock and snorted angrily.

"He abandoned us and you're afraid *he's* in danger?" Tog snarled at Janelia. "I can tell he left on his own. He used a stick to press the words 'Good-bye, fools' into the mud. And then there's a single set of footprints back toward the city."

I winced. Maybe Janelia and Herk did too, but I couldn't look at them right now.

Terrence wouldn't have run away if I hadn't acted crazy, I thought. *He was proud of being chosen to help a princess before that. And then he just saw me as crazy.*

Was it truly that easy for rulers to lose their subjects' trust? Was one slipup, one moment of imperfection, really all it took?

I saw Janelia and Tog lock gazes.

"It was always his own choice whether to come with us or not," Janelia said. She seemed to be trying hard to speak lightly. "We'll do just as well without him."

"Of course we will," Tog said. "I didn't want him to come in the first place."

I wasn't sure if they were trying to reassure me or Herk. I struggled to think of something to say that would sound both regal and as confident as Janelia and Tog.

Herk spoke first.

"Did he at least leave our water gourds behind?" he asked.

"No, but it's summertime! We'll find gourds along the way. And we can make do until we have a chance to dry them. We'll be fine!" Janelia replied.

"We will," Herk said, nodding. "I know we will."

I saw that all three of them were play-acting, speaking just as dishonestly as anyone ever had back at the palace. But this was a different variety of dishonesty than I was used to. It seemed to have nothing but kindness at its heart.

Tog bent down and picked up the last gourd from the ground where Herk had left it.

"I'll go back to the river and at least fill this up, so we have some water with us on the next leg of the trip," he said.

Janelia was scanning the horizon.

"I'll go with you, so I can cut down reeds," she said. "Herk, you can keep watch over Princess Desmia while we're gone, right?"

Herk nodded eagerly.

I had no idea what Janelia was talking about. Reeds? Why would she need to cut reeds? Tog and Janelia were probably going off to confer and figure out what to do without Terrence—and maybe to discuss the deeper, darker motives or dangers behind his leaving. Leaving me behind meant they were treating me like a child, like Herk: someone who needed to be kept in the dark and protected from unpleasant facts. As a princess, I should demand, *Oh no, no, no. You do not leave me out of important conversations! You send* Herk *down to the river for water and we'll have the important conversation right here. You tell me what you know and then you do what* I *decide.*

But I still felt drained and wobbly and unsteady from my moments of screaming uncontrollably under that terrifying dome of sky. I didn't trust my own brain to think clearly right now; I didn't trust my own mouth to speak or hold back the necessary words.

Could it be that right now I trusted Tog and Janelia more than I trusted myself?

Was that safe?

18

The whole time Tog and Janelia were gone, Herk insisted on "standing lookout," as he called it. He climbed up the rocks and peered out at the landscape for miles around—the same landscape that I hadn't been able to bear seeing.

"Your Highness, I see no danger approaching from the east," Herk called down to me. "I see no danger approaching from the north."

He scrambled down from that rock, scurried over to another formation, climbed it, and called down, "No danger from the west or south!"

And then he started over again with the east.

It's just a child's game, I told myself. *To keep him amused.*

Except it wasn't. I remembered Herk and Tog being outside the prison house at the exact right moment when I crashed through the glass and escaped from Madame Bisset. That hadn't been a matter of luck. Herk—and Tog—had been standing lookout then, too, watching and waiting for proof that I was still there, watching and waiting for the right moment to rescue me.

Lying on my stretcher now, with my bandaged feet and aching, muddled head, I felt less proud of my own role in escaping. If Herk and Tog hadn't been there to help, I would have been caught again instantly; my greatest efforts only would have tipped off Madame Bisset that I didn't trust her.

On my own, I never would have had a prayer of getting to Fridesia to search for Cecilia and the others, I told myself. *Of course . . . I'm not sure how much of a prayer I have of getting there with Herk and Tog and Janelia.*

Above me, Herk called out, once again, "No danger approaching from the east, Your Highness!"

Herk was so high up—and I was angled so deeply into the lower rocks—that I could see almost nothing of him scampering around. He stopped climbing for an instant, and I had a momentary view of his bony ankles, sticking out of the bottom of his ragged pants. Herk's ankles looked so scrawny and fragile that I wondered that they could hold him up. And yet those scrawny ankles had carried him all the way out here; they'd held him up while he was carrying *me.*

I was surprised by tears stinging at my eyes.

You've never gotten sentimental about servants helping you before, I told myself.

Except, Herk and Tog and Janelia weren't my servants. I'd never even offered to pay them.

When all this is over, I'll reward them generously, I decided. *I'll announce the reward as soon as Tog and Janelia get back. I should have talked about it from the start. Maybe then Terrence would have stayed, if he'd known he was facing a big reward at the end.*

But did I really want my life to depend on someone who only cared about getting my money?

Maybe it was better not to talk about rewards.

Tog and Janelia came back with grim expressions on their faces. Janelia crouched beside my stretcher while Tog climbed up on the rocks alongside Herk.

"Do you think you might be ready to start moving along now?" Janelia asked hesitantly. "Tog and I both think . . . well, it's not likely that Terrence would hunt up any of your enemies back in the city and tell them where to find you, but . . ."

But what if he did? I thought. *What if he convinced them to come out looking for me on horseback or by carriage? How quickly could they reach us?*

"I'm not even sure who my enemies are—how would Terrence find them?" I asked.

"You and the other princesses put Lord Throckmorton in prison. But you didn't restrict who comes to see him. His wife and sons visit him every day," Janelia said. "And then there's . . ."

I could feel my lips start to tremble.

Strong visage! I ordered myself. *Keep a strong visage!*

"Never mind," Janelia said. "No need to talk of enemies now. All we have to worry about for now is the trip to

Fridesia. We'll need to stay off the road completely now, but that will work out."

Janelia paused, as if she couldn't decide how to bring up the true problem.

"I won't start screaming again," I said, lifting my chin. "I promise." Holding my chin higher meant that I could see a patch of sky over the top of the rocks overhead. I made myself stare at it, just as I'd always tried to stare at the things that scared me.

No different from looking at the sky from the balcony back at the palace, I told myself. *No different at all.*

Only, it was. Because I knew that this sky was completely open and empty. And because, when I'd looked at the sky from the balcony back at the palace, that was before some unknown enemy had burned down the entire palace, before my sister-princesses vanished, before Madame Bisset claimed that all the other princesses were dead.

Somehow in my mind, all of those things were connected to the empty sky.

I couldn't help myself. I began to quake.

I lowered my chin.

"You'll have to carry me with the sheet over my face," I said, my voice clotted with shame. "I'm sorry."

Janelia surprised me by drawing me into a big hug.

"Oh, Desmia, *I'm* sorry," Janelia murmured into my hair, which, now that I thought of it, probably reeked of sweat and dirt and maybe even vomit. "I'm sorry we couldn't get

a carriage for you to travel in, in comfort. I'm sorry that
you have to make this trip at all, worrying about the other
princesses the entire way . . ."

I lifted my arms, willing myself to hug Janelia back.

But I could hear in my mind how Lord Throckmorton
would have viewed the action: *Yes, yes, make her think that
you care about her, too; make her think that you view her as a
true sister and you believe her story completely, and you're not just
using her and Herk and Tog to get what you want.*

And then that thought made it impossible for me to move
at all. I just sat still, absorbing Janelia's embrace, while my
own arms dangled half-up and half-down, caught between
impulses.

It was only later, when I lay back on the stretcher, the
sheet covering my face, that I realized Janelia could have
announced a different choice entirely.

*She could have said, "We have to give up. There's no way the three
of us can carry you to Fridesia,"* I told myself. *She could have said,
"We'll take you back to the capital, but that's it, we want nothing to
do with you after that. You put us in too much danger."*

Janelia and Tog and Herk could have even made the same
choice as Terrence: All of them could have run away.

Why didn't they? I wondered.

It was odd: I could easily understand why someone would
want to harm me. Why was it so hard to understand why
anyone would help me instead?

19

I dozed through a hot, sweaty afternoon under the sheet. Janelia, Tog, and Herk were probably sweating even more than me, so I didn't let myself call out for water. Even when I wasn't actually sleeping, I pretended I was so the other three wouldn't try to talk to me. It was too hard trying to communicate through the cloth over my face, too hard trying to talk to the others as they walked so casually through scenery that terrified me and left me cowering under a sheet.

And they're beggars and I am a princess, I thought. *Don't forget that difference!*

I didn't forget, but I couldn't feel quite so superior about it.

It's like I'm just a thing they're carrying, I thought. *An object, weighing them down.*

It struck me that for most of the time I'd lived in the palace, I'd just been a thing there, too. I'd been a thing that Lord Throckmorton displayed whenever he wanted to awe the rest of the kingdom: *Don't you see? I represent the true princess, who, of course, is a young girl and therefore cannot speak for herself. So you must do everything I say!* I'd been a thing when I'd stood on the balcony every day, waving like an automaton at the commoners in the courtyard below. The palace officials might as well have hung a sign over my head that said, THIS IS YOUR PRINCESS, ALWAYS OUT OF REACH, BUT ALWAYS YOURS. YOUR OWN LIVES MAY BE DESPERATE AND POOR AND PATHETIC, BUT YOU'RE A SUALAN; YOU HAVE THIS AT LEAST! Before Cecilia and Harper came to the palace, I had been a thing even to them, just a placeholder sitting on the throne.

We all forced out the truth, I thought. *The three of us, plus Ella. I wasn't just a thing when we were all working together to find out what was going on!*

But had I gone back to being just a thing in the past month? Hadn't I stood back and let the sister-princesses take charge the way I'd once let Lord Throckmorton run the palace and the kingdom? Hadn't I gone back to smiling prettily and hiding what I truly believed and felt and wondered?

Hadn't I failed to tell the others to watch out for danger?

I can't be just a thing when we get to Fridesia, I told myself. *I'll have to act. I'll have to find all the sister-princesses, or find out what happened to them, or . . . or . . .*

"We're stopping for the night," Janelia said above me.

I realized that I'd tuned out everything the others said for hours. I'd started automatically rolling right or left with the motion of the stretcher, and not even noticing. I'd been so lost in my thoughts that I'd forgotten the outside world.

"Already?" I murmured.

"It's practically pitch-black out!" Janelia said incredulously. "We can barely see where we place our feet! And Herk looks so tired he might as well be sleeping standing up!"

"No, I'm not," Herk said. But he spoke in such a slow, hypnotic voice he could have been talking in his sleep.

"Oh," I said. "I . . . wasn't paying attention."

I hadn't noticed the darkness, but it felt like a comfort now, a relief from the sunlight blazing down on me, baking me even through the sheet.

"Don't worry, we'll camp for the night in a place that's sheltered from the sky," Tog said from above my head. "I've had my eye on a particular overhang alongside the mountains for the past three hours. We're almost there."

"Mountains?" I repeated.

I thought of the topographical map of Suala that always hung in Lord Throckmorton's office. When I was little and he scolded me, I always stared at the peaks of the mountains on the map and imagined myself there—or, really, anywhere but Lord Throckmorton's office.

It hadn't quite occurred to me that they were real.

"Here we are!" Janelia announced.

I felt my stretcher eased down to the ground, the sheet sliding away from my face. "Close your eyes. I'll drape this over the rocks, and then it will be like a tent," Tog said.

I heard him scurrying about. A moment later, he said, "There. Done."

I opened my eyes. "Tent" was too elegant a word to describe the enclosure I was in, with filthy dark rocks on three sides, and the sheet hanging down at the front. But there was no danger that I would glimpse the sky, and I was grateful for that.

"Thank you," I whispered, sitting up.

It was so dark I didn't realize Tog was still standing right beside me until my shoulder brushed his leg.

"I have to go make the fire now," Tog said hastily, backing away. "We're having stew tonight. Maybe you heard, maybe you weren't asleep when this happened—Herk made a slingshot, and, well, it's hardly a royal feast, but he was so proud when he hit a weasel, and—"

"A *weasel?*" I repeated. "People can eat that?"

Tog went instantly silent. Even in the darkness, I could tell that I'd offended him.

"I mean, that's wonderful," I said, trying to recover my manners. "I'm sure it will be lovely."

"No," Tog said stiffly. "It will probably be tough and bristly. But it's food, so—"

"I'll be sure to thank Herk," I said.

Tog bowed out past the sheet. I couldn't tell if I'd placated him or not.

A few moments later, Tog started the fire outside my "tent," and so every motion the others took was silhouetted against the sheet. The contrast between firelight and shadows made even the most ordinary motion seem dreamlike: Janelia placing a small pot over the flames, Tog pouring in water from the gourd, Herk dropping in what must have been the weasel meat . . .

It's no different from eating venison or wild boar, I told myself. *Why did you have to say anything?*

I wondered if the other three would bring food and then leave me alone. But when Janelia came by with a dented cup of stew (which actually did smell good), Janelia ducked under the sheet and took a seat on a rock beside me.

"We only have one spoon," Janelia said. "We had to sell the rest last night to buy supplies. So—you eat, and then the rest of us will take our turns."

It had never struck me as unfair in the palace that royalty and palace officials ate first, and then, if there was anything left, the ones who had actually prepared the food got their chance. But I'd never spent time in the presence of the people who prepared the food.

I pushed the stew away.

"Why don't the rest of you eat first?" I asked. "I haven't been walking, and you have, and . . ."

Herk was already shoving his way in under the sheet.

"All right!" he said. "I'll take that serving."

"Herk! Manners!" Janelia protested.

"It's fine," I said, handing over the dented metal cup. "You provided the meat. And I appreciate that."

Clutching the cup, Herk backed out past the sheet again.

"I am showing manners! I know not to eat in front of people who are still hungry!" he called over his shoulder.

Janelia laughed. But she made no attempt to follow Herk. She lifted something from her lap that I hadn't noticed before—some sort of long, flat, slender leaf? Some sort of reed, still dripping water? Janelia twisted her hands. In the dim light from the fire, it was hard to tell exactly what she was doing, but it was something like a braiding motion. Was it possible to braid reeds?

"What's that?" I asked.

Janelia held out the pair of reeds in her hand, twisted together into what looked like a flat surface.

"This is my plan for raising money as we go—I picked up reeds down by the river, and now I'm making baskets," she explained. She paused, and the clump of reeds threatened to slip out of her hand. "That is, if I can remember how to do it. My mother taught me so long ago . . . Our mother, I mean. I'm sure she planned to teach you someday, just as she taught Rebecca and Lyssie, and Cala . . ."

"Those are your other sisters who died?" I asked.

"*Our* other sisters," Janelia corrected.

She fell silent for a moment, evidently needing all her concentration for the slippery reeds. She blinked, as if it took great effort to get her eyes to focus in the dim light.

She walked all day, she hasn't eaten yet—you'd think she'd be too tired to work, I thought. *But she's working anyway.*

Meanwhile I felt jittery with having done nothing all day long. Even back at the palace I would have walked from my chambers to the meeting rooms to the dining hall. I would have worn myself out with pacing, if nothing else. Lying on a stretcher all day doing nothing but worrying left me with excess, useless energy.

"Show me how to do that," I said impulsively. "Please?"

Janelia looked up, startled.

"All right," she said. She moved closer and handed me the coiled reeds. "I'll let you work this one, since it's already started, and starting's the hardest part. The pattern is over two, under one, like this. . . ."

I watched, then imitated the pattern myself.

"Oh, it's kind of like needlepoint, isn't it?" I asked. "My friend Ella—the one girl I know I can trust in Fridesia—she says needlepoint was invented because corsets weren't *enough* torture for royal women. But I've always liked it. The way the patterns always made so much sense, and if you messed up, you could see it right away and fix it . . ."

"Desmia, you almost never messed up," Janelia said softly. "Even when you were first learning."

I jerked my gaze from the reeds to Janelia's face.

"What?"

"I'm the one who taught you needlepoint," Janelia said. "When you were three."

I shook my head—not in denial, but because this

seemed so disconnected from my own memories. Was it possible? I didn't actually remember the first time I'd grasped a needle and pressed it through cloth. I couldn't remember *not* knowing the chain stitch, the split stitch, the wheat stitch, the French knots . . .

For a moment I had the same sensation I'd had in Janelia's basement home, of *almost* remembering, of feeling a memory squirm away without quite surfacing.

"Think hard," Janelia said. "Can't you remember? I told you the needle was like a fish, swimming through the cloth. . . ."

"Mmm . . . I don't know," I admitted.

Trying to remember bothered me. Even the innocent image of the fish made me think of danger. It made me want to shout, *Swim fast, little fish! There are men on shore with spears and hooks and fishing lines! Swim away to safety! Now!*

Was this the same instinct that had made me want to warn my sister-princesses back at the palace? That made me want to tell them, *Watch out for vipers! Watch out for their fangs!*

I should have warned them. I'd failed them. If I'd warned them, they would have been on guard at the ball that night. They would have been safe right now.

I shook my head again.

"Why didn't you teach me basket-weaving back at the palace?" I asked.

"Oh law, where would I have gotten the reeds?" Janelia asked. "Even if Lord Throckmorton and the other palace officials would have approved of a princess knowing a common skill like basket-weaving—and having all those tiny cuts on your hands from the reeds . . . well, you saw. It was a half day's journey to the right kind of reeds."

"Oh," I said. "I didn't think of that." I had the sudden feeling that I didn't know anything about my kingdom. I'd never seen the Sualan Mountains or the wheat fields of the east or the swampy lands where the reeds and rushes grew. And as long as open sky terrified me, I never would.

"How did your—our—mother learn how to weave baskets, anyhow, living so far from reeds?" I asked.

"Mam grew up in one of the river villages," Janelia said, starting a second basket. "She and Da both did. They were already married before they moved to the capital city. You can start working on the sides of that basket. You keep the same pattern, just pull the reeds tighter together."

I nodded and tilted the reeds slightly, increasing the tension.

"Why did they go to the capital? Why didn't they stay in their village?" I asked.

I wasn't thinking of Janelia's parents as truly having any connection to me. Indeed, I was asking about them to keep Janelia from bringing up more immediate, less comfortable topics.

"There wasn't much in their village," Janelia said, her head bent over her basket. "It's not like they were seeking their fortunes in the capital, exactly, but . . . they wanted a better life. For themselves and their children, in the future."

"And did that happen?" I asked, concentrating mostly on the pattern of reeds in my hands.

Janelia looked up and smiled ruefully.

"It would appear to most people that *you* made out all right," she said.

Herk pushed back in at the sheet again before I had a chance to answer.

"Mam! Mam!" he cried, and I feared that the snakes or wolves he'd talked about earlier had materialized beside the fire. But he went on, "It's your turn to eat!"

"Thank you, Herk," Janelia said, with exaggerated patience. "Next time you enter Princess Desmia's private chambers, make sure you have permission, all right?"

"'Private . . . chambers?'" Herk repeated in puzzlement. "We're outside!"

Janelia pointed at the sheet.

"This is the most privacy we have to offer her, so please respect it," she said.

"Sor-ry," Herk said, backing away.

Janelia patted him on the head, as she slipped out past the sheet.

"You're forgiven," she said.

Janelia and Herk weren't actually related, but was this how normal mothers and children talked to one another? If the queen had lived, would she have treated me with that same bemused but proud affection?

I reminded myself that if the queen had lived, she probably would have had more natural-born children of her own. Ones that didn't die at birth. She wouldn't have had to engage in that desperate charade of passing off orphaned pauper babies as princesses.

And what would have become of me then?

What was going to become of me now?

20

It was the middle of the night, and I could not possibly have been wider awake.

Actually, I was only guessing about it being the middle of the night. Out here in the wilderness, far from the palace clock (which no longer existed, anyway), I had no way of knowing the exact time. But it was dark out, and it had been dark for hours. And the darkness weighed on me in a way that made me feel certain there were hours more of darkness ahead of me.

You're surrounded by a sheet and three walls of rock—it's not like you're missing any lovely view in the absence of light, I reminded myself.

If I'd been back at the palace—if it still existed—I could have lit a candle and opened a book of poetry. Or whiled away the rest of the night by hunching over needlepoint.

The thought of needlepoint reminded me of the basket Janelia had started me on. I used up a moment or two groping for it, but I'd only just learned basket-weaving—I couldn't trust myself to do it in utter darkness.

Wasn't there light anywhere?

My eyes prickled, searching for it. Wait—was there a hint of light over at the bottom edge of the sheet?

Yes, and if there's light, it's outside the sheet, out where the landscape and the sky will terrify you, I told myself. *Just go back to sleep.*

I closed my eyes.

They popped back open.

A jagged rock dug into my back, and when I squirmed to avoid it, another one just as sharp dug into my side. My wounded feet throbbed. But my muscles screamed for me to just get up, just *do* something that wasn't lying still, wasn't waiting, wasn't worrying.

Something that wasn't imagining my sister-princesses dead. And wasn't imagining Terrence bringing all my enemies galloping after me.

I turned over.

The slight glimpse of light at the bottom of the sheet was more definite now that my right eye lined up with the ground.

You can keep yourself from screaming long enough to look out for a moment, I told myself. *Just to see where that's coming from. Just to know.*

I got up onto my knees on the stretcher, and shoved the opposite end of the stretcher to the side. I was pretty sure that that would enable me to crawl the length of the stretcher to the edge of the sheet.

But crawling was awkward, and I wasn't used to feeling awkward. I was used to gliding across the polished floors of the palace in silken dresses that whispered of grace and refinement. I hadn't crawled since . . .

Since the fire, I thought, slipping back into the memory of falling to my knees to avoid the smoke and gracelessly hiking up my ball gown to crawl toward the unconscious Fidelia.

That memory reminded me to hitch up my rough-woven skirt now, and perhaps that saved me from pitching forward and smashing my face against the jagged rocks. I froze, seeing in my mind how easily that could still happen: One moment of losing my balance and then I'd have a cheek or even an eye bloodied by the rocks surrounding me. . . .

Don't be such a coward, I chided myself.

That propelled me to scoot forward along the stretcher until my outstretched hands brushed the sheet. I inched it back, cautioning myself, *Don't scream, don't scream . . . Even if you start to panic, don't do anything to let anyone else know. . . . Just drop the sheet and go back to sleep. . . .*

The first glimpse I got beyond the sheet puzzled me. Were those . . . sparkling jewels studded in some rock wall at a distance far beyond me?

I pulled the sheet back farther and gaped.

No, not jewels . . . stars.

The empty sky that had terrified me at high noon was no longer empty or terrifying. It was a velvet dome studded with stars everywhere I looked—stars so abundant and wondrous and beautiful that it was like seeing thousands of diamonds scattered across the sky and glittering back at me. I craned my neck and peered side to side, horizon to horizon.

"Desmia?" a voice whispered. "You have need of . . . help? Shall I wake Mam?"

It was Tog. I blinked, my eyes struggling to make out his location, halfway between me and the two slumbering lumps that had to be Herk and Janelia, out on the flat expanse nearby. Tog was beside the embers of the fire he'd built earlier. That fire must have been the source the glow I'd noticed before, from behind my sheet. In my awe over the stars, I'd forgotten that that was what I'd been searching for.

I realized Tog was asking an indelicate question.

"No, I have no need of a . . . chamber pot," I said, even though we had no chamber pot with us. I had discovered earlier in the day that my only option was squatting over the ground, with Janelia's help—an embarrassing procedure made even more difficult by my wounded feet.

I went back to staring at the stars.

"The sky doesn't frighten you now?" Tog asked.

I shook my head.

"How could it?" I asked. "Not when it's . . ." There were no words to fit what I wanted to say. I settled for gesturing and murmuring, ". . . like *that*."

Tog laughed, but it was a friendly laugh.

"Your eyes are as big as globes," he observed. "Have you never seen stars before?"

"Of course I've seen stars," I snapped indignantly. Tog looked hurt, and I softened my tone. "But . . . I don't think they looked like this from the palace."

The truth was, I couldn't remember even one moment at the palace that I'd spent gazing out the window at stars.

Probably Janelia would tell me that she used to watch the stars with me, when I was little, I thought scornfully.

But the thought tickled something in my brain—maybe I had watched stars with Janelia, years ago. Maybe I had just forgotten.

"Probably all the torches around the palace were too distracting," Tog offered. "I don't remember stars looking like this from Mam's basement, either. Maybe you have to be out in the wilderness to see stars properly."

"Maybe," I said. I kept gazing at the stars. "In the chapel, back at the palace . . . there were gilt stars painted on the ceiling, and it was supposed to be a marvel. Whenever we had foreign dignitaries visit, we showed them that, and they were always amazed. But those painted stars were nothing compared with this."

I wondered now if the foreign dignitaries had only been pretending to be amazed—yet another show of falsehood in the palace full of lies. For surely, traveling to Suala, they'd seen the night sky in the wilderness for themselves.

Or maybe they hadn't, I thought. *Maybe they'd gone from carriage to inn to carriage and never looked up.*

That's how I would have traveled to Fridesia, if I'd had my way. And would I have had even a moment of noticing the stars in the night sky, on that kind of trip?

I sneaked a shy glance at Tog.

"Are you staying awake just to admire the stars?" I asked. Perhaps he wasn't just a beggar boy. Perhaps he had the soul of a poet.

Tog snorted, then stopped himself.

"Uh, you may believe that if you wish, princess," he said.

"But it's not true, is it?" I asked, suddenly annoyed just by the word "princess." Or maybe it was the way he said it.

I could barely see Tog's face, because it was shadowed even so close to the fire.

"No," Tog said. He turned, and I could see his face more clearly. The dim light made his features stand out more than the dirt covering them. He had a nose as straight as any courtier's. His eyes were a nice shade of green.

"Tell me," I said.

"Mam and Herk and I are taking turns standing watch through the night," Tog said. "Mam took the first shift. I have until the moon reaches there"—he pointed toward what I thought might be the west—"and then it's Herk's turn."

I should have been able to figure this out. After a long day of walking and carrying me, of course Tog wouldn't stay up for something as frivolous as gazing at the stars.

"You think we're in danger, even way out here," I said. "You could have told me."

"I wouldn't have thought I needed to," Tog said.

Was he calling me stupid? Was this the kind of insubordinate insult that any royal should quash immediately?

"But . . . the stars *are* beautiful," Tog said, and somehow that made it impossible for me to scold him. It was enough that he appreciated the stars as much as I did.

He twisted something in his hands, and I realized he was weaving the same kind of basket that Janelia had shown me.

"You're almost done with that?" I asked in surprise.

"Oh, Mam did most of it," Tog said. "I'm probably making it *less* valuable, because I'm not as good at this as she is. But I thought she'd be happy to have at least one basket done."

"I could do some of it," I offered.

Instantly I worried that I'd offended him yet again, but he walked over and handed it to me. Even in the dim light, I could tell that the last two rows of weaving were pulling the basket lopsided.

"Keep in mind, I was trying my best," Tog said apologetically.

"I think, if you just don't pull so hard . . . and let out the tension of what you just did . . . then maybe . . . ," I murmured. I sat down and began tugging on the reeds.

Tog crouched down beside me.

"You *are* making it better!" he announced.

"But here, can you pull this reed this way for me, while I pull back on it . . . ," I asked.

We worked together for a few moments, then Tog suggested, "Put it down flat, and let's see if it looks better now."

It did.

"Mam will be so happy if we finish this!" Tog cried. "She worries, you know, about food. . . ."

I shifted uncomfortably. Maybe I could have found a way to tap into the royal treasury for money for the trip. Maybe there would have been a financial adviser I could have trusted.

Maybe I'd been unfair to Herk and Tog and Janelia expecting them to take me to Fridesia in the first place.

"Do you want me to finish the basket?" I said.

"Be my guest," Tog said, grinning.

I expected him to go back to the fire and leave me alone. Instead, he slid down to the ground beside me, leaning his back against the rock.

"Maybe if I watch, I'll learn how to do it right," he said.

I fell into a rhythm with the reeds and the weaving. In no time at all, I reached the end of one of the reeds, and Tog and I agreed that the basket was tall enough.

I leaned my head back against the rocks and started giggling.

"If anyone from the palace could see me now," I said, "they'd . . . they'd . . ."

I couldn't finish the thought; it was too absurd. I could imagine Cecilia, for instance, gawking at the sight of me sitting on a bare, dirty rock in the middle of the wilderness, wearing a cheap, rough-woven peasant dress instead of silk or satin, my hair neither brushed nor combed by any servant in days, not since . . .

Since the night of the fire, I remembered. *Since Cecilia and the other princesses and I sat in our chambers together, getting ready for the ball.*

Something twisted in my giggling. If it changed much more, it might be sobbing, rather than laughter.

Tog began pounding me on the back. Evidently he thought I was choking.

"Are you all right?" he asked. "Should I get my mam?"

"No, I—"

"Is the empty sky scaring you again?" Tog asked frantically. "Do you need to go back into your tent?"

"No," I said. "No."

I looked back at the starry sky above, and somehow this steadied me. It made it possible for me to be silent again. After a moment I felt composed enough to explain.

"This sky is too beautiful to scare me," I said.

"The sky is beautiful in the daytime, too," Tog said. He looked at me out of the corner of his eye. "Maybe you need to work up to appreciating it. Just glance at it a second or two at a time. Then a little more each day."

I squinted at Tog. It had never occurred to me that I

could stop being terrified of the daytime sky.

"Is that what the soldiers you know do?" I asked. "The ones you said I was acting like? Do they force themselves to get used to scary things gradually?"

"Some of them," Tog said, tilting his head thoughtfully. "The ones who survive."

And the others die? I wanted to ask. I found myself wanting to ask how many soldiers he knew in each category. What was the likelihood of each outcome? What were my chances of being cured of my fear?

And was death the only other option?

I didn't ask any of those questions.

"It's probably very strange for you, out here," Tog said. He brushed his curly hair back from his face. Somehow that just made his hair messier. "You probably miss the palace."

Was he being like Madame Bisset and assuming that I would miss the palace more than I missed the other girls? For a moment, something like fury threatened to overcome me. But then I heard Tog add, ". . . and everyone in it. You must miss everyone you love. Being out here is strange for me, too, but at least I still have Herk and Mam with me."

But not Terrence, I thought but didn't say.

I tilted my head back, gazed up at the stars, and whispered, "I don't miss the palace. I'm glad it's gone."

Tog jerked his head toward me. His eyes bugged out.

"What? You wanted it to burn?"

I looked down at the dark rock beneath me. Why had I admitted that out loud? Now I had to explain.

"I didn't want it to burn," I said. "Because . . ." I had a moment of remembering the screaming, the running, the panicked crowd in the ballroom. And then, just like that, I walled off that memory in my mind. "I'm afraid people got hurt. I don't believe my sister-princesses died, but . . . I think some people might have."

Somehow I needed the cover of darkness to actually admit that. Tog was still staring at me in confusion.

"But you're glad—" he began.

"About losing the palace," I said. "Yes."

Tog's confused squint only deepened.

"I was never inside it, of course," he said. "But Janelia said it was beautiful. I thought you liked beautiful things."

I gazed out at the horizon, where the dark, formless land met the glory of the starry sky.

"The palace . . . ," I began. "I think everything about the palace was designed to make you feel small. To make anyone who stepped foot in there feel small. All those mirrors were so big . . . it was like they were there to whisper, *You're not good enough. You're not worthy.* I think the idea was that if people came to petition the king—or, in my time there, Lord Throckmorton—the palace made it so that they would feel so low and humble that they'd forget they wanted anything, except to get out of there alive. But I always wondered, did the palace make kings and queens feel small too? My ancestors? Did they have to keep adding on and making the turrets taller and the spires higher because that was the only way they could say back to the world, *See, I do deserve this palace! I am the master of it all! Look upon me and tremble!"*

Tog tilted his head, listening intently. And thinking. He seemed to be thinking hard.

"Mam would say those weren't your ancestors," he said. "Not your real ones."

"I always believed they were my ancestors," I said. "And the way everything turned out, they might as well have been."

Tog opened his mouth, then shut it.

"Were you going to tell me that isn't true?" I asked.

He looked away. His gaze seemed to be aimed toward the horizon too.

"Mam's been fretting about you for the past ten years," he said. "I mean, she fretted about me and Herk and the other boys, too—she's such a *mother*. But, you, the way she talked about you, it was like you were right there with the rest of us, growing up. Only, you were always still a four-year-old."

I let out a barking laugh.

"Lord Throckmorton always treated me like a four-year-old too," I said. "Like I didn't have a mind of my own. Like I was a puppet."

"A puppet wouldn't be on her way to Fridesia right now," Tog said. "Only someone who was truly brave would be going to Fridesia."

I had had courtiers tell me that my face was lovely; I'd had music masters tell me that my lute-playing was exquisite;

I'd had ladies-in-waiting ooh and aah over the perfection of
my needlepoint stitches. Back at the palace, everyone from
the lowliest servants up to the most influential advisers and
counselors felt it their duty to blanket me in compliments
all day long. It was like any pathway I stepped down had to
be first lined with layers of praise. Perhaps once upon a time
I had believed it all. But once I took to listening at palace
doors from the secret passageways, I'd quickly learned to
trust none of it: the same music master who praised my
skill to my face called me tone-deaf when he thought I was
out of earshot; the ladies-in-waiting gossiped and nitpicked
and carped behind my back; even the courtiers, on their
own, complained that my eyes were just a tad too big for
their taste and I was probably too prissy for kissing.

But *this*—this was a compliment.

And somehow I was sure that Tog meant it.

21

In the morning when Janelia came to wake me, I considered saying, *You can take the sheet down and I can eat breakfast out in the open with the rest of you. I'll travel today sitting up on the stretcher, with nothing covering my face.*

But the world looked different by the light of day. I saw the pile of rocks I might have fallen into the night before, and they really could have destroyed my face. How could I bear seeing the dangers all around me every moment of the day?

Gradually, I told myself. *Tog said the soldiers he knew worked up to facing their fears gradually. So that's how I'll do it too.*

Janelia peeled the bandages from my feet and examined the wounds.

"Oh, everything is healing so well!" she exclaimed. "You'll be able to walk again long before we get to Fridesia."

Then she glanced up, wincing at her own words.

"I mean—when you're ready otherwise," she added.

"I'll start going without the sheet over my face for short periods of time today," I told her. "I'll be able to go completely without it by the time my feet heal."

It was strange: Back at the palace, I had made a habit of keeping my plans to myself. Even after Cecilia and the others arrived, I shared very little. But something about Janelia's hopeful, expectant expression made me tell her things.

The other three packed up and moved out before the sun was fully over the horizon. I knew this, because I'd peeked out from the sheet soon after I'd settled onto the stretcher.

And I'd managed not to scream.

I also noticed, in that glimpse, that Herk and Tog were working incredibly hard to erase every trace of the fire, every sign that four people had camped there.

Of course, I thought. *They don't want anyone following us. They don't want anyone knowing which way we went . . . or that I'm going to Fridesia at all.*

It was so boring lying flat on the stretcher for hours on end, unable to see a thing. When the others took their first break, I asked hesitantly, "Do you suppose I could weave my basket sitting under the sheet, while we travel?"

"Of course," Janelia replied, her voice seeming to come from so far away, just from the other side of the sheet. "Why would that be a problem?"

"I don't want to make the stretcher any harder to carry," I replied.

"Having you sit up and work won't matter for that," Tog said, almost brusquely. I could hear the weariness in his voice.

At least if I weave baskets, I'm doing something, I thought.

I was able to finish not one, but two baskets by the end of that day of walking.

"But—they're exquisite, Desmia," Janelia said, examining them that evening.

This night we were all camped out in a cave together. They'd given me a section off to the side, which Herk kept calling the palace room.

"So we've got three baskets to sell?" Tog said, coming into the cave with a pile of firewood on his shoulder. "It looks like there's a village just a mile or so to the east, and it's still light out—do you want Herk and me to go into the village and see if we can trade the baskets for food?"

"Sounds wonderful," Janelia said. "You should go right now—I'll start the fire."

After the boys left, I shyly watched Janelia stacking the firewood beneath a hole in the ceiling that I guessed was the cave version of a chimney. Janelia tucked twigs and dried leaves between the larger branches, then began rubbing what looked like stones together.

"What does that—" I began. A spark leaped from the stones to the wispiest, driest leaves. "Ooh. How did you know how to do that?"

"Start a fire, you mean?" Janelia asked. "Didn't you ever notice who lit the fireplaces at the palace?"

I hadn't ever paid attention. But I could guess where Janelia was going with this.

"The maidservants?" I asked. "So you learned how to start fires when you were attending the queen?"

Janelia laughed.

"No, I learned *how* when I was a small child helping my mam," Janelia said. "But I got a lot of practice serving the queen. Of course, the idea was to never let the fire go out so you didn't have to go to all this effort, but . . ."

But it's not like we can carry fire along with us, traveling, I thought.

Janelia put a pot of water on the fire to boil. Then she went over to the mouth of the cave and peered off into the distance.

"I hope the boys are all right, going to that village so late in the day," she murmured, clutching at her apron.

"There's nothing else left to eat, is there?" I asked. I'd noticed when we stopped for lunch that we were down to only crumbs.

Janelia bit her lip, as if trying to decide whether to tell the truth. A moment passed before she finally said, bluntly, "No."

Some of the panic I'd felt the day before threatened to come back, but I tamped it down.

"Oh, I'm sure when we get back into a wooded area, Herk can hunt more," Janelia said. "But we were walking through such scruffy areas today—there were barely any plants, let alone animals."

Janelia was kneading pleats into her apron. For all that I'd never thought much about money in the palace, I could see what a constant worry it was for Janelia.

"How did you have money for food in the first place?" I asked.

"Oh, you heard us talking about this—we sold all but one of our spoons, and we sold that fancy nightgown you were wearing. . . . Terrence was the one who handled that, and I worry now that he made contacts with bad men doing that, because what honest tradesman would buy a royal-looking nightgown from a beggar boy?" Janelia fretted. "Without suspecting it was stolen? We're lucky no one called the magistrate on him, but . . ."

"Maybe our luck would have been if someone *had* called the magistrate on him," I said sharply. "Then we wouldn't have had to worry about him carrying news to my enemies, and we would have brought a more reliable third boy with us."

Janelia seemed almost ready to bite clear through her lip.

"I do still worry about Terrence," she murmured. "He's not a bad boy, just . . . easily misled."

I remembered Tog and Janelia arguing about Terrence from the very start. Janelia probably wasn't the right person to talk with about Terrence.

I shook my head.

"I know all that about how you got money for this trip,"

I said. "I actually meant, years ago, after you left the palace, how did you have money to take in and raise all those boys?"

Something changed in Janelia's face—was she shocked that I asked that?

Too late, I realized that just as asking about someone's wealth was rude in the palace, asking about someone's poverty was probably an improper question outside.

The problem was, I was truly curious. It was much easier to avoid rudeness when you weren't curious.

"I should have told you the rest of the story already," Janelia said. "It's just . . . it's sad. You have enough sad things to deal with right now."

"My sister-princesses *aren't* dead!" I said. "I'm going to find them!"

Janelia gave me a look that I couldn't quite read.

"We'll help you as much as we can, doing that," Janelia said. She came away from the mouth of the cave and checked the pot of water on the fire. I could see steam starting to rise.

"You're showing a lot of faith that Herk and Tog are going to come back with food soon, if you're already boiling water to cook it," I said.

"This water is for boiling rags, to clean your wounds again," Janelia said. She pulled the pot off the fire. "But we need to let this cool a little now."

She seemed a bit at a loss about what to do next.

"Tell me the story while we wait, then," I suggested.

Janelia winced, then nodded and sat down beside me.

"I got fired from my job at the palace when you were four," she said.

Ten years ago, I thought. I couldn't think of any memory I could definitely identify as being from that long ago. I hoped Janelia would move quickly to talking about events that had nothing to do with me.

"It was . . . It was awful," Janelia said, staring down at the cave floor. "A footman accused me of stealing a silver vase. A lady-in-waiting said I'd been rude to her. And that was just the beginning of the accusations. They kept coming, one after the other. None of it was true, and nobody had ever accused me of anything before that, but . . . it was like suddenly I was the worst person in the palace!"

I stirred uncomfortably. This sounded like regular palace life to me. Someone fell out of favor, and instantly everyone piled on, listing all the misdeeds that person might be guilty of. But I had always stayed above the fray. I'd never had to wonder what it would be like to be the target of such false allegations.

At least, not until rumors started flying that I had supposedly killed my sister-princesses.

Nobody could believe that! I thought. *Surely . . .*

I made myself concentrate on Janelia's story.

"Someone just wanted to get rid of you," I said. "They didn't come up with any solid proof, did they? They were probably hoping the accusations would scare you, and you'd leave the palace on your own. And then they wouldn't have to bother disposing of you."

"I wouldn't have ever left, if I'd had a choice," Janelia said, and her voice still carried the despair of a decade earlier. "Not when it meant leaving you behind."

"But you did leave me," I said, and even though I didn't mean them to, the words came out sounding accusatory.

"I stayed as long as I could!" Janelia said. "I tried to fight the accusations—I told anyone who would listen that I was innocent, that I'd never done anything wrong. But then I was summoned before Lord Throckmorton."

I could picture this: Janelia, ten years younger and wearing a maid's simple dress, cowering in the entryway to Lord Throckmorton's imposing suite; Lord Throckmorton's corpulent frame towering over her, his eyes narrowed in disapproval; the cold eyes of the kings and queens and lords and ladies in the portraits behind him seeming to glare down on Janelia as if they, too, disapproved of everything about her.

I could picture all this because of the times I'd been summoned by Lord Throckmorton. I always felt scorned and guilty, thoroughly guilty, even as I racked my brain to think of a single thing I might have done wrong.

"I still don't understand how it all happened," Janelia said. "How could I, a mere maid, have done anything worth the attention of Lord Throckmorton? Even if any of the accusations were true, why would Lord Throckmorton get involved? I've been trying to figure that out for ten years!"

I gasped and put my hand over my mouth.

"What?" Janelia said. "Do you understand? Did he tell you anything about me?"

I slid my hand back from my mouth.

"I didn't know anything about this at the time. I don't even remember you being at the palace," I said. "But if this happened when I was four . . . I think that was when Lord Throckmorton found out I wasn't the true princess. That I was just an impostor. And—he wouldn't have wanted anyone else to know."

I remembered everything my sister-princesses and I had pieced together about our own stories. Every other princess had had a royal item with a secret letter from the queen tucked inside. In Cecilia's case, the royal object had been a harp; some of the other girls had had a pendant or a silver chalice or a bowl. By the time I met my sister-princesses, I had no special item—why should I, when I had a palace full of royal things? But I could remember a crystal globe that broke when I was little. Though of course Lord Throckmorton never confessed, I was certain that he'd found my letter from the queen, and discovered the secret about me that I hadn't even known myself.

But if I could remember the crystal globe, why couldn't I remember Janelia?

Janelia gaped at me.

"If that was Lord Throckmorton's reason, why didn't he

just have me killed?" Janelia asked. "Why didn't he silence me once and for all?"

I felt the danger in that question. I knew how Lord Throckmorton's mind worked; he'd probably considered that possibility.

"Did he ask any odd questions when he summoned you before him?" I asked. "Anything that seemed unrelated to the false accusations?"

"Everything seemed odd and terrifying to me then!" Janelia said wryly. "But . . . he did dwell on exactly when I'd been the queen's serving girl, and whether I was with her until her very last day."

"Because in the queen's letters to her fake-princess daughters, she didn't give the name of the servant who'd gotten the babies from the orphanage," I said. "The queen probably did that to protect you, in case any of the letters fell into the wrong hands. Which they did."

I brooded on this a moment longer.

"Lord Throckmorton must not have been certain you were the right girl," I said. "He had to interrogate you to find out."

"But he never came right out and asked, *Did you get babies from the orphanage for the queen? Did you substitute your own baby sister for the queen's dead daughter?*" Janelia objected.

"Oh, Lord Throckmorton almost never asked a direct question," I said. "He preferred playing cat and mouse. So you'd never know, answering him, if you were accidentally boxing yourself in or backing into one of his traps."

"That's exactly how I felt!" Janelia said. "He had me so confused I felt like saying anything would be like confessing to a crime."

I had always assumed that everyone always felt like that at the palace, at least in the years before Lord Throckmorton was vanquished. But maybe Janelia, as a lowly serving girl, had been oblivious for most of her time in the palace. Maybe she'd been too focused on building fires and emptying chamber pots to see the palace intrigue around her.

"You didn't say anything about me, did you?" I asked. "You didn't tell him I was really your sister, or—"

"No, no—of course not!" Janelia said. "I wouldn't endanger you like that!"

"So you didn't even speak my name to Lord Throckmorton," I asked, and I winced at how much I sounded like Lord Throckmorton, drawing someone into one of his traps.

Janelia's eyes darted to the side.

"Well . . . ," she began. "I didn't give away your identity, but . . . I begged to be allowed to stay in the palace, to take care of you."

"So he knew I was important to you," I said, tapping my chin thoughtfully.

"Was I supposed to lie?" Janelia asked, flashing me an uncertain smile.

Yes, no, maybe, I thought.

"Any action you chose had risks," I said. "Lord Throckmorton was very good at telling when people lied."

"So what could I have done?" Janelia pleaded. Somehow the tables had turned, and it felt like Janelia was the younger girl and I was the older, wiser sister she was begging for advice.

I shrugged.

"Nothing," I said. "Lord Throckmorton would have found you out, no matter what. If it served his purposes to banish you, he would have banished you from the palace no matter how much you lied or pleaded or pretended to have something to barter with."

But he left Janelia alive, I thought. *Why did he do that?*

Either Janelia was lying now, or she'd left out some key portion of the story. Or I was missing something. Lord Throckmorton never left loose ends that might threaten his power.

Unless . . .

"Did Lord Throckmorton pay you?" I asked abruptly. "Did he give you money to keep my true identity secret?"

"What? *No!*" Janelia said. "He didn't know I knew your true identity! Er—not that he let me know about."

Janelia looked confused. Lord Throckmorton usually did have that effect on people.

I slumped back against the rock wall of the cave.

"But the money you used for raising Tog and Herk and the other boys . . . ," I prompted.

"I was getting to that," Janelia said. "After Lord Throckmorton talked to me, he kicked me out of the palace once and for all. He said if I so much as showed my face at the palace door, I'd be executed. He said I was lucky he didn't execute me on the spot for stealing that silver vase. And I pleaded with him—I said you'd gotten used to me. I said it would be devastating to you to lose your most familiar caregiver, when you'd already lost your parents."

"He wouldn't care about that," I interrupted. But I had to harden my heart to get the words out.

I thought about the bitter old woman I remembered as my earliest nanny: Grechettine. She'd been the first to tell me that people wanted to kill me and steal my throne. She'd give me nightmares and beat me when I woke up screaming in the night.

But had she really been part of my life from the very beginning? Was it possible she'd replaced Janelia when I was four?

Was I maybe screaming for Janelia when I had those nightmares, and that was why Nanny Grechettine beat me so violently?

I couldn't remember. But my words made Janelia wince.

"It's true—Lord Throckmorton didn't waver, no matter how much I pleaded," she said. She had her back firmly against the rock wall too. "He didn't even let me tell you good-bye. I was glad then that I'd at least told you about us being sisters as a kind of fairy tale, something to keep secret between the two of us. I thought you'd figure it out as you got older, and come looking for me."

"But I didn't even remember you, let alone—" I began.

Janelia patted my arm.

"It's not your fault," she said. "I failed too, trying to send messages to you, or finding a way to visit you in secret. All I could do was have Tog and Herk and Terrence and the other boys watch over the palace for me, and keep their ears to the ground to hear any news or gossip about you. . . ."

It was strange how comforting I found that, to think that for the past decade people I hadn't even known were watching over me.

I remembered that one of those people was Terrence, who had betrayed and abandoned me only yesterday.

"Were you paying the boys to spy?" I asked hesitantly. "Paying them with—"

Janelia held up her hand, as if to warn me about the rest of the story.

"When Lord Throckmorton threw me out, I was hysterical," Janelia said. "I was standing there in the courtyard, sobbing like crazy, hitting my fists against the door, and a man I'd never seen before pulled me aside."

"I knew it! One of Lord Throckmorton's agents," I muttered.

Janelia's eyes widened in surprise.

"No," she said, shaking her head emphatically. "It couldn't have been. He saved my life. He kept me from going so crazy that Lord Throckmorton just had the guards kill me."

"Oh, I'm sure this man said he was someone else—" I accused.

"Desmia, listen," Janelia insisted. "It wasn't someone connected with Lord Throckmorton. It was the queen's former physician."

I turned my head and stared at Janelia.

"You mean—"

"Right," Janelia said. "The only person besides me who knew from the beginning that you weren't the true princess."

22

I rubbed my hand wearily across my forehead. Wasn't it enough that I had to wonder if my sister-princesses were alive or dead? Wasn't it enough that I was in the dark about who had set the palace on fire? Wasn't it enough that I had to flee to Fridesia, the land of my former enemies, and that I was wounded and had only paupers to rely on?

How was it that the ancient history from fourteen years ago was haunting me even now?

Because it isn't finished, I thought. *It won't be finished as long as any of the other princesses or I keep the throne. And as long as the losers from the queen's deceptions yearn to get their power back.*

"The queen's physician was banished," I said. "After he delivered the baby princess who died. The princess who truly would have deserved the throne, had she but lived."

I was annoyed that I had not thought to wonder about the fate of the queen's physician. How could I have overlooked both major loose ends in the queen's story: the serving girl *and* the physician? When my sister-princesses and I sent Lord Throckmorton and his henchmen to prison, why hadn't the other girls or I asked, *Hey, any of you know what country that physician was banished to? Any of you know any more angles to this story we need to keep track of?*

I knew the answer to that. None of us would have trusted anything Lord Throckmorton or his henchmen might have said. I didn't even trust anything I'd heard from advisers we didn't send to prison.

I sighed.

"No matter who that man *said* he was," I told Janelia, "I'm almost certain he was in Lord Throckmorton's employ."

And then I could see it clearly, how Lord Throckmorton would have planned things.

"Lord Throckmorton wanted to keep you nearby," I went on. "Just in case he ever needed to get rid of *me*. If I ever rebelled against his authority. He would have called you in and tricked you somehow into admitting that I really wasn't the princess, that it was a lie all along. And somehow he would have worked it to come off that *he* still needed to be left in charge."

"I never would have betrayed you like that!" Janelia protested.

"Not even if the choice was betray me, or betray Tog and Herk and all the other boys you were taking care of?" I asked.

Janelia opened her mouth, shut it, opened it again. She looked like a helpless fish, caught on a hook.

"I couldn't have made that choice," she whispered. "I would have . . . escaped. I would have made sure Tog and Herk and the others rescued me."

In spite of myself, I found myself admiring the fact that Janelia hadn't instantly protested, *Oh, naturally, Desmia, it's you I care about the most! I'd throw all those beggar boys to the wolves before I'd do anything to harm a hair on your head!*

But hadn't Janelia put Tog and Herk and the others at risk, rescuing me? Weren't Tog and Herk at risk right now, traveling to Fridesia with me?

I went back to trying to figure out Lord Throckmorton.

"But if you ever came forward with your secret before Lord Throckmorton wanted it out, he could say, *Look, that woman is just a liar and a thief. She must have stolen that silver vase and probably lots of other precious items from the palace,*" I speculated. "His proof would be the argument, *How else would she have gotten money to live on ever since?*"

Janelia had a puzzled squint on her face.

"I guess . . . I guess what you're saying *might* be true," she said. "But that man was so nice—Lord Constantine, that was what he said to call him. He said he'd been looking for me for four years, but it was hard because he had to travel in disguise, and he couldn't step foot into the palace without fear of discovery. He said the two of us had to watch out for each other, since we knew things other people would kill for. I thought . . . I thought it was God's providence that Lord Constantine found me the very day I lost my job."

Lord Throckmorton's scheming is more like it, I thought darkly.

"Lord Constantine wanted me to leave Suala with him," Janelia said. "He said our lives were in danger as long as we stayed in the kingdom. But I said I couldn't leave you behind. I said I had to find a way to get back into the palace to you. He promised, as long as you were on the throne, he'd never reveal the truth about your background. He'd never do anything to harm you. And—he said he respected my decision so much that he'd arrange for me to have enough money to live on."

I saw Lord Throckmorton's fingerprints all over that conversation. Of course Lord Throckmorton would want Janelia to stay close by the palace, in case he ever needed her testimony to discredit my claim to the throne. I shivered. My life had been in even more danger in the palace than I'd believed. If Lord Throckmorton had ever decided I was irredeemably recalcitrant, no doubt Janelia would have been brought in and tricked into revealing the truth. And her story would have been convincing, because it *was* the truth.

And then this fake Lord Constantine would only need to show up with some other girl who he could say was *the true princess he had been keeping safe,* I thought.

"But why did this Lord Constantine tell you to start taking in beggar boys?" I wondered out loud. "How did that connect?"

Janelia flushed.

"He didn't tell me to do that," she said. "That was

my decision. I just had so much money . . . I think Lord Constantine's notion of how much I needed to live on was very different from mine. Once I had all that money, I couldn't stop thinking about the little boy babies left in the orphanage when I rescued the baby girls. I felt . . . responsible once I had money."

"Why?" I asked. "They weren't your children! They weren't your brothers and sisters!"

"But once I had money, I could do something to help," Janelia said. "That did make me responsible."

My mind was reeling.

"So Tog and Herk and Terrence and all the other beggar boys I saw in your basement—you're saying all of them were babies at the orphanage the same night you took the baby girls away? So they're all fourteen?" I shook my head emphatically, thinking of how short and scrawny Herk looked. "Maybe the others are, but you cannot tell me Herk is fourteen!"

"No, you're right, he's only ten," Janelia admitted. "Almost eleven. But even as an infant, he followed Tog around like a puppy, and Tog refused to leave him behind. And then . . . well, you've seen Herk. How could anyone leave him behind?"

I could think of dozens of people who would have stepped past Herk in the streets without giving him a second glance. In fact, the only people I could think of from the palace who would have noticed Herk were my sister-princesses. And I wasn't sure about all of them.

"So are Tog and Herk brothers, maybe?" I asked. "Is that why they were so tight?"

"No, that's impossible," Janelia said. "Because Tog's father died before he was born. In the war, just like ours. And I already told you how his mother died, when he was a baby."

I looked at her blankly.

"Lena was Tog's mother," Janelia said.

For a moment, the name made no impression on me. But then I recognized it: Lena was the servant girl who'd been killed bringing firewood for the king and queen. The one Janelia had mourned for fourteen years, believing Lena had died in her place. The one whose death I had shrugged off with the comment, *It was her own fault, for tarrying on the stairs.* And then Janelia had snapped, *Don't you dare ever tell Lena's son that!* And I had thought there was no chance of meeting some random servant's child from fourteen years earlier.

But the servant hadn't been random, and neither had the child.

"Is *everything* connected?" I asked, and it came out sounding like a complaint. "Is everyone?"

Janelia smiled faintly.

"Sometimes I think so," she said. "Like . . . the fact I took in all those orphan boys, thinking I was helping them, but then they became my spies for helping you . . ."

"And Herk and Tog rescued me from Madame Bisset," I said. "And now they're helping me get to Fridesia."

Janelia nodded.

"And here's another connection you might be able to figure out," she said. "Every month for the past ten years, a packet of money mysteriously showed up on my doorstep on the first day of the month, just like Lord Constantine told me to expect. This month nothing came."

"Because the truth about me was finally out!" I said. "And Lord Throckmorton and his henchmen were in prison. Isn't this proof that the money was actually bribes to keep you silent?"

Janelia frowned, clearly reluctant to agree.

"And you said Lord Constantine left the country," I argued. "There wouldn't have been time for him to have heard the news and stopped sending money because of that!"

"But . . . I guess I expected a letter, or some other explanation," Janelia said slowly. "Even if it was really Lord Throckmorton sending the money, wouldn't he have wanted to fake that? Even from prison?"

"Why would he bother?" I asked. "He was totally defeated!"

Footsteps sounded near the entry to the cave just then, and Janelia sprang up.

"Tog and Herk are back!" she cried, running to the mouth of the cave.

But as soon as I saw the two boys, I could tell they didn't have good news.

"Nobody needed baskets," Tog said dejectedly, holding up the three I had been so proud of. "We couldn't sell any of them."

"I guess we're still too close to the river," Janelia said. "Too close to the supply of reeds, so people can make their own."

"No—I think it was more that people just didn't like us," Herk said. "Those villagers were *mean*. As soon as we got close to the first house, the people were like—" He made his eyes narrow and creepy, and turned his head as if he were trying to watch Tog's every move.

"We'll get food tomorrow," Janelia said. "I'm sure of it."

I glanced back toward the mouth of the cave. I couldn't have said if I was trying for one last "gradual" healing view of the daytime sky, or if I was hoping for a glimpse of the same beautiful starry sky I'd seen the night before with Tog. But I saw neither of those things. Instead, I saw a strange glow that reminded me uncomfortably of the fire at the palace.

"What—" I began.

Before I could even finish my question, I got my answer. An angry voice shouted from outside, "Beggars, begone! We want none of your type abroad in our land!"

And then a crowd of men holding torches swarmed into the cave.

23

"Out! Out!" the men screamed. "Begone from here!"

"Please!" Janelia begged. "Leave us alone! We wish you no harm! We only plan to sleep here for the night! We'll be on our way by morning's light!"

"Of course—after you thieve from our village!" one of the men screamed back at her. "After you steal our sheep and swine and cattle!"

"We won't allow it!" another hollered, swinging his torch so close to Herk's arm that I was surprised his sleeve didn't catch on fire. Then the man began reaching for Tog.

He's reaching for Tog's neck, I thought, mesmerized with horror. *He's planning to strangle him.*

Was this how Cecilia had felt seeing Lord Throckmorton prepare to strangle me? Before she stopped him?

No, I thought. *Cecilia would have seen me as a rival then, a rival who was about to be eliminated. And she* still *stopped him.*

Tog had rescued me and protected me from Madame

Bisset and carried me toward Fridesia for the past two days. He'd been nothing but heroically kind.

Save him! screamed through my mind.

I wanted to scream it at Janelia and Herk, but other men already had a tight grip on them. Both of them were pinned against the wall. I was the only one still free, the only one not surrounded—maybe the men hadn't even seen me in the darkness at the back of the cave. Maybe I had the element of surprise on my side.

But I can't walk! I wanted to protest. *And I'm not near a big, heavy harp like Cecilia was when she decided to fight back against Lord Throckmorton. I don't have anything to use as a weapon.*

I had the stretcher beneath me, but there was no way I could lift it by myself, let alone swing it at Tog's attacker.

My gaze fell on the pot of boiled rags Janelia had pulled off the fire. It was just a few paces away.

Can I—?

There was no time to think through a possible plan. The man's hands were already around Tog's neck.

I rose up on my knees and shuffled forward, my skirt getting tangled around my legs. I almost fell, but my hands landed on the pot handles.

No time to think, no time to practice. Only one chance to do this right. . . .

I grunted, lifting the pot. And then I turned it sideways and threw it as hard as I could at Tog's attacker.

Two men dropped their torches in surprise, the flames

whistling out as they plunged toward the ground. Other men screamed, "What manner of weapon is this?" when wet, slimy rags and a sloshing dribble of hot water hit them. The pot itself bounced uselessly on the floor of the cave. But someone else screamed, "Boiling oil! Is it boiling oil? Men, mind your flames!"

That gave me another idea. I yanked the skirt of my dress out of the way and crawled on my knees toward the fire Janelia had built in the center of the cave. I grabbed the end of one of the half-burned logs and raised it over my head.

"That *was* boiling oil!" I screamed. "Let us go or I'll set you all afire!"

I could barely hold the log aloft—I was in danger of dropping it and setting myself afire. A single moment of thought would have led any of the torch-bearing men to the conclusion that they were dripping with hot water, not oil. But I could see Tog, Herk, and Janelia all pulling away from the men who held them.

That was when I realized my mistake.

Tog, Herk, and Janelia now had a clear path to the mouth of the cave. They could run away. I had a fire and a cluster of angry men between me and any escape.

And I couldn't run. I couldn't even walk. I was doing well to be upright on my knees.

I waited for Tog, Herk, and Janelia to save themselves and abandon me. I waited for the angry men to figure out my mistakes and lies, and swarm around the fire to attack.

That wasn't what happened.

Janelia shoved Herk out of the cave. Then, as if they'd had time to plan, she and Tog ran past the men and around the fire and grabbed me by the armpits.

"Keep waving that log at them," Tog muttered, as he and Janelia half carried, half dragged me past the fire and the men.

Some of the men were starting to recover, starting to figure out that they were soaked with water, not oil. Still, Tog, Janelia, and I reached the mouth of the cave.

"Now throw the log at them, and climb on my back!" Tog whispered in my ear.

My "throw" was pathetic—I mostly just dropped the log. But at least it provided an obstacle right at the cave's mouth, something the men had to avoid. Tog and Janelia paused just past the log, just long enough to hoist me onto Tog's back.

And then he was running out into the darkness. I clutched his shoulders and curved my legs around his waist. He held on, his hands pressed against the bare skin at the back of my knees.

Indecent, whispered in my mind, some remnant of palace gossip echoing in my mind.

But what is indecency when someone's saving your life?

I couldn't see what lay ahead of us and had no idea how Tog could keep running so quickly, so blindly. I could hear Tog's gulping, panting breaths. They echoed, and his footsteps echoed . . .

No, I thought. *I'm hearing Herk and Janelia beside him, running and panting too.*

That made me feel better and gave me the courage to look back over my shoulder.

The torch-bearing men were chasing us.

"Away from our village!" they screamed. "Never let us see you back in our village again! Or in this cave! Or anywhere nearby!"

Tog, Janelia, and Herk scrambled over the rocky ground in the front of the cave. They kept stumbling and barely managing to stay upright. Tog had the worst of it, with me on his back throwing him off balance.

"I see a path to the right," I screamed, squinting into darkness, "where you won't trip so much . . ."

Tog lurched in that direction, with Herk and Janelia at his side. But even the path was dark with shadows.

I glanced over my shoulder again. The line of torches were several yards back.

"They're going to let us get away!" I called to Tog and Herk and Janelia just as Tog stumbled over some unseen rock and almost toppled over. "You can slow down and be a little more careful!"

"Don't . . . want to . . . test that," Tog muttered back. He was breathing so hard now, almost gasping for air. "Don't . . . want them to see . . . where we're going. . . ."

He kept running. So did Herk and Janelia.

"We can hide and wait nearby and then go back for—" I began. I looked over my shoulder once more. The torches were farther away, but somehow they seemed brighter now, with two or three joined together.

Oh. They were burning my stretcher.

"Never mind," I muttered. "I don't think they'll leave anything for us to go back to."

Tog, Herk, and Janelia kept running, their breathing ragged, theirs steps uneven. I was ready to drop with exhaustion, and all I was doing was clinging to Tog. But the others kept going.

Then we crashed into woods that had seemed like only a dark smear on the horizon when we'd first left the cave. Branches swiped against my arms and legs. I ducked my head down behind Tog's back.

"I think . . . it's safe . . . to stop . . . ," Janelia panted.

She and Herk collapsed to the ground. Tog took one last swerving step and almost fell over. I slid down off his back, twisting so I landed on my side, not my feet.

For a long moment all four of us did nothing but lie in the midst of leaves and twigs. I turned my head so I could see back toward the cave. Either there were too many tree trunks and branches blocking my view, or the men with torches had extinguished their flames and gone back to their own nasty village.

"We're . . . all . . . still . . . alive," Janelia whispered. "We . . . survived."

I had reigned over dozens of ceremonies commemorating war victories; I'd sat through hours of supposedly stirring military marches. But somehow this was the most victorious sound I'd ever heard: Janelia whispering, *We're all still alive.*

Even in the dim light, I could see Janelia reach to the right and hug Herk close to her side. Then she reached for Tog and me. And I let Janelia draw me near. I let Janelia hug me just as tightly as she was hugging Herk. I hugged her back.

"You saved us," she whispered.

"You were . . . brilliant," Tog mumbled in agreement. "Fearless."

I basked in their praise. I hadn't been fearless. But it hadn't mattered.

"And you saved me," I whispered back. "Thank you. Thank you for not running away and leaving me behind."

"Never," Janelia whispered back.

"Didn't even think of it," Tog muttered.

"*I* would have come back for you, if they hadn't," Herk added drowsily, almost as if he was talking in his sleep.

The four of us huddled together for a long while. But my triumphant feeling began to slip away. Later, long after Tog had gone off to take the first watch of the night and Janelia and Herk had slipped off into sleep, I lay staring up at the dark branches blocking the starry sky. I wondered, *How will we ever get to Fridesia now? How can we rescue my sister-princesses when it was all we could do to fight off poor, stupid villagers?*

And I kept reliving the same moments over and over again: seeing Tog about to be strangled, throwing the pot of boiled rags at his attackers, clinging to Tog as he held on to me.

How was it that those moments that had made me feel so

terrified also made me feel . . . brave? And—safe?

What those moments really made me was stranded. We were in a woods in the middle of nowhere. I couldn't walk, the stretcher was gone, and there was no way Tog could carry me all the way to Fridesia.

What did finding courage matter now?

24

"Here."

I woke to see Tog standing over me, handing me something I couldn't quite make out because of the contrast with the bright sunlight behind him.

I sat up woozily. He was holding out a pair of tied-together sticks.

No. Crutches, I corrected myself, noticing how the branches angled and curved and twisted together at the top. He'd wrapped swaths of fabric along each branch top, as if trying to add padding. I recognized the fabric—it was the bottom half of his shirt. He'd apparently tried to tuck what remained back in to his breeches, but as soon as he held out the crutches the shirt came untucked and I could see the muscles beneath the shirt.

And last night he held on to my bare knees, I remembered, blushing.

"I *think* these are the right length to fit under your

arms," Tog said. "I tried to measure while you were still sleeping, but luckily we do still have the knife. So I could cut them down if you wanted."

"Oh, um, thank you," I said, blinking in a way that I was pretty sure looked stupid.

"Even if both your feet aren't healed yet, I remembered that the left one wasn't cut up so bad, and I thought you could support your weight on it, with a little help," Tog explained. "I thought, with crutches, you'd be good to go. Watch out, Fridesia, here we come!"

He grinned, and for a moment I wondered if he was making fun of me.

Yeah, watch out, Fridesia. Here comes Suala's crippled princess, I thought mockingly. I wished I'd been kinder to poor, clumsy Princess Elzbethl.

Tog kept grinning. He *wasn't* making fun of me.

I found I could alternate my stupid blinking with vapid staring. And stammering, "You . . . you still think we can go to Fridesia?"

"Sure," Tog said, shrugging. "Isn't that the plan?"

"Desmia, is that still what you want?" Janelia asked quietly. I saw that she was sitting nearby. "It isn't going to be easy. And we might encounter more hostile villages. Especially once we get to Fridesia."

I gulped.

"Tog and me, we think those villagers must have been doing something they weren't supposed to," Herk chimed in from beside Janelia. "Like selling weapons to the Fridesians during the war. Or smuggling food past the royal tax agents."

I remembered Cecilia telling me that she had thought many times during her secret trip to the capital with Harper, *Oh, how can people treat me this way? When they find out who I really am, they're going to be sorry!*

I understood that feeling completely. But I also thought, *How could we have allowed there to be a village in our kingdom that treats beggars—or anyone!—so badly? And if they really are smuggling weapons or food or breaking the law some other way . . . I want to have royal agents investigate and stop them! It isn't right! It isn't fair!*

But how could I do that if I just limped back to my own capital city without my rescued sister-princesses beside me? Without them, how could I stand up to the cruel villagers or the plotters who'd set the fire at the palace— or anyone?

How could I accomplish anything without going to Fridesia?

"*I* want to keep going," I said. "I just didn't think that the three of you . . ."

"We sure don't want to stay around here!" Herk said. His voice came out in a chirp, making him sound as carefree as a bird. I wondered if he was really that calm, or if he was play-acting again for my benefit.

"I'm not sure we would want to go back to the capital

right now, anyhow," Janelia added. "Not if Terrence has been spreading rumors about us to your enemies."

I glanced quickly at Tog, and he nodded.

"I've trapped you here," I said, my voice anguished. I'd been the princess of Suala practically my entire life, but somehow I'd never felt so responsible before for any of my royal subjects' lives.

"No—we *chose* to go to Fridesia with you," Tog corrected. "We all made our own decisions."

I thought about how simple everything had seemed to me back at the beginning of the trip. I'd told Janelia, Tog, and Herk I wanted them to carry me to Fridesia as if I had the right to order them around, to get them to do anything I wanted. Royalty did have that right with commoners.

But that wasn't why they'd come. That wasn't why they were still by my side right now.

I used the crutches Tog had made for me to prop myself up—first onto my knees, then into a standing position. My left foot, the less injured one, sent back a stab of pain at temporarily bearing all my weight. My head was woozy, probably from not eating the night before. And the patch of open sky I could see through a clearing in the trees worried me.

What if I lose control of myself and simply start screaming again? I wondered. *What if I can't walk even with Tog's crutches?*

Annoyed with myself, I inched the crutches forward, leaned against them, and swung my right foot up and over a log that lay in my path.

There, I told myself. *I took one step.*

"Let's go," I told the others. "I know I'll slow us down—we might as well get started."

Herk clapped. Tog's grin grew even wider. Janelia put out her hands to steady me on the crutches.

"Actually," Janelia said, "you can have breakfast first. Herk found some berries over in that clearing. The rest of us already ate."

If I sat back down, would I have the gumption to get back up again?

"No," I decided. "I can eat while I walk. Er—hobble. Let's go."

And I took another leap forward.

That first day on the crutches was rough. Even with the remnants of Tog's shirt as padding, the skin under my arms was chafed raw by mid morning. Tog and Janelia took turns letting me lean on them for a while instead—Herk offered as well, but he was a foot shorter than me, and leaning down to hold on to his shoulder threw me off balance. By noon, when we all stopped to take a break and share the last of the berries, every muscle in my body ached.

"Seeing the sky doesn't bother you anymore?" Tog asked, handing me what I guessed might be more than my portion of berries.

"I've been so busy trying not to trip, I haven't even noticed the sky!" I admitted. "I only look at the ground."

"Well, that's good, then," Tog said, as if he was trying too hard to keep my spirits up.

My eyes met his, and both of us quickly looked away. I began to regret the fact that Herk and Janelia had gone to look for more food and left Tog alone with me as a guard against danger. What was I supposed to say to him? How was I supposed to act? To cover my embarrassment, I let myself fall back flat on the grass behind me. This time I did look straight at the sky. Ominous dark clouds hovered to the west. I had to struggle to keep my breathing normal and even.

"Now, see, that's a kind sky," Tog said gently beside me. "See those clouds? That means we're going to get a refreshing rain this afternoon. That's going to cool us off after all this heat."

How could two people look at the same sky and see such different things?

But Tog's words made it possible for me to keep staring at the sky without screaming.

A moment later, Herk and Janelia came back, Herk holding three dead animals by their tails. Were they more weasels? Squirrels? *Rats?* I really didn't know. I fought against gagging. But Herk was chanting, "We've got fo-oo-od! We've got fo-oo-od!"

And Janelia held up four gourds and proclaimed, "We've got something to carry more water again, as soon as we can dry them! And we found a river and I cut down more reeds—we *will* be more careful about selling our baskets the next time. . . ."

"It's our lucky day!" Tog cried.

His eyes lingered on my face as he said this.

This time I didn't look away. I smiled back instead.

25

We'd been on the road for two weeks when we reached the Fridesian border. I could walk on both feet now, but I'd discarded only one of the crutches. Tog had cut down the other one to make it into a cane for me to use in the afternoons when the last stubborn wound on my right foot began to ache. When I wasn't using the cane, Herk used it as a prop for an entire skit he'd made up, pretending to be an old man. He'd kept the rest of us laughing at his nonsense.

Or is that really how old men act? I wondered. *Old men who aren't Lord Throckmorton or the other bitter, cruel palace advisers?*

There was so much I hadn't known, living in the palace. I saw fields of grain and amused the others by asking, "What kind of trees are those?" I learned how to use the knife, first to cut the reeds for making baskets, and then—wincing—to skin the random animals that Herk kept bringing back for meals. I hadn't looked in a mirror since my last night in the palace, but I knew from glancing down at my arms and hands that the skin

of my face had probably turned as brown and tough-looking as
Tog's, Herk's, and Janelia's.

I hadn't even known that would happen, being out in the
sun all day.

For the last several miles before the Fridesian border,
we traveled through a strange landscape where trees were
broken off and dying, and the grasses were just green sprouts
barely poking up through acres of scorched earth.

"Was there a fire?" I asked hesitantly as dead leaves
crumbled like ash beneath my feet.

"It's the battlefield," Tog said.

"This?" I asked. "This is what war looks like?"

"No," Tog said curtly. "This is what the *land* looks like
after a battle. The people . . . well, even if they don't have
scars you can see, they're carrying this inside."

I thought of the military officials I'd met at the castle,
droning on about strategy and advantages and territory
gained and lost. I'd only met generals and other commanders,
I realized. The ones who sat in tents far from the battlefield
and gave orders for other men to die.

"I wanted to end the war," I told Tog. "I stood up to Lord
Throckmorton about that. Even before Cecilia and the other
princesses came to power. That was how everything started
to change."

"I know," Tog said. And then he surprised me by falling to
one knee before me, and kissing my hand. "In the name of my
dead father, I thank you."

I blushed. I had had dozens of courtiers kiss my hand before, but somehow this was different. Somehow, even after he let go of my hand, I could still feel the touch of his fingers, the mark of his lips. I was glad that Janelia spoke next, so I didn't have to react.

"In the name of our dead father, I thank you too," Janelia said.

"And I don't know how my father died or who he was—I don't know anything about my mother, either—but I thank you too," Herk said, putting on a comical expression. "Just in case."

I appreciated him clowning around, because then I didn't have to admit that I hadn't known what I was doing, stopping the war. I mostly wanted to stop it just because Lord Throckmorton wanted it to go on and on.

"The war won't start again, will it?" Herk asked, balancing on a burned log. "Even if no one from Suala shows up to sign the treaty?"

"Don't worry—Cecilia will be there," I said.

"And you," Tog added. "We're going to get you there in time."

I walked a little faster.

There was no actual borderline for us to cross. We weren't on any road, so of course there were no border guards. But we knew we were in Fridesia when we came across a crude sign that pointed only to Fridesian cities.

"We're in enemy territory," I whispered, staring at the

sign. "I never thought I'd step foot in enemy territory."

"It's not enemy territory anymore," Tog said.

"But, maybe, just in case, we shouldn't tell anyone who we are," Janelia said, glancing around. The territory around us was just as eerily empty and dead as the land we'd left behind in Suala. "And maybe try to talk with more of a Fridesian accent?"

"Loik dees?" Herk attempted. He sounded ridiculous.

"Ella always said we Sualans sounded like we were holding marbles under our tongues," I said. "So maybe we should just try to talk with our tongues flat on the bottom of our mouths as much as possible. Like this?"

"Oh, that was good!" Janelia said. "You sounded totally different. We're just lucky Fridesians and Sualans speak the same language. I heard they used to be part of the same country a long time ago, and that's why we can understand each other."

"I never knew that," I said.

I thought about the Sualan history I'd learned at the palace—I'd had to memorize the names of every king and queen for sixteen generations. But of course, while Suala was at war with Fridesia, it probably would have been treason for my governess to claim even a long-past connection between Suala and Fridesia.

The empty landscape around me was starting to give me the panicky empty-sky feeling again. I quickly fastened my gaze on Janelia and Tog, walking in front of me.

"Look—everything's green ahead of us," Tog said, as if he knew I needed help. "And isn't that the strangest tree you've ever seen?"

He pointed to an apple tree that grew at a diagonal slant from the ground.

"Do you suppose the ground tilted after the tree started growing?" Herk asked. "Or was it struck by lightning? Or are all the trees in Fridesia like this?"

I stopped in my tracks.

"Those are . . . those are apples on that tree, right?" I asked.

"Uh . . . yeah," Tog said, as if he wanted to make fun of me but thought I sounded a little too serious to be mocked.

"And is that a path beside it?" I continued.

"Maybe it used to be," Janelia concluded, gazing at a trail beyond the tree. It was overgrown with new grasses.

"Then I know this tree!" I exclaimed. I could feel a smile breaking over my face, stretching my sunburned skin. "This is the marker for the camp Ella and Jed built for the refugees from the war." I grabbed the others' hands and pulled them toward the overgrown trail. "Come on! If we're lucky, they might even be there right now!"

26

A moment ago, my legs had ached and my feet had throbbed and I would have said I wasn't capable of walking any faster than a slog. But now I ran down the overgrown trail, pulling the others along with me.

"What—?" Herk began.

"Could you—?" Janelia added.

"Explain?" Tog finished.

I laughed and told them everything even as I ran.

"I didn't even think of this as a possibility before!" I cried. "See, this is what Jed cared about most when Ella met him—taking care of war refugees. And she told him, well, the best way to take care of them would be to end the war. And then they won't be refugees. And—"

I paused long enough to leap over a gully in the path. I landed on my sore foot and didn't even waver.

"And I know Jed and Ella were going to stop at the refugee camp on their way back from Suala, before they went to the Fridesian capital for their wedding and the treaty ceremony,"

I went on. "I didn't know how long they were going to stay before moving on, but maybe, maybe . . ."

Maybe all of this can be over today! I thought. *If Ella and Jed are here, I can tell them everything that happened, and they'll know what to do. They'll find out what really happened to my sister-princesses, and they'll take care of rescuing them for me. Ella and Jed will take care of everything!*

I rounded a corner and caught my first glimpse of a long, low building ahead. No—there was a row of buildings, neatly tended and surrounded by tidy gardens. A little farther on, I could see a gate and, behind the gate, a small building with a carefully lettered sign that said, OFFICE.

I ran faster, closing the distance. With the others right behind me, I burst through the office door.

"Ella? Jed?" I called eagerly.

A plump, middle-aged woman turned around and dropped a stack of towels.

"Oh, no," she moaned. "It's started again, hasn't it? Oh, you poor, poor dears." She picked up four towels and held them out to me and the others. "Well, don't you worry. You're safe now. We'll get you fixed right up. You can wash up, first thing."

She reached out and brushed a smudge of dirt from Herk's cheek.

"What's started up again?" I asked in bewilderment. "You mean the war? No, the ceasefire is still in effect. I think. We just—"

Could it be—did the woman think *we* were refugees? I remembered that that had happened to Ella when she first arrived at the refugee camp. But Ella had said she looked awful then. I looked down at myself, at my sunburned skin, my ragged dress, my holey shoes with the bandages sticking out.

Maybe I looked worse than Ella ever had.

I shook my head, and tried to think how to explain. This must be Mrs. Smeal, a camp worker Ella had told me about. Ella had said Mrs. Smeal could be really nice if you stayed on her good side.

"We just had a long trip," I said, trying to smile in a respectable, not desperate way. It was hard to do through the sunburn. I also reminded myself to keep my tongue flat and sound more like a Fridesian than a Sualan. "We were so eager to see Ella and Jed we, um, didn't stop to wash up or change out of our, um, traveling clothes."

Mrs. Smeal frowned disapprovingly.

"Well, Ella and Jed aren't here," she said. "And they might have warned me that they were going to invite company to drop by! I'm not happy with those two right now. Not even giving me the pleasure of attending their wedding!"

She sniffed.

Janelia had never even met Ella and Jed, but I wasn't surprised that she stepped forward to try to smooth over Mrs. Smeal's anger.

"Oh, I'm sure they *wanted* to invite you," Janelia said. "They probably thought of it as a kindness, not asking you to travel all the way from here to the capital just for the ceremony."

Mrs. Smeal sniffed again.

"You think I wasn't invited?" she asked. "*That's* not the reason. Of course they invited me. But then——" She leaned in as if she was about to impart some shocking gossip, and she wanted to see our reactions close up. Her eyes glittered. "They went and canceled the wedding! They're not getting married after all!"

27

I jerked back from Mrs. Smeal as if the woman had punched me. It certainly felt like someone had knocked the air out of my lungs. Or like the earth had suddenly tilted wrong on its axis.

"Ella and Jed love each other!" I protested. If I couldn't count on that, what could I count on?

"Well, now, that's what I thought too," Mrs. Smeal said. She patted my arm, almost as if she were viewing me once again as some devastated refugee. Or a comrade in sorrow. Maybe the glitter in Mrs. Smeal's eyes was unshed tears, not gossipy glee. "You just never know sometimes. Those two are both so headstrong—when they get something into their minds, they're like dogs holding on to bones. Two stubborn people like that really shouldn't marry each other, I guess. Nobody ever gives in."

Jed and Ella are the type who never give in, I thought. *Or give up.*

I remembered the hours of peace negotiations with Jed, the way Ella had stuck by my side when I whispered to her about secret princesses locked in the dungeon. I remembered the way Jed and Ella looked into each other's eyes.

And that's why they wouldn't call off their wedding. Unless . . .

Unless something else was going on.

I had prickles at the back of my neck, as if my skin understood better than I did that the news I'd just heard was tragic.

I looked helplessly toward Janelia and Herk and Tog.

"But . . . Ella and Jed are still in Fridesia, right?" Janelia asked. "Back at the capital?"

"So far as I know," Mrs. Smeal said. "They left here a week ago and all the plans were set. Everything *seemed* fine. Then new supplies arrived yesterday, and the wagon driver brought me this."

Mrs. Smeal picked an embossed card from the desk in front of her and held it out to us. The script was as fancy as anything from back at the palace:

We regret to inform you that the intended nuptials between Jedediah Reston and Ella Brown shall not take place as previously planned. Pray do not inquire further as to details, as this is a painful time for us both. And we pray that you will not be insulted if we do not contact you again for many a month, as we require a period of silence and introspection as we recover.

It didn't sound like Ella or Jed. The handwriting didn't look like Ella's or Jed's either, but perhaps it had been copied out by a scribe.

"As long as I've worked with them, and I don't even get the courtesy of an explanation?" Mrs. Smeal complained. "Just a 'leave us alone, please, so we can suffer in silence'?"

I handed the card back to her.

"I'm sorry," I said. "I suppose we should just be on our way, then. We've got a long walk ahead of us, all the way to the capital."

Somehow my legs and feet had gone back to aching even worse than before. I remembered Ella describing her walk from the Fridesian capital to the refugee camp, and it had taken her weeks. We probably had more time ahead of us on the road than we'd already spent walking from the Sualan capital.

"Could we at least have something to eat first?" Herk said plaintively behind me. I turned and saw that he had his face pressed against the window. He was staring out at the hundreds of bean pods hanging from the plants outside.

"We could work for you, in payment," Tog added quickly.

Mrs. Smeal frowned.

"You think I would have sent you off hungry?" she asked incredulously. "And—so filthy? What kind of an establishment do you think we're running? The four of you are going to wash up, and then you're going to have a big meal while I have some of our girls who are training to be laundresses tend to your clothes. . . ."

She touched the sleeve of my dress and pulled her hand back as if it pained her.

"Er, no," Mrs. Smeal decided. "I'm not sure those clothes would hold up to being pounded against the rocks in the river. It may be the dirt actually holding them together. So we'll give you new clothes instead."

"We couldn't possibly accept all that," Janelia said. She had her fists clenched, as if it was a struggle to say the polite thing. "We have nothing to pay you with."

She, too, looked longingly toward the garden outside.

"Enh, with the war stopped, it's been a little slow around here," Mrs. Smeal said. "A lot of our refugees moved back to their homes as soon as they could. And the supplies we got yesterday were more than we needed. Some of the food is just going to rot if nobody eats it."

"That would be *awful!*" Herk said, and even Mrs. Smeal laughed at the way he said it.

"Right, right, just what I thought." Mrs. Smeal nodded as if she and Herk were sharing a secret. "We might even have to send some of it along with you when you get back on the road."

Mrs. Smeal was *good*. I'd had fourteen years of experience sifting lies from truth, and even I couldn't tell if Mrs. Smeal really did have a lot of extra food or if she was making that up to get us to accept it.

Or was I just out of practice with my lie detection after two weeks away from Suala's palace?

Mrs. Smeal put her arm around Herk's shoulders, as if she planned to lead him off to some elaborate feast. Then she froze.

"Oh, I should have thought . . . ," she began.

She raised her face toward the same window Herk had peered through, and she must have seen something, because she instantly went dashing for the door.

"Hold on! I'll be right back!" she called over her shoulder as she shoved her way out.

We all looked at one another and shrugged. None of us understood what was going on. But Herk went over and held the door open behind Mrs. Smeal.

Now I could see a man hitching a pair of horses to a wagon.

"—promise it won't delay you more than another hour," Mrs. Smeal was saying to the man.

The man lifted his hands in resignation.

"No skin off my nose," he said. "And I know you'll keep nagging me until I say yes, anyway, so I might as well start with that."

Mrs. Smeal hugged him, and then came racing back toward me and the others.

"You don't have to walk all the way to the capital, after all!" she announced joyfully.

"Yes, we do," I countered, sounding just as stubborn as Ella and Jed. "If that's where Ella and Jed are, then . . ."

How could I explain without giving away that we were from Suala?

"I'm not trying to stop you from going to the capital," Mrs. Smeal said, her eyes dancing. "It's the walking part you don't have to do. Because the wagon driver who brought our supplies yesterday is going back that way, anyhow. You can ride in style and be there the day after tomorrow!"

28

Riding "in style," was a bit of an exaggeration, considering that we were sitting in the open air in the back of a rough wooden wagon. Budley, the wagon driver, had the odd habit of chewing on dried leaves—maybe it was a Fridesian custom? But every time he'd had enough of a particular dried leaf, he spat it out in a huge glob. During my first moments in the wagon, I'd learned that ducking was a good idea whenever I heard Budley start to clear his throat.

But the others and I were all freshly scrubbed—Herk's face was actually pink under all that dirt he'd been carrying around. And we were wearing fresh new clothes that Mrs. Smeal had insisted would have just gone to waste otherwise. Two weeks ago I would have sneered at my new pink cotton dress as too simple and peasant-like. Definitely beneath me. But it didn't smell like sweat, and it didn't have smears of dirt and ash on it, and it was soft against my skin. . . . Right now it felt like the most luxurious item I'd ever worn.

And we had sandwiches stuffed with thick slices of roast chicken and a pot full of cooked beans and a whole sack full of raspberry tarts and enough bread and cheese and potatoes and grapes to last us not just to the Fridesian capital, but for two or three days afterward.

"Heaven," Janelia murmured beside me. "We have died and gone to heaven."

"No, we haven't," Herk corrected. "I'm too *clean*. In my heaven, there's going to be a lot more dirt."

"But all the girls in the Fridesian capital will fall in love with you, looking so clean," Tog said.

I met his eyes and looked away. I'd spent practically every moment of the past two weeks in his company—and he'd seen me screaming and sweating and limping and covered with nearly as much dirt as Herk. But ever since we'd climbed into the wagon together, I felt strange just sitting near him. Cleaned up, he didn't look like a beggar boy anymore. He looked . . .

Royal? My mind suggested.

No, that wasn't it. But I didn't know how to describe it, even to myself. I felt funny just trying.

"You want to impress the ladies in the capital, you need to stop calling it 'the Fridesian capital,'" Budley the driver said, turning around from the front of the wagon. "Like there'd be any capital besides Fridesia's! Best you just call it by its name, Charmeil."

He made the word roll off his tongue so elegantly that

for a moment I forgot he was old and fat and balding and prone to spitting plant juices.

"Shaar-may-eeell?" Herk repeated, drawing out all the vowel sounds.

The driver winced.

"Where are you people from?" he asked. "I've never heard anyone talk like the four of you before!"

I put my hand over Herk's to make sure he didn't blurt out the truth.

"We've moved around a lot," I said. "I guess we picked up some odd accents."

"I'll say!" the driver said, shaking his head. "So you're, what, itinerant basket weavers?" He nodded at the pile of reeds Janelia had placed beside us.

I had to hold back a snort. I was glad that Tog answered for us: "That's probably the best way to describe it."

Budley flicked the horses' reins to get them to move a little faster.

"Well, any friends of Ella and Jed's are friends of mine, too," he said. "You may not have encountered many swell types like I have, but I'll tell you, not many of them are like Ella and Jed. Sure, he's a lord and I guess she's a lady, but they still treat people like us like . . . like we're practically equal or something. Most swells act like I might as well be a horse or a cow."

For a moment, I was afraid I might choke on my roast chicken.

I treated servants like they might as well be horses or cows, I thought. *That's kind of how I saw Janelia and Herk and Tog at the beginning of this trip.*

I thought about how most of my sister-princesses were always friendly with the servants. I'd thought the other girls just needed to learn how to act royal.

It's not fair if they're the ones who died while I got to live, I thought.

As long as we sat in the wagon, I couldn't talk with Janelia, Tog, and Herk about our plans for once we reached the Fridesian capital—*No,* I corrected myself, *Charmeil*—because we couldn't risk Budley overhearing. So we feasted and wove baskets and slept. Once or twice Tog or Janelia offered to take the horses' reins so the driver could sleep.

I told myself we needed to rest up before Charmeil. But the empty sky above us started seeming frightening to me again. I had to bend my head forward and concentrate on weaving basket after basket to block out the fear. But I couldn't weave constantly. And every time I closed my eyes to sleep, my mind began racing with questions.

What if we can't find Ella and Jed?

What if Cecilia and Harper don't show up for the treaty signing?

What if I can't rescue any of the other sister-princesses?

I always tried to stop that thought from continuing, but sometimes a worse one sneaked in anyhow.

What if they were all dead from the very start, and this whole trip has been for nothing?

And then there were more.

What if even Janelia and Tog and Herk give up on helping me?

Even if I get my throne back, what if I'm all alone on it— *again?*

What then?

29

We arrived in Charmeil late on a Friday afternoon. If I had counted my days right, the treaty signing was scheduled for the following Tuesday, and Ella and Jed's wedding had been intended for the following weekend.

But if the wedding date changed, anything else might have changed too, I thought, looking around anxiously at the strange houses and stores of Charmeil. It wasn't as if I had seen that much of my own country's capital except for the palace, Janelia's basement, Madame Bisset's prison house, and the other houses around the palace courtyard. So I didn't have much to compare. But Charmeil looked as if it was trying too hard, with too many decorative sconces on its walls, too many lacy-looking wrought-iron fences around its trees, too many pointless frills on its women's dresses.

Janelia and Tog were looking around just as silently as me. Herk, meanwhile, commented on everything.

"Can you imagine climbing that fence?" he asked. "Do you think I could stand on that point at the top? And why are all the men wearing hats that make them look ten inches taller? Or do their heads really go up that high?"

Budley didn't even try to answer Herk's questions. He just threw out his arms and proclaimed, "Welcome to Charmeil! You could travel the entire world and never see a finer city!"

I was pretty sure I'd heard Budley say that the refugee camp was the farthest place he'd ever traveled from Charmeil. So how did he know? But I decided not to point this out.

"What if the Sualan capital is nicer than Charmeil?" Herk asked, before rest of us could stop him. "Huh? Did you ever think of that?"

"You mean *Cortona*?" Budley asked, pronouncing the word like it left a bad taste in his mouth. "Piffle. I've talked to soldiers coming back from the war. Up in Suala, people pretty much just live in pigsties."

"But that's not—" Herk began.

"—any way to live," Tog interrupted.

"No. Of course not," Budley agreed. "Why else do you think they're giving up on the war? It's not like *they* could ever defeat *us*."

Behind the driver's back, Tog put his hand over Herk's mouth.

"I'm sure everyone will be glad to have peace again," I said, and even though I was trying to talk with more of a Fridesian accent, I felt for a moment as though I was back in the Palace of Mirrors. I spoke with the same modulated voice I'd always used there, the one that hid all signs of anger, annoyance, or fear.

Budley glanced at me in surprise. It was almost as if, for the first time since I'd stepped into his wagon, he suspected I might not be the simple peasant he'd been told.

"Enh," Budley said, shrugging. "You know how those royal types never seem to stay out of wars for long. I think they get bored. I expect we'll be fighting Domulia next."

Janelia flushed as if she was the one fighting to hold back anger now.

"But don't you think it matters?" she asked. "Don't you think children should grow up knowing their fathers, wives should be able to live with their husbands for years and years—not just long enough for them to always be getting killed in some war?"

"Sure," Budley said, shrugging again. "But you know it doesn't matter what *I* think."

Budley let us off at a street corner not far from the Fridesian palace. We all shook hands and thanked him, but something had changed when we were talking about the war. Now he just seemed glad to be done with us.

Even after he flicked his reins at the horses and they trotted on, the others and I stood still for a moment.

Does everyone else feel as foreign and out of place as I do? I wondered. Even though we were surrounded by a bustling crowd and tall buildings with frilly spires that mostly blocked out the sun, I was starting to get the empty-sky feeling again. I remembered how foreign dignitaries always looked so impressive arriving at the Palace of Mirrors: dressed in their fanciest clothes, riding the showiest steeds, accompanied by large entourages.

I had none of that. I was on foot once again; if I had to walk very far, I'd probably start limping. Tog, Herk, and Janelia hardly counted as an entourage. And, now that we were in the city, my simple cotton dress no longer felt luxurious just because it was clean. Now it seemed like a sign around my neck announcing, *I'm poor! Maybe even a beggar! Cross the street to get away from me!*

Then I felt Tog slide his hand into mine.

"You're not going to tell anyone who you are until after you talk to Ella and Jed, right?" he asked.

My mind cleared.

"No," I said. "I'll need Ella to help me get the proper clothes, first thing."

I was careful not to say "royal clothes," but people in the crowd were glancing oddly at us anyhow.

What if someone here knew what a Sualan accent sounded like?

"And you think the best way to find Ella and Jed would be . . . ?" Janelia began in a hushed voice.

It would have been easy to let this question panic me. But I kept a firm grip on Tog's hand and answered calmly, "Jed works at the palace. So we'll go over there, and . . ." I remembered that there'd undoubtedly be guards. Even that didn't deter me. "If we wait outside, surely eventually we'll see him going in or out."

I thought of the odd letter Mrs. Smeal had shown me— the letter announcing that Ella and Jed's wedding was off. It hadn't said anything about Jed changing jobs.

And it would have if that had changed too, I told myself. *Right?*

"That could work," Janelia said, patting my back. I couldn't tell if she truly believed that or was just trying to sound encouraging.

She seemed to be glaring a bit at Tog, then looking pointedly at my hand clutched in his.

Tog didn't let go, and I didn't pull away.

He's just helping me for now, I thought. *Just as it was acceptable for him to touch my bare knees when he was saving my life from the angry villagers, the rules are a little different right now. Because we're in enemy territory.*

We walked toward the palace square and soon came to a broad boulevard full of carriages. I remembered Ella's story of coming to a ball at the Fridesian palace and paying a driver to make it look like she'd come the whole way by carriage rather than walking. I was glad I wouldn't have to attempt a charade like that. But I wished my own plan involved something a little faster than standing around waiting until we spotted Jed.

"You know," Herk said, coming up behind me. "If the palace guards here are like, um, *others*, uh, someplace else—you know what I mean?" He was being so careful not to say, *back at the Palace of Mirrors in Suala*. "Then maybe one or two of them might be nice, and they might answer questions about Jed or even take him a message. I could go talk to them."

My heart beat a little faster at the thought of Herk with his poorly disguised Sualan accent actually talking to a Fridesian palace guard.

"Maybe you're right," I said, trying to keep my voice light. "But why don't I be the one to go talk to the guards? I've got the most experience talking to palace types."

Neither Janelia nor Tog objected, which surprised me. Maybe they thought I had the best fake Fridesian accent. Or maybe they saw some danger in my original plan that I'd missed.

Is it worth the risk of trying to talk to a palace guard, if that could mean we get to Jed and Ella faster? I wondered.

We entered the palace square, which was filled with extravagant flower beds of pansies and asters and ostentatious orange blooms that I didn't recognize. The aroma was overwhelming. But I didn't have time to stand around smelling flowers.

Which of the palace guards over there looks the most approachable? I asked myself.

None of them did. They all looked fierce and forbidding, standing before palace doors that rose the height of two or three men.

If you sound like a Fridesian, you'll be fine, I told myself.

I took a deep breath and stepped past the last flower beds.

And then Herk yanked me backward. No—he tackled me, smashing me down flat onto the cobblestones.

I lay with grit on my face and pebbles pressing into my skin.

"What did you do that for?" Tog scolded Herk, trying to pull the little boy away from me.

"What if you'd hurt her?" Janelia asked.

Herk held on tight. And for some reason, he kept pressing my face against the ground.

"You can't go over to the palace right now!" Herk hissed in my ear.

"Why not?" I asked.

"Because," Herk whispered, "Madame Bisset is standing right by that front door!"

30

Tog reacted first. He scooped up Herk and me and pulled us to the other side of the flower bed. And then he peeked out from the behind one of the giant orange blooms, toward the palace.

"Herk's right," he reported. "That is Madame Bisset."

"What's she doing here?" Janelia asked, crouching alongside me.

"Is this proof that she's the same Madame Bisset Ella told me about?" I whispered. "Because she's back in Fridesia, back at the palace where she was so mean to Ella?"

"Then why was she in Suala with you the day after the fire?" Tog asked.

No one seemed to have answers for these questions.

Madame Bisset was trying to manipulate me, but I don't know why, I remembered. *And she said all my sister-princesses were dead, but then there were those rumors that they were all going to Fridesia. . . .*

What was the connection between those facts?

I raised my head just high enough to peer out past one of the giant orange flowers. I studied the scene before me. Madame Bisset was most recognizable for her posture: I had never seen anyone else stand so erect and prim and proper. She wore what seemed to be a gray silk gown, and carried a gray parasol to keep the sun off her face. The parasol looked so severe I could imagine it being used as a weapon. Though she stood near the row of guards, she acted as though she were entirely alone. She also looked past the crowd of commoners in front of the palace as though they were all beneath her notice.

"She probably wouldn't even see me if I walked past her to talk to the guards," I suggested. "It's not like I look like a princess anymore."

"Yes, you do," Tog said softly.

My heart beat a little faster. I wanted to ask, *You think so? Even in this cotton dress, even with sunburned skin, even with ragged bandages still on my feet?*

"Don't worry," Janelia said, patting my back. "*I* can go up and ask the guards about Ella and Jed, even if the rest of you can't. Madame Bisset has never seen me, like she did you and Herk and Tog."

This was true.

"But Madame Bisset would recognize a Sualan accent—" I reminded her.

"I won't talk like I have stones in my mouth," Janelia said, demonstrating her best Fridesian imitation. "I've got it."

She stepped out from behind the flower bed before the rest of us could offer any more advice. Watching Janelia walk away brought me an oddly familiar feeling. It took me a moment to identify it.

This is like being back in the fire, worrying about Cecilia and Harper and the other sister-princesses, wanting to get all of them to safety . . .

I saw that Janelia had the sense to approach the guard the farthest away from Madame Bisset. Janelia's light green peasant dress looked all the poorer next to the guard's spiffy blue-and-gold uniform. Janelia was saying something. . . . Was she succeeding? The guard *didn't* instantly grab her by the arms and scream, *Impostor! How dare you try to pass yourself off as a Fridesian! I can tell you're from Suala!* Actually, the guard barely seemed to be listening to her.

"She looks so small by those guards and those giant doors," Tog whispered beside me. "I guess it's true, what you told me about palaces."

I opened my mouth to object. I'd only described the way the Sualan palace made people feel small; I hadn't been talking about palaces in general. I'd only ever been in the Palace of Mirrors. But maybe the Fridesian palace was the same. Maybe all palaces were.

I tilted my head back, taking in the entire view. For the first time I noticed black bunting hanging from all the palace windows—why? And though the front part of the palace looked very similar to the Palace of Mirrors, the back part of it looked more like a fortress. Maybe the Fridesians had first built a castle for defensive purposes, then decided to go in for frills and furbelows when they expanded. That was different from the Palace of Mirrors, which had never had any purpose but showing off.

Maybe we Sualans should have thought about defending our palace a bit more, I thought ruefully.

Just then somebody grabbed my shoulder.

"What are the three of you doing?" a bearded man in some sort of police uniform barked at us. "Pickpockets looking for your next mark, I'll warrant! I'll haul you off to prison, I will!"

31

"Please, no!" I cried. "You've misunderstood!"

But how was I supposed to explain? Saying we were from Suala would probably land us in prison too.

"We're only waiting on our mam," Tog said. He pointed toward Janelia and the guards. "See, we lost our father because of the war, and our farm, too, and Lord Jedidiah Reston helped us so much, with his refugee camp and all, and we came to the cap—er, Charmeil, to thank him."

"But none of us have palace clothes, exactly, and Mama was ashamed of how we look, so she told us to wait here," Herk added. He poked his finger into a hole in his shirt—how had he already gotten a hole in his new shirt? "See?"

The police officer—some sort of constable?—looked confused. Then something like disgust slid over his face.

"And your mam wanted to see Lord Reston all by herself?" he asked. "She wanted to entice him to some pub, I'll warrant, and then—"

"No, no," Tog interrupted. "That's not—"

The constable clapped his hand over Tog's mouth.

"Silence!" he growled. "I don't want to hear your lies. I can tell you've got the gift of gab, you and your brother both. I want to hear from *that* one."

He was pointing at me.

I made my eyes wide and innocent. And maybe ignorant, too. This was a look I'd perfected with Lord Throckmorton, although I'd always wondered if he could see right through it and was just toying with me.

"What, sir?" I asked, as if I were slightly stupid and hadn't followed the question. Or his implications.

"Why did your mam want to see Lord Reston alone?" the constable asked, slowing down his words a bit. So maybe he did believe I was stupid.

I thought fast.

"Why, sir," I said. "She heard he was getting married. She wanted to meet his bride and offer to be her . . . washerwoman."

The constable tugged at his beard. Did he believe me? Would he ask some other question to trap us in our lies?

"Sir? Is there a problem?"

It was Janelia, coming back toward the flower bed. I couldn't tell from her expression what she'd heard from the guards. Or if she'd heard anything the constable or I had said.

Wouldn't Jed come and save us from this constable? I wondered.

What if the constable threw us all in prison before Jed and Ella even knew we were in Fridesia?

"Are these your children, ma'am?" the constable asked.

"Oh, yes. Please—"

"Just tell me this," the constable said. He'd switched to stroking his beard in a crafty way. "I understand you're a widow. How is it that you earn money to support your family?"

Why didn't I make up a different story? I agonized. *Why didn't I talk about the baskets we're carrying?*

Out of the corner of my eye, I saw Herk making fists behind the constable's back. The constable probably outweighed him by a couple hundred pounds. Did Herk think fighting was a good idea?

I wanted to frown and shake my head, but the constable was looking right at me and Janelia.

Herk didn't hit the constable. Instead, the little boy began moving his fists up and down, pantomiming scrubbing his shirt.

Did Janelia even see him?

Her expression didn't change.

"Why, sir," Janelia said, "I wash clothes. I'm a laundress."

The constable's face fell.

"So I reckon you were telling the truth, after all," he mumbled. His countenance brightened a bit, as if he'd thought of something else. "But I'll warrant that Lord Reston and his new wife won't be hiring you."

"Er, no," Janelia said. "The guards said Lord Reston is still in Suala, of all places."

Was that true, or just something Janelia was making up for the constable's benefit?

The constable looked more confident.

"Then begone with you," he said sternly, pointing away from the palace. "The likes of you don't belong in this part of town. Don't let me see you back here. Now go!"

"Yes, sir," Janelia said.

She grabbed Herk's and my hands and began walking away. Tog followed close behind.

"Don't look back," Tog whispered to me. "Don't give him a reason to change his mind and arrest us after all. . . ."

And don't give Madame Bisset a chance to get a glimpse of us, I reminded myself.

I already felt as if everyone on the street was watching us. We walked a block away, then two, then three.

At the start of the fourth block, I felt safe asking, "Was that true? Did the guards really say Jed's still in Suala?"

Janelia collapsed against the side of a building.

"Yes," she said. "They said he hasn't been in Charmeil in months."

I wanted to weep. I wanted to scream every bit as loudly as I had back in the desert, with that first glimpse of empty sky.

Instead, I pulled Janelia back from her slump. To my surprise, Tog was doing the same thing.

"Don't make us stand out," Tog whispered.

We already stood out. We were four Sualans in the Fridesian

capital. We were four people dressed in country-peasant clothes on a street full of dandies in brocaded jackets. We were carrying baskets that looked plain and rustic and simple, in a place where everything was frilly and overdecorated and complicated. We were children and women, and I didn't know where Fridesia kept their women and children, but it mostly wasn't in the blocks surrounding the palace.

Except for Madame Bisset, who stood on the palace steps like she owned it.

"Did you ask about Cecilia and Harper—or any sort of delegation from Suala?" I asked Janelia. "Is *anyone* we know here besides Madame Bisset?"

"No, I didn't ask," Janelia said, "I saw the constable grab the three of you, and I thought you needed help." She made a wry face. "I'm not sure the guards would have told me the truth, anyhow. I'm not sure even *they* believed what they said about Jed and Ella. They were just trying to get rid of me."

"So we wait to go back after Madame Bisset and the constable are gone," Tog suggested. "This time I'll go up and talk to the guards."

"There could be some other constable there then who doesn't like us any better," I said. "What are the laws here? That man acted like it was a crime to be poor!"

None of the others bothered to reply. They didn't even look surprised.

Because . . . people always treated them like it was a crime to be poor back in Suala, too, I realized.

That was the danger Janelia and Tog—and even Herk—had seen in my original plan. That was why, if I ever got back to my own kingdom, I needed to change how people in Suala were treated.

I couldn't think about any of that right now. I went back to focusing on our immediate problems.

"And, even if we don't see Madame Bisset standing outside the palace, she could be inside, looking out a window," I continued. "It's too dangerous to go back to the guards."

"Do you have any better ideas?" Tog challenged.

I tried to think, but my mind kept looping back to, *You stand out. Worry about that first! Look at all these people watching you!*

Tog had asked me weeks ago if I missed the palace, and I said I didn't. But I did miss the secret passageways, where I could hide and watch and not be watched. I needed that now, a place to observe and think and figure things out.

It's a pity I can't just sneak into the Fridesian palace, I told myself. *I bet they have secret passageways too.*

I didn't have my sister-princess Ganelia's knowledge of architecture, but something clicked in my brain. The one section of the Fridesian palace looked so similar to the Palace of Mirrors. What if it was completely similar—even down to the secret passageways hidden inside?

"We don't need to ask the guards anything else," I told the others. "We're going to sneak into the palace instead."

32

The others stared at me like I was crazy.

"Right, because the guards don't think it's their job to stop people *sneaking* into the palace," Tog said. "Just the ones who ask permission."

He tried to put his arm around my shoulder, but I pushed it away.

"I may be wrong," I said. "But I think I know how to do this without anyone seeing. I remember back at the Palace of Mirrors . . ."

Janelia was looking at me even more curiously now.

"Oh," she said. "You mean, go around to the side, down into that gully, and then..."

"And then there *should* be a secret entrance," I said. "One that even the Fridesians might have forgotten."

"We can try," Janelia said.

We waited until dusk.

Tog tiptoed close to the palace first and came back to report that Madame Bisset was out of sight and the constable seemed to have a regular pattern of sweeping through the three blocks closest to the palace every ten minutes. That didn't leave enough time for anyone to go speak to the guards without the constable seeing, but it was enough time to circle around the palace.

"I don't see any doors on this side," Herk complained in what he probably thought was a whisper. "And the lowest window is two stories up. How can you go inside without a door or a window?"

"Shh," Janelia and Tog said together.

"Watch," I said. I took an apple from the bag of food Mrs. Smeal had given us back at the refugee camp. "See that rock in the wall up there, the one that's a little different color than all the others?"

"Yeah," Herk said.

"Let's see what happens if I hit it," I said.

I reared back my arm. I couldn't remember the last time I'd thrown anything, even a ball—why would I, a princess, have ever thrown a ball? But I remembered this motion. And either my muscles remembered it too, or I simply got lucky: the apple hit the stone exactly, with such a soft thud that I didn't worry about anyone hearing it.

I didn't worry *much*, anyway.

For a moment nothing happened, and I wondered if I'd imagined everything—not just about the Fridesian palace, but in my memories of the Palace of Mirrors back in Suala as well.

And then, just above my head, a door in the wall swung open.

"How did you know that was there?" Tog asked incredulously.

"I started thinking maybe the same person who designed the Palace of Mirrors had designed this palace, too," I said. "And designed it the same way. With secret entrances and exits and passageways."

Tog was still shaking his head in disbelief.

"But—"

"Hush," Janelia hissed at us. "Let's move fast—that door is like a beacon, as long as we leave it open. Herk, go look past those trees and make sure no guards start patrolling in this direction. Tog, you go up first and make sure it's safe."

She put out her hands, cupped like a stirrup, and Tog stepped into them. The doorway was high enough up that he still had to prop himself on his arms and shimmy in across the threshold. He disappeared into the darkness. A moment later, he looked back out.

"I don't know if it's safe or not," he complained. "I can't see anything in here."

"Put me up next," I asked.

"Desmia—" Janelia began.

"I know what the secret passageways are like back in Suala," I said. "Or—what they were like. I won't need a light."

Janelia still looked doubtful, but she cupped her hands again. They were trembling.

"We'll be fine," I said, hitching up my skirt and putting my foot against Janelia's hands.

Janelia lifted me, and Tog reached down and pulled up on my arms. Something flashed in my memory.

I was so little then that Janelia could boost me up to stand on her shoulders so I could see inside the secret door we found. And then I crawled inside. . . .

As soon as I was safely inside the doorway, I whirled back around and hissed at Janelia.

"Janelia! I remember!" I whispered. "The two of us found the secret passageways back at the Palace of Mirrors together. When we were playing ball and the ball hit the stone just by accident. . . ."

Even in the dim light, I could see Janelia beaming at me.

"Yes, that's right!" Janelia whispered back. "I thought, of all the things we did together when we were little, that might be something you remembered on your own."

An owl hooted over by the tree where Herk was watching. Tog pulled me back from the door.

"That's Herk's signal!" he hissed. "Janelia, shut the door and hide!"

"Try to meet us back here at midnight," Janelia said. "Stay safe!"

And then the door shut and I heard the faintest sound of footsteps, walking away.

Tog and I were in total darkness. I fought the impulse to reach for his hand. Somehow it would mean something different if I reached for his hand than if he reached for mine. It would be . . . cruel.

"Put your hand on my shoulder," I said, speaking as quietly as I could, directly into his ear. "I'll lead the way. But we need to be quiet. If this secret passageway is like the ones back at the Palace of Mirrors—well, the way they used to be—then we might be just a few feet away from someone on the other side of a wall."

"Right," Tog whispered back. Somehow in the darkness I thought I could hear something extra in his voice.

Fear, I thought. *He's afraid too.*

His hand landed on my shoulder. I didn't know how much it helped him, but it gave me the courage to start moving away from the door. I ran my fingers along the wall to guide myself.

"When we get to any occupied rooms—the ones that are brightly lit, anyway—we'll probably see glimmers of light where there are peepholes," I said, trying to sound brisk and unafraid. "That will help."

Tog was so close behind me that I could feel the movement when he nodded his head.

We took several steps forward before Tog whispered in my ear, "If Janelia knew about a secret doorway into your palace, why didn't she use it to get back to see you after Lord Throckmorton sent her away?"

"Because . . . ," I began, thinking hard.

Had Janelia maybe not cared as much as she pretended? Was this proof that part of her story wasn't true, after all?

Then I realized the actual reason.

"Back at the Palace of Mirrors, there were always guards along the wall," I said, still walking forward in the darkness. Somehow the darkness made it easier to remember. "It was the only place I was allowed to go outside to play, and so it had to be guarded. And then Lady Throckmorton heard that the Domulians had a giant lily pond at their palace, and so Lord Throckmorton had a lily pond put in where Janelia and I used to play. . . . Honestly, I was afraid we were going to have to swim to find the door here. I thought the Fridesians might have gone in for a lily pond too."

Things were getting confused in my mind—or maybe they were straightening out. Maybe the story about Lady Throckmorton and the Domulian lily pond had been another lie, and Lord Throckmorton had really just wanted to end my playing outside. It probably wasn't just to keep me away from Janelia. Once he learned I had no royal blood, he wanted to hide me so no one outside the palace would recognize a substitute princess if he got rid of me.

I had a memory of standing in the secret doorway, peeking out through a crack at workers digging deep into the ground, then building high walls around a pond. It had been the autumn—I could remember because of the dying leaves on the trees the men chopped down. Janelia wasn't with me, and neither was anyone else. So how had I gotten up to the doorway?

By then I'd found entrances to the secret passageways from inside the castle, I thought. *Was I . . . was I saying good-bye to that secret doorway and the special yard where I'd played with Janelia?*

I could picture myself as a little girl standing in the doorway whispering, *Don't think about her ever again. She left you. You shouldn't even remember her name.*

"I think I forgot Janelia on purpose," I whispered to Tog. "Because it hurt too much to remember."

"She didn't forget you," Tog whispered back.

"I know," I said. "We'll have to make sure we get out of here alive so I can apologize."

Tog didn't answer right away, and I was afraid I'd violated some rule of bravery. Maybe it was best not to even mention the possibility of death?

But then Tog whispered in a husky voice, "Janelia would like that. She would especially like us staying alive."

We inched forward until my foot struck a step. I stopped, then slid my foot to the right, where the floor dropped away.

"This *is* like the Palace of Mirrors!" I hissed back to Tog. "This is the exact right place for a stairway. We can go up to the main level of the palace or . . ."

Or climb down toward the dungeon.

I had a flash of remembering how I'd found all my sister-princesses except Cecilia in the dungeon of the Palace of

Mirrors. I thought about the strange letter that Mrs. Smeal had received back at the refugee camp; I thought about the palace guards saying Jed had never returned from Suala, when Mrs. Smeal said he and Ella were in Charmeil.

"Maybe this is foolish, but I want to check the dungeon first," I whispered to Tog.

"Lead the way," he whispered back.

I began to climb down the stairs, with Tog right behind me.

Was it this dark in the secret passageways back at the Palace of Mirrors when Cecilia and Harper were escaping? I wondered. *They knew the secret passageways—they could have escaped anyhow. Right?*

Before the fire, Cecilia and Harper had been in the secret passageways only during the dangerous time when Lord Throckmorton was still in power; only when Cecilia, Harper, Ella, and I were trying to figure out what was going on and why there were extra princesses down in the dungeon and knights trapped in the torture chamber. Once the secrets came out, Cecilia and Harper were more interested in exploring the open areas of the palace and working with everyone together. Not skulking around still hiding.

I was the only one who couldn't make the transition to doing everything out in the open.

I clutched the railing of this stairway and kept going.

The floor leveled out, and I ran my hand along the wall.

"There should be a door right over here," I whispered back to Tog.

Just as my fingers brushed against an iron door handle, I heard a gravelly voice growl on the other side of the wall: "No, of course the prince doesn't know you're down here. More's the pity for you!"

33

Tog tightened his grip on my shoulder, so I knew he'd heard too. Each of us pressed an ear against the stone wall, listening for some answer to the gravelly voice, some indication of who might be in the dungeon that the prince didn't know about.

I heard barely a mumble in response, as if the speaker was too weak or too fearful to speak loudly. Or simply too far away, on the opposite side of the dungeon. It could have been Ella or Jed or Cecilia or Harper or any of my other sister-princesses . . . or, really, anyone at all, for as much as I could tell.

"Right," the gravelly voice spoke again. "You can demand an audience with the prince all you want. Ain't going to happen. Now, shut your yapper, lest I beat you for annoying your jailer."

Silence.

Was the imprisoned person—or people?—too terrified

to speak? Or could I just not hear what he or she—or they—was saying?

I reached for the door handle, just as Tog put a cautioning hand on my arm.

"I'm just going to open it a crack, just to see," I whispered, shoving against the handle.

The door didn't budge. It was locked. And—I ran my fingers all along the edges—both the lock and the hinges were on the other side.

I stood still, desperately trying to remember if there'd been more than one secret passageway leading down to the dungeon back at the Palace of Mirrors.

"Desmia, that could be just some ordinary prisoner the jailer's talking to," Tog whispered in my ear. "Whoever that is may have nothing to do with you or Suala. From what we saw back in Suala, when Janelia had us watching the palace and trying to get a message to you . . . there could be all sorts of people imprisoned, for all sorts of reasons a prince or princess wouldn't know about."

I winced, because back in Suala, I'd been the ignorant princess for so long. And then, even after the other sister-princesses and I ousted Lord Throckmorton, we'd acted like we could just paper over the past. None of us had wanted to investigate his crimes thoroughly. We'd just put him and his coconspirators into prison and pretended the past was over.

I had known better, even if the others were all too innocent and naïve. But I had been too paralyzed to do or say anything.

Just as I felt paralyzed right now.

"Desmia?" Tog whispered. "Shouldn't we find out what's going on elsewhere in the palace and then come back here if there's time?"

"All right," I said reluctantly. I still wanted to know who was in that dungeon cell. I still wanted to be sure it wasn't Ella or Jed or any of my fellow princesses.

But Tog had a point. Maybe the answers we wanted lay in some other part of the palace.

We turned and began climbing back up the stairway. Not long after we passed the hallway that would have led back to Janelia and Tog, the stairway curved around and broadened.

"Light!" Tog whispered behind me.

I felt his arm extend past me, pointing toward the top of the stairs. It was almost like he was starting to put his arm around me.

Then he dropped it.

"I told you we'd eventually see some light," I whispered back. "That means there are peepholes."

We kept climbing, and the light transformed from a vague, distant glow to distinct pinpoints along the wall. Because I'd studied these things back at the Palace of Mirrors, I knew there were probably little eyeholes scraped out at intervals in the mortar between the stones in the ballroom we were approaching. But from this side, in the darkness, the glimmers of light looked as miraculous as the starry sky Tog and I had seen out in the mountains.

We climbed higher, and I could hear dance music. A violin, perhaps, the brief blare of a horn . . . That song ended and another one started.

"Oh," I gasped, stopping in my tracks.

"What's wrong? Are you hurt?" Tog asked.

"No, it's just . . . ," I choked back the cry I wanted to give. "This is the galliard. The last dance the musicians played that night at the ball. Before the fire."

I sniffed as if I expected to smell smoke.

"I'm sorry. But the music didn't *cause* the fire," Tog said soothingly. "It's . . . just a song."

I still felt my stomach churning. I still had to force myself to keep climbing toward the music and lights.

You were brave during the fire, I told myself. *You can be brave now, too. You pushed Cecilia and Harper out of the ballroom. You went back for Fidelia and wanted to rescue her, too.*

But my view of the night of the fire had shifted like a kaleidoscope. I had done my best to save Cecilia and Harper. But had I really been that brave, going back for Fidelia? Or had I just used her as an excuse—even to myself—because I was terrified of leaving the palace, terrified of stepping outside?

You weren't afraid to go outside to get away from Madame Bisset, I told myself.

But wasn't that just because her news—that all my sister-princesses were dead—was even more terrifying than the thought of escape? Had I been brave or just a coward running away?

How could I hope to figure out what was happening at the Fridesian palace when I couldn't even see myself true? When I'd gone years without letting myself think of Janelia, the one true thing from my childhood?

Think about now, not the past, I told myself. *Don't get paralyzed again.*

I reached the level of the first peephole and put my eye against it. I gazed out at the most highly decorated ballroom I could possibly imagine. Every wall, every cushion, every tapestry was covered with bows and frills.

"It looks like a dress shop exploded," Tog whispered beside me, putting his eye up to another hole.

"This isn't how Ella described the Fridesian ballroom," I whispered back. "I wonder what—"

I broke off because suddenly a man's face appeared just inches from my eye. It was a handsome man's face—maybe even the most handsome face I'd ever seen. This man had perfect blue eyes and perfect blond hair and a perfect angle to his jawline.

Prince Charming? I wondered.

I wasn't sure. I knew the king and queen of Fridesia had one son; because the royal couple were old and decrepit and possibly even senile, Prince Charming was viewed as the true ruler of the land. Ella had always described him as unbelievably handsome but also too vacant and dim to think or feel anything deeply. And this man looked . . . well, I wouldn't call his expression profound, but there was a certain fervency marring the beauty of his perfect face. Maybe even despair.

"It's too soon," he murmured, so close to me that for a moment I feared he'd seen me and for some reason had decided to pour out his anguish to me.

"Your Highness." The voice came from beyond the prince. "I know you are still mourning Princess Corimunde, but . . ."

Mourning? I thought. I remembered the black bunting I'd seen at the front of the palace, and for the first time it made sense. Maybe that was a Fridesian custom at times of grief. *And the person who's dead, Corimunde, that was . . . his wife?*

I remembered the crazy story Ella had told about how Prince Charming ended up marrying Ella's despised stepsister. So now Corimunde was dead?

And apparently Prince Charming had truly loved her?

"I am mourning my wife and my baby son," Prince Charming snapped. He turned, and for the first time I could see the man standing behind the prince. It was an elderly gentleman with a neatly trimmed beard and a look of keen intelligence.

Lord Twelling, I thought, remembering how Ella had described the prince's main adviser.

I knew exactly the look of advisers who thought they knew more than their royalty. Lord Twelling had been a bit of a villain in Ella's tale of her time in the Fridesian palace. Just not as bad a villain as Madame Bisset.

"I am aware that you have faced a loss," Lord Twelling hissed to the prince. "But you are young, and you are the prince of the land, and you are currently unmarried."

"Widowed," the prince corrected. "I am widowed. There's a difference."

I was at the wrong angle to see the glare Prince Charming directed at Lord Twelling. But I could tell from his voice that it was intense.

"Anyhow," Lord Twelling continued, as if he hadn't noticed. "Sulking won't bring Corimunde—or the newborn infant Charming the twenty-fifth—back from the grave. The babe barely lived a few hours. It's not as if he were someone you *knew*."

Now Prince Charming positively glowered at his adviser. Lord Twelling ignored this, too.

"But in the meantime," Lord Twelling continued, "you have a fabulous opportunity. And for the sake of your kingdom, you must at least pretend that you are over your heartbreak."

"Even when it seems as though it will never end?" the prince asked incredulously. "I wish Jed were here. He would understand."

Jed! I thought hopefully. But I wasn't sure if the prince meant that Jed wasn't in the ballroom, or wasn't in the palace, or wasn't in Charmeil at all.

Watch Lord Twelling's reaction carefully, I told myself. Was it possible that Jed was the prisoner the prince didn't know about down in the dungeon? Was Lord Twelling maybe the one keeping that secret from the prince?

But Lord Twelling didn't have a chance to reply. Trumpet blasts sounded from behind the two men, and both Lord Twelling and Prince Charming turned away from the wall. They both stepped toward the center of the ballroom. The dancers parted before the prince.

"Do you know what that was all about?" Tog whispered.

"I'm not sure," I whispered back. "But—"

Out in the ballroom, the trumpet blasts sounded again, eerily reminiscent of the trumpet blasts that had always welcomed me into court occasions back at the Palace of Mirrors.

Are they trying to imitate the Sualan Royal Anthem, or is it just a coincidence? I wondered.

"King Charming, Queen Gertrude, Prince Charming," a herald announced from across the room. "Lords and ladies of the Fridesian court. Allow me to present our royal guests, the princesses of Suala!"

I thought my heart would stop. Tog clutched my arm.

"It's true!" he hissed. "They did come to Fridesia! You've found them after all. Look!"

A bevy of shimmering beauties came into the room, seeming that much more stunningly gorgeous after my weeks away from the palace and royal clothing and royal servants to make *me* beautiful. There was the lovely russet hair that glowed from the top of Princess Ganelia's head, the statuesque height that made Princess Porfinia the envy of all the others, the same kind of creamy white skin that I had seen against an aquamarine gown when Princess Fidelia had fallen on the dance floor.

"You want to find a door so you can go be reunited with them right now?" Tog whispered. "So they know *you* survived the fire too? So they'll stop worrying about you?"

I stood frozen.

"Desmia?" Tog asked.

"It's all wrong," I moaned. "Wrong!"

"What are you talking about?" Tog asked. "This is what we came for. Your sisters!"

I turned to him, my eyes burning.

"Those aren't my sister-princesses," I hissed. "They're impostors, every single one!"

34

"Are you sure?" Tog asked, squinting harder into the peephole.

"You think I don't remember what they look like?" I asked.

Out in the ballroom, the herald began to introduce each one individually.

"Princess Adoriana . . . Princess Cecilia . . ."

"That's not her?" Tog whispered. "The one you saved . . ."

The girl who stepped forward did look like Cecilia, with similar long dark hair and the same kind of silky lilac dress that Cecilia herself might have chosen. But this girl lacked the flash of the real Cecilia's eyes; she moved too smoothly, without Cecilia's usual awkward enthusiasm.

This Cecilia didn't look like the type of girl who would ever jostle my shoulder with hers.

"No," I whispered back.

"Are you sure?" Tog asked. "They're kind of far away, over on the other side of the ballroom. Maybe you just can't see—"

"Princess Desmia," the herald announced, and another girl stepped forward.

"Oh," Tog whispered, as if the situation had finally sunk in. "They even have a fake version of you."

The fake Desmia curtsied, first for the king and queen on their thrones, and then for Prince Charming, standing alone on the dance floor.

"At least they chose the prettiest girl to pretend to be you," Tog whispered, as if that would be any consolation.

"Why?" I asked. "Why are they using fakes? What are they trying to accomplish? Who set this up?"

My voice rose with each question. Tog put his hand on my arm, a clear reminder that the nearest Fridesian out in the ballroom was barely three feet away.

I pinched my lips together and went back to watching the rest of the introductions.

Then Madame Bisset stepped out from behind the row of fake princesses. Even in the ballroom she wore a more severe dress than the other ladies. It was a silvery gray once again, and unadorned, without a single frill or flounce. She regarded the prince with a confident gaze.

"And which of the lovely princesses of Suala would the prince like to dance with first?" she asked. "It is so fortunate that none of them are yet betrothed. You have your choice!"

My stomach twisted.

"Oh, no," I whispered. "Oh, no . . ."

"Did you figure something out?" Tog asked.

"The Fridesians like their beauty contests," I said. For a moment, I was too horrified to go on. "Now that the war is over . . . if the Fridesian prince is truly widowed . . . if he chooses a Sualan princess for his second wife . . ."

"It'd be good, right?" Tog asked. "If the Fridesian prince had a Sualan princess for a wife, he wouldn't want to go back to war with Suala!"

What was wrong with Tog, that he saw only the happiest outcome?

He hadn't had the palace childhood that I had. He didn't see that everything in a palace was about power, not love; conquest, not conciliation.

"No," I moaned. "No. It would mean Fridesia won the war. They'd take over Suala completely!"

"I don't know how that could happen," Tog said. "Even if he marries one Sualan princess—fake or not—there'd still be twelve other princesses running Suala."

I watched Lord Twelling nudge Prince Charming toward the nearest fake princess. I guessed it was supposed to be Lucia, with her light brown hair and a maroon dress.

"Don't you see?" I whispered back. "If they can just make up thirteen fake princesses, they can easily make twelve of them go away. Their carriage will be lost in a raging river, traveling back to Suala. Or they'll all sicken and die from some mysterious fever. Or . . ."

I slumped down to the floor. I couldn't go on watching the prince and the fake princesses play out their roles. I couldn't go on listing ways princesses could die. For the first time since the fire at the Palace of Mirrors, I stopped wondering if my sister-princesses were alive or dead. What did it matter? Even if the other girls had survived the fire, Madame Bisset and whoever else was orchestrating this would make sure they were dead after Prince Charming chose a fake princess for his bride.

Even if the princesses were right now down in the Fridesian palace dungeon, I couldn't think of a single way to creep down through a different secret passageway, sneak past the jailer, and rescue them before they were killed.

So did I condemn my sister-princesses to death when I first acknowledged them as equals? I wondered in despair. *Was Queen Charlotte Aurora actually signing death certificates when she wrote those letters designating orphan girls as her heirs? Were we all doomed from the very beginning?*

"It's hopeless," I whispered.

I was stunned when something hit me in the leg. No—it was Tog kicking me.

"Aren't you going to stop this?" he asked. "Or did we come all this way for you to just give up?"

35

"What am I supposed to do?" I asked.

Tog pointed out toward the ballroom.

"Get out there and tell those Fridesians the truth!" he said. "Get them to help you find the real princesses!"

This never would have occurred to me. Truth? In a palace?

"Why would they care about helping me?" I asked. "You don't know what royalty and courtiers are like."

"I know what you're like," Tog said. "*You'd* help."

I blinked. *Would* I? If the situation were reversed, would I do anything to help missing Fridesian princesses?

I'd want to, *anyway*, I thought. *I'd just need to see how it was possible. . . .*

After all, back in Suala I had helped Cecilia and the other eleven sister-princesses when they showed up at the palace and I came to understand their plight. Even when it meant sharing my power and prestige.

"I'm . . . kind of not like most people in a palace," I said. "I was lonelier, I guess, and that made me do things differently. Most people in a palace are selfish and obsessed with power. And to get them to do anything, you have to get them to think they're going to get something out of it."

"Oh right, I'm just a stupid beggar boy, so I wouldn't understand any of that," Tog said bitterly. "Outside of palaces there aren't ever any mean people who do things just for their own reasons. No one like Terrence, who runs away from an injured princess. No one like those villagers with torches driving beggars away. No one like that constable outside the palace, who yelled at us just because we looked poor."

I gaped at Tog.

"Oh," I whispered. "I never thought of it that way."

"Royalty and courtiers and normal people aren't *that* different," Tog argued. "There are bad people inside and outside of palaces. And . . . there are good people inside and out of palaces, too. Like Janelia, who was good in both places."

I thought about how Janelia had watched over me inside the palace, and then all the way to Fridesia.

"I suppose I could try to make the Fridesians think it helps them to help us," I said thoughtfully. Then I looked down at my plain cotton dress. I could see cobwebs hanging from the hem. "At least, I could if I had the right clothes. If I looked like a princess again."

"Desmia, you *always* look like a princess," Tog said. "You sound like a princess, you act like a princess—you'll convince them."

I didn't say anything.

"Believe me, the most royal thing I've seen you do was throw that pot of boiled rags at the villagers to save me and Herk and Janelia," Tog said. "And you were wearing rags and bandages then."

Tog thought that was royal? I marveled. But something shifted in my brain. I stood up and put my eye back against one of the peepholes out into the ballroom. Everyone was looking in the other direction, toward the fake princesses.

"You're right," I whispered. "I have to stop this. I have to try, anyway."

I owed it to my kingdom and to my sister-princesses, regardless of whether they were alive or dead. I owed it to Tog and Herk and Janelia, who had worked so hard to get me to Fridesia.

And I owed it to myself. Because I couldn't live with myself if I once again stood back and stayed silent and did nothing.

I walked over to the point in the wall where, back at the Palace of Mirrors in Suala, a hidden door had stood between the secret passageways and the ballroom.

The door I sent Cecilia and Harper through, trying to save them, I thought.

I felt along the wall—yes, there was a release hidden in

one of the stones, just like in Suala. I turned back to Tog.

"If anything . . . bad . . . happens to me, take care of Janelia and Herk," I said. "Make sure they get back to Suala safely."

Then, quickly, before I could change my mind, I pressed the release, and the door in the wall swung open.

36

At first nobody saw me.

You could still change your mind. You could still go back into hiding . . . I told myself.

But I pushed the door shut behind me. It made a soft click, causing a young pageboy holding a silver tray of something orange—salmon chunks speared between melon slices, perhaps?—glance my way. He blinked and looked puzzled, and started to open his mouth as if he was considering screaming. But then he closed it, putting on the bland servant's expression that seemed to say, *You know, I don't actually get paid to think or make decisions. So I'll pretend I didn't notice anything. I'll go on pretending to be just another piece of furniture.*

I was not even dressed well enough to pretend to be a palace servant. But maybe I could take on that same blank expression. Maybe I could just blend in and go around unnoticed for a while eavesdropping and spying on people.

No, I told myself. *You need the element of surprise. Or they won't listen to you at all.*

I cleared my throat. For a moment I still felt paralyzed.

Look straight at what frightens you most, I told myself, starting to scan the crowd for Madame Bisset's steadfast posture. But that technique had backfired for me out in the frightening empty-sky landscape.

Maybe it's better to think about who's rooting for you to succeed, who . . . loves you, I corrected myself. I could feel Tog's concern for me radiating out from the wall behind me; I could feel Janelia and Herk waiting for us outside. I could even draw strength from remembering Cecilia and Ella and Harper and Jed. And all my real sister-princesses. Wherever they were.

This is for them, I thought. *This is what I have to do.*

I stepped forward, proclaiming in my loudest, most regal voice, "I should like to apologize to the royal family and courtiers of Fridesia."

As I expected, every head in the ballroom turned my way. Every eye stared at me. The royal orchestra, which had been playing soft background music while Prince Charming looked over the lineup of fake princesses, screeched to an inelegant halt.

Silence.

I didn't let myself look for Madame Bisset even now. I turned toward the king and queen and prince. I lowered my head and raised it again, a quick royalty-to-royalty acknowledgment of high status. I considered a curtsy for the queen—wasn't that the Fridesian custom? But I decided against it. The dress I was wearing wasn't made for curtsies. It was made for hours of standing beside a cooking pot, or tending to babies, or picking apples from a tree, or some other peasant work.

It would not do for me to begin by splitting my dress.

"I apologize," I repeated, "because you have been lied to. We Sualans have faced unrest and instability because of secrets and lies dating back a generation. Perhaps more than a generation. I regret that some of the liars stirring up the trouble have spilled across your borders, threatening our fragile peace."

The Fridesian king blanched at the words "unrest" and "instability," two terms most monarchs didn't ever want to think about. The queen seemed to be studying my clothing and hairstyle, with a dyspeptic expression on her face that made it clear she didn't approve.

The prince merely looked confused. And—grief-stricken. He still looked grief-stricken.

Lord Twelling, who was standing at the prince's elbow, whispered something into the prince's ear.

"So . . . um, what are these lies you're talking about?" the prince asked.

"Those are not the princesses of Suala," I said, pointing at the bevy of silk and braids and flounces on the thirteen impostors. I purposely did not look directly at them, because I still didn't want to see Madame Bisset's reaction behind them. As long as she didn't rush toward me to push me out of sight, that was enough for me. "They are merely pawns in a game of chess. The liars are trying to trick you into becoming their pawn too."

The prince still looked confused. Too late, I remembered Ella's low impression of his intellect. Perhaps the prince had never played chess? Perhaps he didn't know what pawns were?

Lord Twelling started to whisper in the prince's ear again, but the prince pushed him away.

This gave me hope.

"How do you know?" the prince asked. "Who *are* you, anyway?"

I drew myself up to my fullest height. The change in posture alone made me feel for a moment that it didn't matter that I was wearing cotton instead of silk, that my hair was adorned with twigs and cobwebs instead of gold and gems.

"I am the true Princess Desmia," I said.

The prince looked back and forth between me and all the fake, beautiful, royally dressed women behind him.

"Prove it," he said.

I held back a gasp. I should have planned for this. I should have brought evidence. I should have found my crown after the fire. I should have at least found other allies to bring to Fridesia besides a former servant girl and beggar boys. As it was, I had nothing but my own wits to guide me now.

And my memories, I told myself. *I have memories, too.*

All my guidelines about dismissing the past and focusing

on the present had not exactly been helpful. Right now I needed my past.

I thought about everything I knew and everything I'd guessed and suspected. I did not want to be the typical palace type spinning some grandiose story that was more fiction than truth, and constantly running the risk of getting caught in my own lies.

But I did actually have one bit of information that I was pretty sure would be news to the prince.

I held my regal pose and returned the prince's challenging gaze with a steady one of my own.

"Perhaps the prince would care to accompany me to the palace dungeon?" I asked.

37

I was gambling. If I was lucky, we would find Ella or Jed or one or more of my sister-princesses down in the dungeon, where I'd heard the jailer taunting someone, *Of course the prince doesn't know you're down here.*

If I wasn't quite so lucky, it'd be some other prisoner, maybe even somebody the prince didn't care about.

But I can still say, "Look, this is almost proof. This proves your advisers lied to you. My advisers lied to me, too. Can't you relate? Don't you want to listen to my whole story before your advisers talk you into an even bigger mistake?"

That is, I could say that if the jailer himself hadn't been lying about what the prince did or didn't know.

I saw that the prince, even behind his glaze of grief, had the slightest glimmer of curiosity on his face. That was a good sign.

But it was Lord Twelling who stepped forward first.

"As you wish," he said. "The *two* of us shall accompany you to the dungeon." He favored me with a thin smile. "Of course, it would not be appropriate for the young prince of Fridesia and a young—er—possible princess of Suala to go anywhere alone together, unchaperoned."

"Fair enough," I said, with a confident nod of my own, even though I was thinking, *Oh, no! What if Lord Twelling really is the reason there's someone in the dungeon the prince doesn't know about? What if Lord Twelling is just going along to find out what I know and sabotage my plan? What if he's even in on the fake-princess plan with Madame Bisset?*

I reminded myself that the prince still had ultimate power. He was the only one I had to convince.

And regardless, I couldn't back out now.

I stepped toward the nearest ballroom door. It was all I could do not to cast a glance over my shoulder, to make sure Lord Twelling and the prince followed.

You have to act as though you're sure they will, I told myself.

I heard the prince mumble, evidently to the royal orchestra, "No reason not to carry on with the music and the dancing while we're away."

A violin bow scraped against strings; flutes and trumpets joined in. Then I could hear the stomp of dancing feet behind me.

That's the thing about courtiers, I thought. *They know their roles. If any of them are curious, they'll have to wait. When the prince says they're supposed to dance, they don't ask questions.*

I let myself turn around once I reached the antechamber of the ballroom. I acted as though I were just waiting for the other two to catch up.

"It appears our palaces are very similar," I said to the prince, as if I were only making polite chitchat. Really, I was trying to figure out if I was leading them in the proper direction.

The prince squinted at me as if he didn't understand. It was left to Lord Twelling to cover for him.

"The same architect, Lord Anthony Thrassler, designed both palaces, more than four hundred years ago," he said. "Of course, the Fridesian palace was built first, and Suala merely copied ours."

He is being rude to me on purpose, I thought. *He is seeing what he can get away with.*

"Indeed," I said. "I find that Sualans prefer not to follow every fad and trend. It was generous of Fridesia to build the experimental model so Suala could go with the tried and true, and know what would work and what wouldn't."

Lord Twelling blinked, and I counted that as a victory.

Yes, I am going to be a formidable opponent, I thought at him. *It will be to your advantage to side with me, rather than with the fake princesses and Madame Bisset. Or, at least to make sure the prince sides with me, and never suspects that you were ever part of the conspiracy, if you ever were. . . .*

I was frightening myself, reminding myself of everything I didn't know.

I decided to go back to focusing on the prince. I gave him a sympathetic smile.

"The sad news about Princess Corimunde and your son had not reached Suala before my entourage and I left," I said. "May I offer my condolences?"

I only meant to get him on my side, to use his sorrow to achieve my own goals. But somehow looking at the man made it impossible to keep up my act, as only an act. Some of my own anguish and worry over my sister-princesses—and now Ella and Jed as well—slipped into my voice.

"You must have loved her very much," I said.

"I . . . did," the prince said, looking jolted. "I still do."

Had I made a mistake, touching on something so real before we reached the dungeon? Had I made it impossible to ask what he knew about Ella's and Jed's whereabouts?

"The stairs are this way," Lord Twelling said, smirking. "The prince's grandfather made a renovation of the palace fifty years ago, so perhaps this section is different from Suala's."

I let him lead the prince and me down a dark hallway, which lacked the frilly bows and ornate sconces that had been so abundant behind us. The prince let out a pained gasp. When I glanced curiously toward him, he mumbled, "This is the end of the area that my wife redecorated. I forgot . . . how bare the entire palace looked before she arrived."

So all the crazy decor was because of Corimunde? I wondered. *Good thing I didn't begin by insulting* that.

The prince leaned against the wall for a long moment, as if he had to steel himself to go on.

"It intrigues me that you would choose the dungeon as a place to confide in the prince," Lord Twelling murmured, once we continued forward again. "It is my experience that princesses would prefer to stay out of dungeons. To pretend, in fact, that a palace can exist without such a place."

Was that a reference to Princess Corimunde neglecting to bring her decorating skills to the lower levels of the palace?

Or was it a something deeper—maybe even a threat?

"It is my experience," I countered, "that dungeons are places where hard truths cannot be avoided."

Take that, I thought.

We were descending the stairs now: down and down and down. The stairway narrowed so much that we had to go single file, and further conversation wasn't possible. Finally we came out into a room that felt more like a stone cage. A chamber-pot-scented cage, perhaps. The stench was so overwhelming I could barely breathe.

"The air is so bad down here, even torches don't burn well," Lord Twelling said, indicating a flickering wooden torch in a rusted ring on the wall. It seemed to create more shadows than light. "But this is where you asked to go, and we Fridesians always accommodate our guests. I present you . . . our dungeon."

He made a mocking gesture, almost a bow. And then he lit a second torch and waved it around the room.

I looked around and—there was no one there. No gravelly-voiced jailer, no mystery prisoner or prisoners that the prince didn't know about. All the doors of the row of prison cells before me stood open, the cells empty.

I had begged for us to come down here for nothing.

38

"Does the palace perhaps have some other dungeon space besides this?" I asked desperately.

"You wish to imply that the Fridesian royal family has so many enemies it needs multiple dungeons?" Lord Twelling asked. I could hear the threat in his voice.

"No," I said faintly. "Of course not."

How could I have messed up so badly? If this was the right dungeon, had Lord Twelling arranged to move the secret prisoner or prisoners? The prince and I had been with him every step of the way since the ballroom, but perhaps there'd been some secret signal I'd missed. Perhaps he'd rapped his knuckles a certain number of times against the wall at the top of the stairs and I hadn't even noticed. Or perhaps one of his coconspirators had dashed out of the ballroom the very minute I mentioned the dungeon, and hidden all the incriminating evidence.

For all that I'd spent almost my entire life skulking around the Palace of Mirrors listening to other people manipulate one another, it turned out I was really bad at it myself.

What was I supposed to do now, when I had no bargaining chips left?

You do still actually have the truth on your side, I reminded myself.

I saw the prince wince as he glanced around the empty dungeon, and that made me think of something else I could try. It was a long shot, but it was all I could think of at the moment.

"Well?" Lord Twelling asked.

I took a deep breath, or as much as I could when the air around me felt so stale and lifeless.

"Suala's royal family had secrets that endangered us," I said. "They endangered us when we were hiding them, and they endangered us once everything was revealed. They made us vulnerable to the lies of a woman named Madame Bisset—whom I am sure you both know."

Lord Twelling nodded ever so slightly, as if to encourage me to go on.

The prince only looked blank.

"But the Fridesian royal family has secrets as well," I continued.

Be diplomatic, I told myself. *Handle this as delicately as possible. Watch their reactions.*

Lord Twelling's expression didn't change.

The prince furrowed his brows as if he didn't understand.

"Given Suala's history, I am sensitive to the fact that secrets can be ruinous," I said. "But secrets are my proof that I am who I say I am. *Your* secrets. So I didn't want to reveal them in front of the entire ballroom."

I tried to peer directly into the prince's eyes, to make the connection: *I am a Sualan princess who was used as a pawn, and you are the Fridesian prince who was used as a pawn. I know it got ugly when Lord Twelling and Madame Bisset wanted to force Ella to marry you. You and me, we've both made mistakes. But we are* royalty! *We of all people should be able to control our own lives, make our own decisions—do what is right! If we can't act on our own, who can?*

I was stunned at how quickly the prince responded. He grabbed Lord Twelling by the ruff around his neck and slammed the older man against the nearest slimy stone wall.

"Princess Corimunde yet lives, does she not?" the prince screamed at Lord Twelling. The prince slammed the other man's head against the wall again and again. "This has all been a lie—her illness, her death, the child's death—why else did you refuse to let me see the bodies? Why else did you not let me say good-bye?"

"Prince—" Lord Twelling attempted to choke out. His head lolled side to side, as if he'd lost control of it. No—he was trying to lock eyes with me. "Please, princess, I beg of you—tell him you know nothing of Princess Corimunde!"

I narrowed my eyes, calculating. Was it possible that Princess Corimunde *was* still alive, and *she* was the unknown prisoner I'd heard the jailer talking to? That seemed wildly unlikely—preposterous, even—but could I spin a convincing tale for the prince? Could I make him trust me long enough to get what I wanted?

I peered at the prince's anguished face. I couldn't do it. I couldn't exploit his grief.

"I'm sorry, Prince Charming," I said. "I know nothing about your wife's death. I only meant that I know how you came to marry her. I know you were betrothed to her stepsister Ella first, and Ella changed her mind. I know that Ella was imprisoned in the castle dungeon because of that. And I know these things only because—"

I stopped because the prince wasn't listening.

He'd collapsed into a sobbing heap on the stone floor.

"I still had hope," he wailed. "She made me think there was still hope. . . ."

Lord Twelling stepped over the prince and toward me.

"Ella had a servant girl she was friendly with," he said. He hung his torch carefully on the wall between us. "It was believed that servant girl must have helped Ella escape. Perhaps you are only that servant girl, grown-up and returned to cause more problems."

He seemed to be trying out his story, trying to figure out what would stick.

"No!" I protested. "I know about Ella because she came to Suala with Jed Reston. She's my friend. I'm worried about her! She—"

I stopped this time because Lord Twelling had stepped too close to me—indecently close. He glanced back once toward the sobbing prince on the ground. And then he gave me a shove.

I landed hard on the slimy stone floor and slid backward.

"How dare—" I began.

But my words were drowned out by the sound of a door slamming behind me, then a lock clinking together.

Lord Twelling had just trapped me in a dungeon cell.

39

I sprang up from the stone floor and rushed for the door.

"You can't do this!" I screamed. "This is an act of war! You'll start the fighting between our countries all over again!"

Lord Twelling regarded me calmly through a barred window in the door.

"I am protecting Suala from a pretender to its throne," he said. "I should be made a national hero in your land."

I slammed into the door. It held solid. I wrapped my hands around the bars on the window and shook. Nothing moved.

I decided to ignore Lord Twelling and appeal directly to the prince.

"You know I am the true princess of Suala," I said. "You know that pretending otherwise doesn't change the truth."

The prince didn't raise his head from his sobbing.

"A true princess would never travel to a foreign land alone," Lord Twelling taunted me. "A true princess would never agree to share her throne with twelve other girls who have only scant claim to the crown. A true princess would have such rivals executed."

"I—" I began, and stopped. It would not do to mention Tog or Janelia or Herk, because that would only endanger them.

But there's hope, as long as I know they're out there, I thought.

Except that I had told Tog to think mostly about keeping Janelia and Herk safe.

I decided I couldn't think about the three of them right now. Not unless I wanted to join the prince as a helpless royal sobbing on a dungeon floor.

Lord Twelling leaned close to the bars.

"A true princess would know that truth is worthless," he hissed. "What matters is what you can get people to believe. Who was ever going to believe you?"

Tog, I thought. *Janelia, Herk, Ella, Jed, Harper, Cecilia. And all my other sister-princesses. They believed me and trusted me, even when I didn't trust them.*

It was possible that half the people I was listing were dead. It was even possible that all of them were.

But I felt buoyed by their names anyway.

"A true princess would have known not to challenge *me*," Lord Twelling whispered.

He drew back from the door. Too late I realized that I'd missed my opportunity to scratch his face or grab his waistcoat and reach into the pocket for a possible key.

Now Lord Twelling bent over the sobbing prince.

"We're done here," he said. "I took care of the impostor. Come along."

He reached down to pull the prince upright.

"Prince Charming—you *know* Lord Twelling lies to you," I said. "But *you* are the prince. If you want to see your wife one last time, nobody can stop you. If you want to set me free, you can do that, too. If—"

I stopped because Lord Twelling had pulled the prince around the corner to the stairs and out of sight.

A moment later, Lord Twelling poked his head out again from behind the wall.

"One more thing," he said. "If you decide to search for a chamber pot in that prison cell, or even just a hole in the ground for your, ah, elimination . . . your search will be in vain. We had a bit of a problem with a previous prisoner— perhaps you heard of it?—and so we filled in all possible escape routes from all of the cells. And you have no shovel, anyhow. And, of course, how could a true princess do such filthy work?"

Then he was gone again.

How long will he and the prince still be in earshot? I wondered.

"You say the truth doesn't matter, but it does," I called out after them. "In a palace people start believing that it's just one person's word against another's, and the word of whoever has the most power is considered to be true. But outside the palace, people are truly starving or truly prospering. People are falling in love or having their hearts broken. Things are *real*. People live and people die, and the lies people tell in the palace don't change any of it. But what people *do* in the palace can change things. Prince Charming, I don't know if your wife and child are alive or dead—but don't you deserve to know the truth? Don't I deserve to know the truth about my real sister-princesses? And Ella and Jed?"

No one answered. I listened hard, and could hear nothing but water dripping steadily somewhere overhead.

Trembling, I started to sit down on the floor. Then I remembered Lord Twelling's warnings about the lack of a chamber pot—and what that implied about the condition of the floor. I reversed my motion midsquat, poking my knee against the side seam of my dress.

R-rip!

I stared down at the damage, the broken threads poking out from the skirt that I must have muddied when I hit the floor to begin with.

And Tog says I always look like a princess . . . something else he was wrong about! I thought.

I'd been wrong to take his advice to appeal directly to the Fridesian royalty. I'd been wrong to think that coming to the dungeon would do any good. Probably I'd been wrong to leave Suala in the first place.

But what else was I supposed to do?

Just then I heard footsteps coming toward me. I sprang back toward the barred door in time to see a cloaked figure taking the torch from its holder. The light glowed eerily around the cloak. And then the figure turned around just as a trimmer figure stepped up alongside him.

"Are you sufficiently humbled?" the first man asked. "Shall I take this chance to gloat?"

I recognized the hated voice before I could get my eyes to focus on the face.

It was Lord Throckmorton.

And beside him stood Terrence.

40

"You!" I cried, suddenly dizzy with rage. Everything fell into place for me at once. "The two of you—were you working together all along?"

Lord Throckmorton waved the torch at me in a way that could have extinguished it completely.

"Not *all* along," he said, his voice carrying the false cordiality I knew so well.

"Janelia assigned me to watch for you at the palace a few years ago," Terrence chimed in. "Lord Throckmorton was wise enough to notice a young boy who was present in the courtyard a little too often. . . ."

"A boy who, plied with an occasional treat, could be relied upon to tell all about a former servant I had reason to want to spy upon . . . ," Lord Throckmorton added.

"Janelia was so good to you!" I accused Terrence. "You agreed to spy on her for Lord Throckmorton? You betrayed her—and me!"

"Lord Throckmorton treated me even better than she did," Terrence said, grinning carelessly.

"Only because he was using you!" I cried.

"And Janelia wasn't?" Terrence countered, smirking even more. "I had to spy on the palace for eight hours every day before I earned my supper."

"She shared all the food she had with her boys!" I argued. "She would have given you more if she had it!"

Lord Throckmorton stroked his chin. Or, rather, his *chins*—he had three of them.

"Now, now, children," he said. "You know I can't tolerate childish bickering like that. Though it amuses me, Desmia, to see you defending the sister who abandoned you so heartlessly."

"Only because you kicked her out of the palace!" I replied.

Lord Throckmorton just shook his head in mock surprise.

"Oh, is *that* the story she's spinning?" he asked.

Once that tone of Lord Throckmorton's would have been enough to make me doubt myself. That was how he had controlled me for most of my life. I was surprised that now, even stuck in the Fridesian dungeon, I didn't feel the slightest quiver of doubt, the slightest desire to just give in to whatever Lord Throckmorton was going to tell me.

Maybe I truly had grown up.

I turned to Terrence.

"Were you still loyal to Janelia when you started out with

us, on the way to Fridesia?" I asked. "Or were you a total traitor even then?"

Terrence tilted his head, considering.

"I was still thinking that if I played my cards right, I could end up married to a princess," he said.

"That's not an answer!" I insisted.

"You seemed so . . . royal . . . until you started screaming," Terrence said. "I thought maybe you might still win."

"Until I started screaming," I muttered.

Terrence shrugged, and at least had the grace to avoid meeting my eyes.

"You know you lost as soon as you defied me," Lord Throckmorton chided me. "I thought I taught you better than that! Siding with those anonymous girls and bumbling knights instead of me. You know I always win!"

It was true. I had seen him win against challengers again and again in the palace.

"What possessed you?" Lord Throckmorton asked. He sounded truly hurt, almost as if I had been a beloved daughter who ran away.

"What you were doing—what you wanted—it was wrong," I said, stumbling over my own words. "The war was wrong."

"Oh, and so you became a moralist?" Lord Throckmorton asked. "You, who were always so cold and aloof—you actually began to care for soldiers you'd never met?"

"Yes!" I said.

But had I? I thought back to the first time Ella and Jed had come to the palace, the way they seemed so different from everyone else I knew. And then Cecilia and Harper showed up, and Cecilia screamed and yelled and threw fits and Harper still stayed by her side. And they were different too.

"And . . . maybe I wanted friends," I admitted. "Maybe I wanted true friends, for the first time in my life."

I couldn't separate it in my mind. Wasn't it still good to want to impress friends who were good people, and wanted good things? Who maybe made me a better person myself?

Of course, better person or not, now I was imprisoned in the dungeon of the Fridesian palace, with Lord Throckmorton and Terrence both gloating over my mistakes.

"Why do you care about any of that now?" I asked Lord Throckmorton. "You're out of prison, and I'm in it. You got your revenge! And—are you working with Madame Bisset now? Was it the two of you who conspired to burn down the Palace of Mirrors?"

Lord Throckmorton smirked.

"We found so many people willing to help," he crowed. "Jailers willing to accept the slightest bribe, palace officials whose feelings were hurt when the twelve new princesses had no interest in their advice . . ."

I closed my eyes weakly. I had known the sister-princesses needed to be more tactful. I should have warned them about that, too.

But I'd also been in awe of their bluntness, their energy,

their willingness to do what they thought was right no matter what.

I'd been a little jealous.

"You've won, of course," I murmured. "So you can tell me—are they still alive? The other twelve *real* princesses of Suala?"

I opened my eyes, hoping to see the truth written on Lord Throckmorton's face. But he had even more years of palace experience than I did. I could tell he was keeping his expression carefully unreadable.

"None of you were ever *real* princesses," he said. "Surely you realize that now. And surely you realize how easy that makes it for Madame Bisset and me and our underlings"—he glanced almost dismissively at Terrence—"to replace all of you in one fell swoop. With a fake princess who will serve *our* needs."

"By marrying her off to the prince of Fridesia," I muttered. "Joining the two kingdoms. Leaving you and Madame Bisset to be the powers behind the throne of a country that's twice the size of Suala."

Lord Throckmorton beamed, his eyes greedy.

"I taught you well!" he announced. "You see the possibilities! Isn't it a marvelous plan?" He leaned in close. "We *were* willing to let you play the true princess role, if only you'd cooperated with Madame Bisset. Because you *do* look so much like a princess—you can, anyway—and you'd served that role for so long. But, alas, you chose to betray my goals yet *again*. By running away after the fire."

"And so you started the rumor that I set the fire and murdered the other princesses," I murmured, finally putting this piece of the puzzle together. "As revenge. And—to thoroughly discredit me. So nobody would believe me if I dared to come out of hiding and tried to rule alone."

"Quite so," Lord Throckmorton said, nodding. "Quite so."

It was frightening how well I understood him. I didn't want to. How could I know him so well when he didn't understand me at all?

"But it's too late for you now," Terrence interrupted, leering at me through the bars. "Lord Throckmorton knows not to give you any more chances. Right? And other things could change too. Maybe it won't be Madame Bisset who stays in power as Lord Throckmorton's second in command. Isn't that true? Because there are *other* people you'd rather help?"

Both Lord Throckmorton and I ignored him.

"But did Lord Twelling kill the prince's first wife?" I asked. "Did you kill the other princesses? And what happened to Ella and Jed?"

I tried hard to sound disinterested, as if I was only asking as a point of curiosity. But my voice cracked, letting out the pain and fear. There was too much for me to hold back.

The corners of Lord Throckmorton's mouth twitched.

"I believe I'll leave you in ignorance on those matters," he said. "Consider it the first torture we decide to administer."

Torture?

Was he just toying with me, or did they have that planned for my future?

Terrence tugged on Lord Throckmorton's sleeve.

"Lord Twelling should be pressuring the prince into making a decision soon," Terrence said.

"Ah yes, I believe he is a hasty decider," Lord Throckmorton agreed. "Madame Bisset told me he agreed to marry his first wife sight unseen. Which explains why such a handsome man ended up yoked to such an ugly hag."

I had spent barely a quarter hour in Prince Charming's presence, and for much of that time he had been sobbing and I had been begging to be released from the dungeon. But I still winced at Lord Throckmorton's insult to the prince's deceased wife. I could imagine how hurt the prince would be.

"You won't get away with this," I argued. "Long before the wedding, the Fridesians will realize you're lying. I already planted the seeds of doubt. Eventually they'll come to believe what I told them instead."

"*Will* they?" Lord Throckmorton asked. "When we provide them with the proof you lacked?"

"You won't have proof," I fumed. "Because you're lying!"

Lord Throckmorton tapped his finger against his cheek.

"Perhaps Janelia told you who Lord Constantine is?" he asked.

"The doctor who delivered Queen Charlotte Aurora's baby?" I asked. "Who was exiled because he knew the baby

41

I stared at Lord Throckmorton in dismay.

That would work, I thought. *That would actually work very well.*

I'd seen his strategies in action for fourteen years. A chill struck me as I thought of another angle he could use: All he needed was Janelia to testify that the man claiming to be Lord Constantine really was Lord Constantine.

And Lord Throckmorton could probably get her to do it by making her think it might help me, I thought.

It was all I could do not to scream, *Stay away from Janelia! Don't hurt anyone else! Especially not anyone I care about!*

"Milord," Terrence mumbled beside Lord Throckmorton. I could tell he probably wanted to tug on Lord Throckmorton's sleeve again but was afraid to.

"Yes, yes, I know," Lord Throckmorton agreed. "We need to go back to the ballroom to see who the lucky winner is. I believe we've told Desmia everything she needs to know."

died? The one who supposedly bribed Janelia to stay quiet, when really it was you?"

Lord Throckmorton looked like he was going to object to the last description, but then he only shrugged.

"Conveniently, Lord Constantine is going to show up in Fridesia in, oh, about a week's time," he said. "He'll tell a tale of palace intrigue . . . about how the original baby wasn't dead after all. He'll be able to swear to the true claim to the Sualan throne of . . . well, *whomever* Prince Charming chooses!"

He can tell by my face that I understand, I thought. *He didn't teach me to hide my feelings well enough after all.*

"Put the torch back, boy," Lord Throckmorton ordered Terrence.

Terrence hung it back on the wall, and then the deceitful man and the deceitful boy disappeared into the stairway.

I waited a few moments, because I still had my pride—I wasn't going to let myself cry until I was sure neither of them could hear me. But, strangely, after the footsteps receded on the stairs, my eyes stayed dry. I waited for the empty-sky helpless feeling to overwhelm me once again, but it didn't come.

I felt calm.

Because . . . my brain still thinks there's something I can do? I wondered. *Even if I haven't figured it out yet?*

Could there be some way to escape this dungeon cell, even without a shovel or a hole?

I went around poking at the stones up and down the wall. But they all seemed solid and unmovable.

If a guard or even that gravelly-voiced jailer showed up, could I bribe him to get a message to Tog and Janelia and Herk somehow?

What if a guard or jailer never shows up, and they just let me starve to death in here? What if nobody comes back until it's time to remove my skeleton?

I decided not to think about questions like that.

Lord Throckmorton was acting rather mean to Terrence, now that he's done using him as a spy, I thought. *If Terrence ever comes back down here, could I get him to switch his allegiance once again?*

That seemed like a possibility. But it would require Terrence stepping down into the dungeon once more. And maybe he'd learned a lesson from me: that it wasn't wise to step foot in a dungeon when you weren't with people you could trust.

Just then, I heard footsteps again on the stairs. They were soft and hesitant, not like the confident stomping of Lord Throckmorton or Lord Twelling, or even Terrence or the prince.

"Hello?" I called. "Is somebody there?"

"It's us," a soft voice called back. "*We* believe you."

I saw the gleaming hair and glistening jewels and shimmering dresses first. And then I got my eyes to separate out individuals from all that glittering: It was three girls.

Three of the impostor princesses.

42

"Well, of course you believe me," I said bitterly, before I could stop myself. "You know you're not real princesses."

"But we don't know for sure that you *are*," the blond girl in the middle pointed out. Was she supposed to be Elzbethl? "So it *is* a matter of believing you. Trusting you."

I clutched the bars on my door.

"You're right," I said. "Completely right. I'm . . . sorry."

I squinted at the girls in their finery, so out of place in the grimy dungeon. I knew how Lord Throckmorton would view my apology: as an admission of weakness. Royalty wasn't supposed to admit mistakes. Or make them. But I was experiencing something like double vision—or maybe triple vision. I could see how I'd always thought a princess should act. I could see what behavior had come to seem acceptable during my time with Janelia and Herk and Tog.

Could I also see what I needed to do to convince these girls to help me?

They're already here, I told myself. *They already said they believe you.*

I swallowed hard.

"Who are you?" I asked.

"Sophia, Elzbethl, and Marindia, of course," the one in the middle said. Then she laughed. "No, we're messing with you. We're Catrice, Zuba, and Rose."

She pointed first at herself, then at the other two. So Catrice was the blond in the middle, Zuba was the tall brunette on the right, and Rose was the tiny brunette on the left.

"And you believe me?" I asked. "You really do? Do the other ten believe me as well?"

The three girls exchanged glances.

"We didn't exactly have a chance to ask everyone," Zuba volunteered. "But . . . I think everyone else could be convinced."

"Because none of us wants to die," Rose finished up.

I winced.

"You figured out the same thing I did," I whispered. "One girl gets to live in luxury in the palace, as the wife of Prince Charming. And then eventually she'll be queen—queen of the combined kingdoms of Suala and Fridesia. But for that charade to work, the other twelve girls must be . . ."

"Eliminated," Catrice finished for me. "To make sure we never tell our stories. So no one ever knows the truth."

I wanted to sink down to the ground. Then I remembered

the filth on the floor and just clutched the bars of my dungeon cell even harder.

"What *is* your story?" I asked. "You all look so . . ."

"Real" was the word I wanted to use. They looked as though they had all grown up in a palace—or at least lived in a palace for the past few months. Girls who were peasants wouldn't wear ball gowns with such ease and natural grace. Girls living on paupers' food wouldn't have hair that gleamed like that, or skin that glowed with such health and vitality. Girls who had to work for a living wouldn't have such smooth hands, such perfect fingernails.

I knew this because I could feel how rough and frazzled my own skin and hair had become in the weeks of walking from Suala. I could see the many cuts on my own hands from the days of basket-weaving; I could see all my chipped and broken nails.

Catrice snorted.

"It's *so* easy to figure out," she said. "We're actresses."

I should have thought of that. But I'd only heard about acting troupes from my sister-princesses. Lord Throckmorton had forbidden their presence in the palace because he considered them tacky and low-class. And untrustworthy liars and thieves.

And he wanted to be the only liar and thief in the palace, I thought bitterly.

"I warrant that every acting troupe in Suala is missing its ingénue cast member right now," Zuba added.

"If none of us goes back, I don't know how they'll ever act out a love story again," Rose said, as if this was something to worry about. "It'll just be the pirate and soldier plays they do. And there'll be no kiss waiting for the brave hero at the end. . . ."

"Maybe they'd just start using ugly girls instead," Catrice said calmly. "The ones who usually play servants. Love stories wouldn't die."

I blinked. How did any of this matter? How could they care about the future of theater troupes at a time like this?

"So someone came and—what? Kidnapped all of you?" I asked. "Forced you to act like princesses?"

"They didn't have to kidnap us," Zuba said, shrugging apologetically. "They offered us four times our usual salary."

"For a long journey and maybe just one performance," Catrice finished. "Tonight's performance."

"But whoever the prince chooses—" I began. "She'll have to go on acting for years and years and years."

"You think that one will have a long life either?" Rose asked. "I mean, maybe the prince will like her. But—"

"But since when is it the prince's decision?" Catrice broke in. "Look what happened to his first wife!"

They were all so matter-of-fact about all this: the danger they were in, the casual manipulation of people's lives.

"Does this surprise you?" Zuba asked, watching me carefully.

"I . . . I guess I was a little sheltered growing up in the palace," I replied.

It was true. I had known about lies and manipulation and evil, but I'd almost never seen the messy outcomes. People just disappeared. Whispers just traveled through the courtiers. I'd only seen prettied-up evil, masked by perfume and luxury.

The first true thing I'd seen had been my sister-princesses trapped in a dungeon back at the Palace of Mirrors.

And I did something about it! I wanted to protest.

But that had just led to the fire. It had led to my sister-princesses vanishing.

And it had led to me being trapped in this dungeon now.

So maybe I'm not all that great at dealing with truth?

"If you knew what Madame Bisset and Lord Throckmorton were planning, why did you go along with it?" I asked plaintively. "Why didn't you refuse from the very beginning?"

"Because we *didn't* know what was going on until tonight," Zuba said, shaking her dark curls for emphasis. "We thought we were doing our patriotic duty, fooling our enemies."

"And protecting the real princesses," Rose added. "Don't forget they told us that. We thought we were being noble and brave, standing in for the real princesses in the danger of our enemy's court."

"And then you showed up and . . . we thought about things a little deeper," Catrice said. "We sneaked down here and we heard what you talked about with Lord Twelling and the prince, and then with Lord Throckmorton and Terrence."

So they had help in getting to believe me, I thought. *They had proof. They didn't just trust me outright.*

"Do you know what happened to the real princesses?" I asked. "The other twelve besides me?"

Catrice shook her head.

"Madame Bisset talks like they were still alive after the fire, but—"

"But even if they were dead, she'd lie so you'd think you were protecting them," I finished in despair.

"Right," Zuba said. She twisted up her face and whispered, "Sorry."

Distantly, I heard the chiming of a clock: *Dong . . . dong . . . dong . . .* I counted.

"Is that eleven?" I asked. "Eleven o'clock already?"

The other girls exchanged glances once more.

"The prince is supposed to announce his decision at midnight," Rose said.

And Tog and I told Janelia we'd meet her and Herk at midnight, I thought. *We have one hour.*

"We need a key to get me out of this prison cell," I said. "Maybe the three of you could search around and find it, if you can do that secretly. But what if someone notices you're missing from the ballroom? What would happen then?"

Catrice shrugged.

"We told the others we had to go and powder our noses," she said. "Nobody would expect a princess to do that quickly."

"And there are ten other fake princesses," Zuba said.

"It's kind of hard for anyone to keep track of all of us."

Like I was trying to do the night of the fire with the real princesses, I thought. *I couldn't.*

But tonight I felt responsible once again for other girls: I would need to figure out a way to smuggle out thirteen fake princesses without anybody noticing. Having all thirteen girls disappear at once would be impossible to miss.

Maybe we could get impostors for the impostors? I wondered.

My mind started racing. I shook my head, trying to clear it.

"I changed my mind," I announced. "We're not going to have time for anyone to go look for a key to this door. We've got too many other things to take care of. Does anybody have a hairpin I could borrow instead?"

The three girls looked at me strangely. But Catrice said, "Sure. I've got about sixty of them holding up my hair right now. I don't think anything's going to change if I pull one out."

I held my hand through the bars in the door. When Catrice handed me a hairpin, I reached for the lock on my door and jammed the pin inside.

It took a few moments, but the lock came undone with a *click.* I pushed the door open.

"I didn't know princesses could do that," Rose said, her eyes wide.

"There are a lot of things most people don't know about being a princess," I answered, stepping out of my prison cell.

"So, um, what's next?" Zuba asked.

I thought about how much I'd wanted to find out who had been in this dungeon or some other palace dungeon an hour ago. But that would have to wait. I looked down at my filthy, ripped dress.

"Do you think the fake Princess Desmia would mind trading dresses with me?" I asked. "To save her life and her kingdom?"

43

I stepped back into the ballroom. I wasn't alone. Rose—the fake Marindia—walked alongside me on the left, her dark hair bouncing against her mint-green dress with every step.

And on my right, clutching my arm, was a girl dressed as Princess Elzbethl. But it wasn't Zuba, the actress who'd been playing Elzbethl all evening. It was a servant girl named Mary, who had been friends with Ella when Ella was living in the Fridesian castle. Mary, in fact, had been the one who'd helped Ella escape.

I was just relieved that I'd remembered Mary's name. And that Zuba, Rose, and Catrice had been able to find her quickly.

"I'm way too ugly for this dress," Mary whispered nervously. "We get out of the shadows, everybody'll know I ain't a princess."

"You act pretty, people'll think you are pretty," Rose

whispered, leaning past me. "Beauty's just an illusion. Acting. And anyhow—you've got the greatest prop ever. That golden dress. A *toad* could look beautiful in that dress!"

I didn't think this was helpful—who wanted to be compared to a toad? But Mary stood up straighter and beamed.

"You think so?" she asked. "Even *I* look beautiful now?"

I studied her face. Mary's eyes and nose and mouth weren't exactly symmetrical, and in general her features were all either too big or too small. But—I glanced to my other side, toward Rose—Rose's features weren't perfect either. And yet she had tricked me into considering her beautiful.

"You look perfect," I told Mary. "And—you're doing something good. That counts for more than beauty."

"But what will I say?" Mary fretted.

"Both Fridesians and Sualans tend to prefer their princesses quiet and polite and well behaved," I said. "So 'please' and 'thank you' will probably do it."

And then, later on, none of us will be quiet and polite and well-behaved, I thought grimly. *We'll be running.*

With Mary and Rose on either side of me, I stepped from the shadows to the back of a cluster of the other fake princesses. Rose immediately began whispering to the nearest girls, telling them to leave in twos and threes, and go out and find Zuba and Catrice and the fake Desmia. The three of them were finding servant girls to trade clothes with the fake princesses. And then the servant girls were leaving clothes to change back into in convenient places near the ballroom, for afterward.

Is this going to work? I wondered. *Will any of us get out of here alive?*

I looked toward the opposite wall, toward the secret door hiding the passageway where Tog and I had been together peeking out at the ballroom only an hour or so earlier. Just in case he was still standing there, I put my finger to my lips. I hoped he would understand that that meant, *Don't show yourself. Don't think I need to be rescued right now. Just stay hidden! Stay safe!*

"Might I have this dance?" a voice said in my ear. "I believe you're the only princess I haven't danced with yet."

I turned.

It was the prince.

My first instinct was to drop my head, put on a coy act, maybe let him think me so exceedingly shy that I wouldn't meet his eyes . . . anything so that he wouldn't recognize me. But he was already looking me directly in the face, and his expression stayed blank and vaguely cordial.

He already doesn't recognize me, I thought in amazement. *All I had to do was change my dress and put up my hair and attach a few strings of pearls to my neck and arms and head. And now he has no idea who I am.*

Were all men so dense?

I didn't think it worked that way. As the prince led me

out onto the dance floor, I took the precaution of bending my head, pretending I was overcome with the thrill of dancing with such a heart-throbbingly handsome man.

But we'll be in the brightest part of the ballroom, I thought in a panic. *Lord Throckmorton will see me. Madame Bisset will see me. Lord Twelling will see me. . . .*

"As long as you're dancing with me, nobody will dare to do a thing," the prince said quietly, putting an arm around me and launching both of us into the first steps of a slow waltz.

My feet moved automatically into the proper steps, but I glanced at the prince in surprise. His expression stayed carefully bland, no different from a moment ago. Then, very quickly, he winked.

"You're not as stupid as—" I almost said, *as Ella told me you were.* But then I caught myself. "I mean, not as stupid as you try to make people think."

The prince sighed, the melancholy expression of mourning returning to his face for a moment before he hid it again.

"I think the better way to describe it is, I'm not as stupid as I used to be," he said. "If Ella told you about me, probably whatever she said was true. Then. But now . . ." He shook his head, as if he regretted everything that had turned him into a deeper thinker. "After we left the dungeon, I made Lord Twelling accompany me to the family crypt. You were right—I had the power all along to do that. I was just afraid.

But seeing them just proved that my beloved wife and child are dead. Will I ever know what killed them? *Who* killed them? Will I ever know if God took them from me or if it was murder?"

"I don't know," I said. "I'm sorry." I waited a moment, letting the swirl of the dance steps turn me so I was facing only the opposite wall. So no one who was inclined to read lips could do so. "But . . . wouldn't it help at least a little if you could vanquish the ones who are gleeful about Corimunde's death? The ones who are plotting against us all—Lord Throckmorton and Madame Bisset. And maybe Lord Twelling, too?"

The prince spun to the right, then the left.

"Yes," he finally said. "It would help. But . . . what are you playing at? What are you trying to do?"

Again, I waited until I was facing the opposite way.

"I want the plotters arrested and imprisoned where they can never trouble any of us again," I said. I thought about how Lord Throckmorton had already escaped once. "Maybe somewhere remote, like in the old war zone, where no one would think to look for them. And with guards we know we can trust."

I didn't give the prince a chance to answer before I was finished.

"And I want to rescue my sister-princesses if they're still alive," I continued. "The real princesses, I mean. I want to find Ella and Jed, and make sure they're all right too. I know there

was somebody in a palace dungeon that you weren't supposed to know about. What if it's them? And . . . I want to save my kingdom. And that means signing the peace treaty with Fridesia."

The prince seemed to be pondering all of this. Maybe he wasn't stupid, but he was much too deliberate of a thinker for my taste.

Maybe he just wasn't used to doing much of it on his own.

"You have the power to arrest whomever you want," I reminded him. "Right now. You could take care of Lord Throckmorton and Madame Bisset. We could do everything else in safety."

The prince frowned, adding to the lines of grief marring his handsome face. He and I turned, so now he faced away from the crowd.

"But I don't know if Lord Twelling is one I should arrest alongside the others," he said. "You leave one monster free, it doesn't matter how many others you send away. You're still in danger. No . . . We need to keep up our charade a while longer. To flush out any other plotters."

That actually made sense, as much as I hated having to wait.

Maybe my sister-princesses and I should have adopted a similar strategy back in Suala? I wondered. *Maybe we should have held off letting the truth out, until we were sure of our own power?*

Somehow I didn't think that would have worked either.

Maybe we just needed to go through this whole disaster for everything to work out right?

That could only be true if my sister-princesses had survived the fire.

I realized I was the one frowning now. But the prince was still talking.

"I'll send guards out to look in all the dungeons, and to look elsewhere for Jed and Ella, and to try to get information about your other princesses," he said. "I'll do all that right now. I should have done that for Jed and Ella anyhow when I got word that their plans changed and they weren't coming back to Charmeil."

"*That* was what your advisers told you?" I asked. "That's what you believed?"

The prince winced.

"I know—it sounds suspicious, doesn't it?" he asked. "I was just too . . . bereft to do anything. To care about anything."

Fridesia with its grieving prince and aged, out-of-touch king and queen, I thought. *And Suala with its jumble of unexpected princesses. Of course we were both prime targets for scoundrels and rogues.*

"And about the peace treaty—" I prompted.

The prince spun out, then whirled back to face me.

"Why don't we just sign that tonight at midnight?" he asked. He grimaced. "So I have something big to announce when I *don't* select a new bride?"

44

Dong...

I heard the first chime of midnight. The royal orchestra must have been timing things very closely, because they finished the last notes of the last waltz in exact harmony with the chiming clock.

Dancers bowed to each other, their faces flushed with exertion.

And maybe, in the case of twelve of the girls, they're also flushed with fear of discovery? I wondered.

All the substitutions had been made. Twelve fake princesses had been replaced with even bigger fakes: palace servants dressed in royal clothing. To my eyes, they didn't look all that different. And, to my surprise, I hadn't seen any missteps or etiquette gaffes out on the dance floor.

Probably palace servants knew every bit as much about acting royal as the royalty and courtiers did.

But could it be that everyone in the ballroom has noticed the switch and is just too afraid to speak out? I asked myself. *Or are the plotters just biding their time? Have Madame Bisset and Lord Throckmorton—and maybe Lord Twelling—already planned their retaliation?*

I didn't dare glance at any of them to find out.

"Hear ye, hear ye," the royal herald cried, silencing the crowd of courtiers, royalty, and fake royalty. "The prince has come to a decision."

Prince Charming stepped forward from his position beside me.

"It has been a pleasure this evening to meet so many lovely princesses representing Suala," he said. "Had my ancestors but known the extent of female pulchritude in our neighboring land, I am certain they never would have started our long-simmering enmity."

Oh, that was awkward, I thought. *The prince doesn't need anyone telling him what to think, but maybe a speechwriter . . . ?*

The prince stopped, and for a moment I feared he'd lost track of what he intended to say. But he gritted his teeth, and I saw he was only gathering his strength for what came next.

"It is a delicate moment between our two kingdoms, as we balance between war and peace," he said. "I do not wish to do anything to disrespect Suala, or disrespect our delicate peace. But I also do not want to disrespect the memory of my beloved, my late wife Corimunde."

The ballroom was instantly pin-drop silent. I suspected that not a single person was even daring to breathe. Courtiers froze, as if the slightest movement or rustle of silk would be treasonous.

Then Lord Twelling stepped out from the crowd.

"Your Highness—" he began.

Prince Charming held up his hand.

"Let me finish," he said.

Lord Twelling stood uncertainly, on the brink of insubordination.

Will he—? I wondered. *Is he going to*—?

Lord Twelling didn't take another step.

"It is much too soon for me to marry again," the prince continued. "It would be unfair to the memory of Corimunde. And—" He turned toward the cluster of doubly fake princesses. And then he took my hand in his own. "And it would be unfair to whomever I would marry next. For those reasons, I will not choose a bride tonight."

Whispers broke out in the assembled crowd. Madame Bisset and Lord Throckmorton were too far back for me to see their reactions, but Lord Twelling's face went instantly red with fury. He still didn't step forward but seemed to be mouthing instructions at the prince: *Take it back! Take it back this instant! Say you were only joking! That girl standing right beside you is pretty enough! She*—

Lord Twelling froze, midsentence, his gaze on my face. No, not just on my face—burning into my eyes.

So he really didn't notice who I was until now? I marveled.

It was amazing how much people could be blinded by a simple thing like a dress and a fancy hairstyle.

I nudged the prince, because if we were going to succeed at our plans tonight, we had no time to stall. The prince stayed silent, his lips pressed tightly together, his chin trembling.

He's fighting tears, I realized. *He doesn't think he can speak without crying.*

I squeezed his hand.

"As one of the princesses of Suala," I began, "I want to be clear: We are honored by the way Prince Charming honors his late wife."

All right, then, I thought. *Maybe I could do with a speechwriter myself?*

I kept going anyway.

"And we are more concerned about the future well-being of our kingdom than the possibility of matrimony," I said. That sounded better, didn't it? "To that end, the prince and I have agreed that we shall move up the signing of the peace treaty. To tonight. Perhaps if the prince's adviser would be so good as to——"

I looked straight back at Lord Twelling. I could feel the defiance in my expression, but it couldn't be helped. Maybe it was necessary.

Lord Twelling gave a little jump of surprise, but then he whispered to someone standing beside him. It was evidently another of the prince's underlings, because a moment later servants appeared carrying a heavy wooden table. A parchment, a quill pen, and a bottle of ink lay in the center of the table.

By now, the prince seemed to have recovered his

composure enough to gesture chivalrously at me.

"Ladies first," he said.

A servant uncapped the bottle of ink. I picked up the quill.

Just sign the treaty, I told myself. *Get your signature and the prince's signature down on paper, and then all the doubly fake princesses can run away, the prince can get his guards to arrest Lord Throckmorton, Madame Bisset—and maybe Lord Twelling—and then you can . . .*

I could what?

I had not exactly allowed for how I myself was going to get away safely. If the prince decided he needed to keep up his charade in order to flush out Lord Twelling, then was I still in danger after the treaty signing?

Not if Tog comes back with Janelia and Herk, I thought. *And he will. He will if it is humanly possible.*

It was odd how much this thought filled me with confidence. I'd told Tog to think about the others' safety. And I was fully aware of how many obstacles lay in Tog's path. But I trusted him to do everything he could for me. And somehow that trust was worth as much as certainty about what was really going to happen.

Because . . . because he's someone who looks at me the way Harper always looked at Cecilia? I thought. *And . . . because I wish I could let myself look back at him the same way?*

This was not the right time for revelations of the heart. Not when the entire ballroom was staring at me.

I gripped the quill a little harder, and looked out at the

cluster of doubly fake princesses. I thought the sight of them would steady me, would remind me that I had already managed to make sure thirteen girls would get away safely.

But I got a jolt: There weren't just twelve doubly fake princesses standing in that corner of the room. There were also about a dozen other girls, all wearing various servants' costumes.

The impostor princesses that I had been so proud of saving were back. Back in the ballroom—and back in danger.

45

What is wrong with them? I wondered. Didn't they believe me after all? Did even those girls lie to me? Were they setting me up for betrayal all along?

But then I saw Catrice, the blond girl who had seemed to be the leader of the others down in the dungeon, mouth the words, *We thought you might need our help.*

There was a reason they hadn't let me save them: Because they thought I might need them to save me.

I glanced at the faces of the other girls behind Catrice. Some of them looked just as eager as Catrice; some, I suspected, had come back because they still kind of wondered if maybe there would be an opportunity to marry a prince. That didn't make them insubordinate or evil. That just meant that, like Prince Charming, they had started thinking for themselves.

But it ruins the one thing I was sure I was going to be able to accomplish tonight, I thought.

There was still the peace treaty, but now I doubted even

this. To hide my uncertainty, I began to read the parchment in front of me, starting at the top: *Be it known throughout the world that the kingdoms of Fridesia and Suala shall cease their long-standing war once and for all as of* _____.

I filled in the date and read on. The next section was flowery language describing the glories of both kingdoms, and how decades of enmity should not be allowed to *continue to have a detrimental effect on or inhibit the progress of either kingdom.*

I was only skimming now. Then I tripped over a phrase: *This barrier of land between the two kingdoms shall be subdivided into equal thirds and governed by rulers to be known henceforth as King Eldridge, Queen Estrelline, and King Lochlin.*

I blinked. Was it possible that my enemies' schemes were even more diabolical than I'd suspected? I backed up and reread the previous paragraph, which was as dense as a thicket and even easier to get lost in. As far as I could tell, it seemed to refer to a huge strip of land, perhaps more than of a third of each of the two kingdoms. And that land was to be set aside to keep the warring kingdoms of Fridesia and Suala safely apart.

And who's supposed to be governing that land? I wondered. *Kings Eldridge and Lochlin, and Queen Estrelline?*

It struck me that I had once heard that Lord Throckmorton's given name was Eldridge.

So could I stake my life on the likelihood that Madame Bisset's given name is Estelline, and Lord Twelling's is Lochlin?

Was it a matter of needing to stake my life on that? My life and Prince Charming's and the fake princesses' and the doubly fake princesses' and—how many other people's?

"We can't sign this," I whispered to Prince Charming.

I pointed to the offending phrase in the document.

He looked at me blankly—blankly and dully and as though, even though he was *trying*, he still couldn't care about anything beyond the deaths of his wife and child. He was *trying* not to be stupid and to do his own thinking, but right now he needed a little help.

I remembered that an entire ballroom full of people was watching me. Enemies and friends—and a vast swath of people who might take either side.

Sometimes you just can't worry about what anyone else is going to think or how anyone else is going to react, I told myself. *Sometimes you just have to do what you know is right.*

I snapped the quill pen in half.

"We can't sign this," I said aloud, the words ringing throughout the ballroom, filling up every crevice. My voice was not well modulated; it did not sound palace bred or cultured or pretty. But it was strong and sure and authoritative. And that was exactly how I needed to speak. "This is not the peace treaty we Sualan princesses negotiated with the Fridesian ambassador. The war is over, but this is not the document to seal the peace. Bring us the proper document and *then* we will sign!"

For a moment it seemed that everyone was too stunned

by my words to do anything. But then everything happened fast.

Lord Twelling turned and began trying to shove his way back through the crowd, toward the door. Prince Charming recovered enough to scream, "Guards! Stop Lochlin Twelling!"

Guards appeared out of nowhere and grabbed Lord Twelling by the arms.

"Guards! Get Lord Throckmorton and Madame Bisset, too," I screamed, because I could see them also trying to slip out the back.

And even though I was Sualan and my kingdom had been at war with Fridesians almost my entire life, the Fridesian guards obeyed me, too.

Meanwhile, one of the doubly fake princesses I hadn't noticed missing before came bursting out of the secret door in the wall—wasn't that Ella's friend Mary? The one who had claimed she was too ugly to be a princess?

Mary was screaming, "Wait! Wait! I found them! All by myself! Before the guards did!"

And then Ella and Jed stepped out of the secret passageways too.

"Don't sign anything yet!" Jed was screaming. "I've got the proper treaty right here!"

Ella was just beaming at me.

"Sorry, I'm so sorry I left the ballroom," Mary apologized as she came tripping toward me. "I think I'm better at watching out for Ella than at acting like a princess. When I heard the prince tell the guards she and Jed were missing—I had to go find them. Good thing I remembered all the prisons and extra dungeons Madame Bisset and Lord Twelling like to hide people in, from the *last* time Ella messed up one of their plans."

"You *both* saved us," Ella cried, throwing her arms around Mary and me.

"So you *were* in some secret other dungeon?" I asked. "And the prince didn't know?"

"Right," Ella whispered, hugging Mary and me even tighter.

I tried to figure out how the secret dungeon in the Fridesian palace corresponded to the dungeon system back at the Palace of Mirrors, but quickly gave up. It really didn't matter now that Ella and Jed were free.

I hugged Ella and Mary back, then turned to see if Prince Charming was ready to sign the new treaty—the right one.

The prince had just finished hugging Jed, and now he was staring toward men at the back of the ballroom.

"No!" he screamed. "You do not set *my* palace on fire! Guards! Stop them!"

And then everyone in the ballroom swarmed toward the men who were taking torches down from the sconces. Maybe they would have succeeded in reaching the torches up toward the many frills and bows, but even Lord Twelling was yelling at the men, even with his own arms clutched by guards, "No! No! This is not the time for the flames! You were supposed to wait until *after* that treaty was signed and *after* it was safely out of the palace and *after* the poison toast was drunk . . ."

How many people did our enemies plan to kill? I wondered in horror.

Prince Charming and I yelled together, "Guards! Arrest the men with torches too!"

Just then Tog and Herk and Janelia came rushing out of the secret door, panting and brushing cobwebs from their clothes.

"Desmia! We're here! We'll save you!" Tog cried.

"That's not necessary this time around," I said. "But I appreciate the thought."

For a moment I forgot the other hubbub in the ballroom, and just looked into Tog's eyes. It was so strange to remember the times I'd thought of him as just a beggar boy. The times I'd had to remind myself that he and Herk were so different from me. They weren't. He wasn't. It was true that he wasn't royalty. But he wasn't a beggar, either.

He was just my friend.

Er—was I still lying to myself? Wasn't he actually more than that?

"You could do something else for me instead," I said.

"Um, sure," Tog said. "What—?"

To answer, I leaned in and kissed him.

And he started to kiss me back, but we were interrupted by screaming over by the doors: "Desmia, Desmia—is Desmia here?"

It was Cecilia, with Harper on her heels.

I raced toward my friend and sister-princess, crying, "I'm here! I'm here! You made it too!"

Behind me, I could hear Lord Twelling ranting at the guards who held his arms.

"But I told the entire royal guard to keep out anyone else who claimed to be a Sualan princess," he cried. "You were supposed to take them directly to the dungeons!"

"You aren't in charge anymore," the guards growled back, practically in unison. "You're the one going to the dungeon!"

I grinned at Cecilia. We could hardly stop hugging each other. But I was the first to pull back.

"The other girls," I murmured. "Did you and Harper come straight here after the fire? Or did you find out what happened to any of the others first?"

"We stopped to see Sir Stephen and Nanny Gratine, to tell them to find out for us, and to help the other girls if they could," Cecilia said. "But we knew we had to get to Fridesia to meet you. And to make sure nothing messed up the treaty signing. Or Ella and Jed's wedding."

"Nothing could mess up that," Ella said behind us. "We would have exchanged vows in the dungeon, if we'd had to." Then her face became more serious. "But—I'd like to know what happened to the other princesses. Surely they must have survived the fire too. . . ."

I wondered how much Mary had told her. Or—how much of an optimistic spin she'd put on the tale.

Just then Madame Bisset stopped in front of us as the guards led her out. I was stunned to see that the woman's silver hair was sticking up and a button had come off her prim gray dress.

"'Surely they must have survived the fire, too,'" she mockingly mimicked Ella. "Only because Lord Throckmorton and I had our men save them from the flames. Not that they were worth the bother. Such idiots. Such shortsighted, defiant idiots."

Was she calling the sister-princesses idiots? Was that proof that they had survived?

I put out my hand to keep the guards from pulling Madame Bisset away.

"What are you talking about?" I asked.

Madame Bisset narrowed her eyes at me.

"We smuggled twelve girls out of the fire—all but Cecilia," she said. "We never found her. And you ran away. But we made all eleven of the other girls an offer. Well . . . we did it in declining order of desirability. We offered everyone the opportunity to come here for the chance to marry Prince Charming. We thought we'd set it up with one true princess and all the rest actresses. And of course he'd choose the true princess. But every single princess refused to help us. Everyone said it would hurt her kingdom—and her sister-princesses."

Not a single one of them was a viper, I thought. *I should have trusted them fully, all along.*

Madame Bisset peered disdainfully at Cecilia and me.

"At least the other girls were ladylike enough *not* to escape through cobwebs and roam the countryside with a young man, totally unchaperoned," she said. "Or to jump out a second-story window before I even had the chance to *explain* our offer."

Cecilia looked at me in amazement.

"You jumped out a second-story window?" she asked.

"I had to," I said.

"But you were the princess we were most worried about," Harper said. "Because everyone else had a knight and a nanny to look for them and take care of them. And you had . . . only us. And we couldn't get back into the ballroom because the secret door locked behind us. We couldn't think of any other way to help you *except* by coming to Fridesia."

I cast a glance over my shoulder, at Tog and Herk and Janelia.

"Oh, it turns out I had people of my own too," I said. "And a thirteenth sister."

Janelia beamed at me.

Cecilia looked around, as if noticing for the first time that the ballroom was in utter disarray.

"So," Cecilia said. "Do you think the other girls came here too? Are we just . . . not seeing them in all the confusion?"

It wasn't such a crazy question, given that there were thirteen fake princesses and a dozen servants dressed as impostor princesses milling about.

Madame Bisset turned back to us, jerking away from the guards trying to lead her away.

"You want to know where your sister-princesses are now?" she asked, smiling maliciously. Even with the mussed hair and the missing button, she seemed to have regained some of her usual dignity. Or usual cruelty, anyway. "You want to know if they're dead or alive? You could go to your graves wondering that. Because *I'll* never tell."

Epilogue

The first strains of the wedding march sounded from the pianoforte at the back of the chapel. A flow of harp music quickly joined in, providing an unusual harmony.

It was Tuesday morning, the time that had been set aside for the official signing of the peace treaty between Suala and Fridesia. Prince Charming, Queen Gertrude, King Charming, Cecilia, and I had already done that late Friday night—or, actually, an hour or two into Saturday morning—after things had settled down a little and we'd all agreed that, to prevent further scheming, we should make the *real* treaty official.

After a lifetime of war and countless lives lost, we finally had peace. Real peace.

But Tuesday was still set aside as holiday celebration day for both kingdoms, and so Jed and Ella had decided to use the day for a different happy purpose: as their wedding day.

"Mrs. Smeal will never speak to us now," Ella had moaned in the palace ballroom in the early hours of Saturday morning, as they planned everything. "Letting her think we canceled our wedding and then having it anyway on a different day . . ."

"We can have a second ceremony out at the refugee camp for her and any refugees who are left," Jed suggested. "I just . . . don't want to delay any longer. And the faster we get married, the faster we can help the Sualans find their other princesses."

They were still missing. It appeared that Madame Bisset was the only one who'd ever known where all of them were taken, and she still wasn't talking.

Now I sat in a pew with Cecilia, Janelia, Tog, and Herk, with a space left for Harper as soon as he finished his part of the wedding music. The sped-up wedding plans meant that there'd been little time to think of clothing. Catrice and the other fake-princess actresses had offered us their ball gowns from their one night of pretending to be Sualan royalty, but Cecilia, Janelia, and I had turned them down— after all, they were all invited to the wedding too, and that would have left them with nothing to wear. They were all officially out of work now, and far from their acting troupes. And Lord Throckmorton, Lord Twelling, and Madame Bisset had of course never paid them for their convincing performances. So we couldn't disadvantage them further.

I'd feared that that would leave Janelia, Herk, Tog, and

me wearing the peasant garb Mrs. Smeal had given us at the refugee camp, and Harper and Cecilia wearing the slightly ash-stained suit and ball gown they'd brought from that last tragic night at the Palace of Mirrors. But then Prince Charming offered the boys outgrown clothing from when he was their ages. And, in the spirit of the new peace treaty, he offered Janelia, Cecilia, and me clothes that had been delivered for Princess Corimunde, which she'd never had a chance to use.

Princess Corimunde had been quite a large woman. And though Ella's friend Mary had proved quite skillful at sizing the dresses down, nothing could be done about the fact that the former princess had also gone in for rather bizarre fabric designs: Cecilia's dress was covered in a pattern of life-size green cabbages—or maybe those were supposed to be giant, oddly colored roses? Janelia's dress seemed to have a repeating pattern of giant scissors and mine, a similarly garish pattern of huge orange spinning wheels.

It was a good thing we weren't still in the Palace of Mirrors, or I might have had to fight giggles all through the wedding ceremony, seeing those crazy designs reflected again and again.

The strange thing was, Tog was staring at me as though I were wearing the most beautiful dress in the world.

He really did seem to be wearing the most handsome suit in the world. He could easily be mistaken for royalty now. And yet, staring at him, I could understood why he'd said I'd looked most royal back in the cave, when I was heaving the pot of boiled rags at the men who were about to strangle him.

As handsome as he looked now, I still thought he'd looked even better in that same cave, when he and Janelia ran back to save me.

Cecilia dug her elbow into my side.

"Hey, I know you're all googly-eyed with the newness of this love thing, but you really should be watching the bride and groom, not your own beloved," she whispered.

Googly-eyed? Love thing? Beloved? I wondered.

I realized I'd totally missed Ella walking down the aisle.

"Oh . . . right," I murmured.

I glanced back once more at Tog and noticed that Herk was digging his elbow into Tog's side and maybe saying the exact same thing. Tog glanced my way once more, guiltily, and then turned to face the front of the chapel.

I reached out and firmly grasped his hand anyway, because at least I could have that at Ella and Jed's wedding. How could I not want to hold Tog's hand as we listened to other people speak of love?

"Do you, Jed, take Ella . . . ," the chaplain was saying.

Jed and Ella peered into each other's eyes as if they were the only two people in the world.

"Of course," Jed murmured.

I remembered that the chaplain was actually Jed's younger brother. There wasn't much family resemblance:

The chaplain was a stuffy palace type without a single hair out of place, while Jed, even on his wedding day, looked wild-eyed and wild-haired. But the chaplain beamed at Jed and Ella as though he was as happy about their marriage as they were.

Ella got her chance to promise to love and honor Jed, and then the chaplain was finishing up with the words, "What God has joined together, let no man put asunder." But he got no further into it than "asun—" because suddenly there was screaming outside.

"Wait! Wait! Don't give up on the treaty! I'm here!"

"And me!"

"And me!"

"And—"

A cluster of disheveled girls spilled into the chapel—girls and aged, decrepit knights and arthritic old women I recognized as former nannies.

"I'm Princess Sophia of Suala, and—"

"I'm Princess Fidelia of Suala, and—"

"I'm Princess Rosemary, and—"

I counted, which was hard to do because everyone was jumping up and down in amazement and exultation. And they were also sweeping each other into hugs.

"Oh, so you survived!"

"I thought I'd never see you again!"

Some of the girls had no crowns on their heads, and some had broken crowns, and one—Porfinia—seemed to have fashioned a replacement crown out of bits of charred wood and burnished jewels. It was amazingly beautiful.

. . . eight, nine, ten, eleven . . .

They were all here, all my sister-princesses. Every single one had survived. Every single one had escaped whatever hiding place Madame Bisset had trapped her in, evidently with the help of the ancient knights and former nannies. And every single one had cared enough about the peace treaty—our sole true joint accomplishment—to risk everything and find her way to Fridesia to make sure it was properly signed.

They'd all managed to arrive exactly at the moment they thought the treaty was to be signed.

In the hubbub, none of them had yet noticed Cecilia and me sitting in our pews. They were still exclaiming about each other's survival. Evidently, none of them had known that the others had also escaped and traveled to Fridesia.

"Oh, Marindia, I was so worried about you!"

"Oh, Elzbethl, did you pass out in the smoke and then wake up in a strange house the next morning too?"

"Adoriana—is Adoriana here too?"

"Where's Lucia?"

It appeared that none of them, even numbers-obsessed Florencia, had thought to use my approach of simply counting. I guess I just had more experience with that.

I stood up. Out of the corner of my eye, I saw Cecilia doing the same thing.

Cecilia looked over and flashed me a grin that was even wider than the one she'd had on our coronation day.

"Go ahead, you tell them," she said. "I gave you my proxy vote, after all——you might as well have *some* chance to use it!"

I had permission to speak, but for a moment I was too overcome to use it.

Partly that was because I could still see the whole scene the way Lord Throckmorton would view it: *What a bunch of disorganized, disheveled, disreputable girls!* He would sniff. *What an embarrassment! So they survived one challenge to their crazy unprecedented reigns——so what? They don't have a palace anymore! Most of them aren't even wearing shoes! And who knows what shape they left Suala in, every single one of them thinking she had to traipse all the way here?*

I could see how Lord Throckmorton would view everything——but that didn't mean I had to agree with him.

Incredibly enough, I could see how lots of other people would see things too. Just as soon as Porfinia noticed Cecilia and me and saw what we were wearing, she would think, *Oh, my goodness! This kingdom needs my fashion advice!* Ganelia would think, *Wonderful! All thirteen of us are here——I can bring out my sketches for how we should rebuild our palace.* Sophia would be ready to assure us, *Don't worry, don't worry! If we show a united front when we get back to Suala, there won't be a rebellion there at all. . . .*

I knew my sisters. I trusted them. But that didn't mean I had to agree with them all of the time either.

Like Prince Charming, I'd learned to think for myself. And I had some ideas growing in my head about a better way to run our kingdom when we got back to it:

Maybe I can talk Ganelia into designing our palace to be more open and approachable this time around. . . .

Maybe we can take our advisers now from outside the palace, from out in the countryside even, so we know what's really going on in our kingdom. . . .

But first, I needed to get my sister-princesses' attention.

"Girls!" I cried. And I was sorry, but it was simply not possible to speak in a well-modulated bell-like voice when I was trying to speak over so many excited, jabbering girls. Maybe I would never again speak in a well-modulated, bell-like voice. It just wasn't worth it. "Girls, I am so happy to see you all! Cecilia and I both are. I am so glad all of us survived, and we will be able to continue reigning together. I assure you, everything is taken care of with the peace treaty. And, with Prince Charming's help, we have also vanquished the ones who masterminded our palace's destruction. I can't wait to hear all of your stories of how you escaped and came here. But right now we are being very rude to our Fridesian hosts."

All eleven of the newly arrived sister-princesses stared at me with a mix of astonishment and confusion and delight. For that matter, Cecilia, Harper, Janelia, Tog, and Herk looked a little confused too.

I went on.

"The treaty signing is over, but you've arrived just in time for the best part of Ella and Jed's wedding," I said. "Don't you think we should let them finish, and *then* straighten ourselves out?"

I pointed toward the front of the chapel.

Even the chaplain looked confused for a moment. Then he grinned in a way that, for the first time, made me see a resemblance to his brother Jed.

"Oh, right!" he said, jerking to attention. "Really, it's all over except for, 'I now pronounce you man and wife!' And, Jed, you get to kiss the bride. And . . . live happily ever after."

"This," Jed said, "is going to be worth the wait."

And then all of us—Fridesians and Sualans, royalty and servants, courtiers and actresses and paupers—watched Ella and Jed kiss. Both of them had their eyes closed and wore blissful expressions on their faces. They once again seemed to have forgotten that the rest of us existed. They already had everything they needed for their happily ever after.

Tog squeezed my hand, which I knew meant, *When we get a chance to kiss again, and it's not in the midst of a ballroom and a crisis and lots of surprise people dropping by—that's going to be worth the wait too.*

I squeezed back, and I was pretty sure he would understand I was saying, *I totally agree.*

I thought back to the coronation day with all the other

princesses, when I'd wondered how I would survive when I didn't know who my enemies were. I hadn't even been asking the right question. Because survival didn't just depend on knowing my enemies.

It also depended on knowing whom I could count as friends. And I had that now. I had friends and sisters and a beloved and a kingdom and a friendly neighboring kingdom and even—if you counted Herk—a little brother.

And those were the ingredients for *my* happily ever after.

MARGARET PETERSON HADDIX

is the author of many critically and popularly acclaimed books for children and teens, including the other books in this sequence, *Just Ella* and *Palace of Mirrors*; as well as *Game Changer*, *Claim to Fame*, *Uprising*, the Missing series, and the Shadow Children series. A graduate of Miami University (of Ohio), Margaret Peterson Haddix worked for several years as a reporter for the *Indianapolis News*. She also taught at the Danville (Illinois) Area Community College. She lives with her family in Columbus, Ohio. Visit her at haddixbooks.com.